Stars of Antrana

Book One of the Erskan Trilogy

First Edition

K. McVey

Stars of Antrana

Book One of the Erskan Trilogy

First Edition

Published by The Nazca Plains Corporation
Las Vegas, Nevada
2007

ISBN: 978-1-934625-00-2

Published by

The Nazca Plains Corporation ®
4640 Paradise Rd, Suite 141
Las Vegas NV 89109-8000

PUBLISHER'S NOTE
Stars of Antrana is a work of fiction created wholly by *K. McVey's* imagination. All characters are fictional and any resemblance to any persons living or deceased is purely by accident. No portion of this book reflects any real person or events.

Editor, Karen Martin
Cover Art, Michael Manning (www.thespidergarden.net)
Art Director, Blake Stephens

Acknowledgements

Thanks to Clive, Chrysty, Selena, Virgina, Lisa, and Karen for their support & encouragement.

Stars of Antrana

Book One of the Erskan Trilogy

K. McVey

Contents

Introduction

Mom used to tell me, "To be a good police officer, there are two things you have to do right. One: you have to survive. Two: be able to tell a good story."

Coming from four generations of cops, she knew of what she spoke. She had a strong sense of ethics, pride, loyalty, courage and morality. All were traits she cultivated in me. Strongest of all, though, was a feeling that you could make a difference in people's lives.

You might remember historical accounts about me. It occurred about one-hundred years after the accidental discovery of the corona space drive, in the era you now call the "Outward Expansion". To those of us that lived back then, we just called it the "Expansion" – because we could hardly keep up.

Mankind was journeying to previously unheard of and unnamed destinations. A modern space craft could get to Earth's closest stars in a matter of days or weeks. Expansion was, initially, the canvas of the very wealthy and of military craft of the Earth Alliance. But technological advances brought a palette of relatively inexpensive and fast space crafts to the upper middle-class and medium-sized businesses.

I grew up in Metroplex City, in north Texas, watching my Mom dress at night for her patrol duties. She often remarked that only professional scuba divers took more time to get ready for work. Her equipment ritual was completed when she eased her StacGun into its polished leather holster. I can still smell the scent of her leather boots, leather gloves, and faint perfume... I can close my eyes and remember the burning embers in her eyes: full of purpose, confidence, and vitality. Well...

What made the news accounts about me memorable is not that another Ranger was lost. (No, those were dreary times for us, when several of my friends had fallen.) It was the fact that I became *missing*. Of course, you can ask your grandparents to recount what they recall. Of course, you can obtain detailed news accounts from back then. Of course, finally, all of those accounts end with my disappearance – without a trace.

I managed to survive; now I'm going to tell you the story.

Chapter One
The Pursuit of the Day

"SON," I said, looking through the clearsteel at the orbiting transit station. "Run pre-separation diagnostics. Advise when complete."

"Received," the soft female voice replied, amplified over the cockpit speaker.

My police cruiser was a top-of-the-line model. Ten years ago. But it did have several upgrades and could, at least, keep up with anything the bad guys would have. The basic design of the Tamagra cruisers had been unchanged for two decades. A large, 3,000 foot by 100-foot section contained the corona star drive, food, water, and air supplies. Shrouded by heavy layers of armor plate and external defensive systems, the corona section could be detached from the much smaller and maneuverable crew section and left to defend for itself. The Systems Operations and Navigation computer, or SON, was master on the crew section, with an autonomous slave SON running on the corona section. They functioned best when together, but could function well when apart.

"Diagnostics complete. All clear."

"Thanks," I replied. Then I touched a button on my steering wheel. "Celion base, this is Earth Alliance Ranger Charlie Three Oh Eight, requesting permission to leave my corona section with you."

After a half-second gap, "Ranger Charlie Three Oh Eight, granted. Bay Edward Nineteen is available."

"SON, lock on and display," I told the computer.

The liquid electrical display inside the panoramic clearsteel illuminated a glowing green highlight on a "top" docking bay.

"Celion base, received," was my reply.

Absent mindedly, I rubbed the tips of my fingers of my left hand onto the flight recliner. It was jet black, rich leather, and was one of the several upgrades I had ordered and installed. Synthetics were fine for most people, but the real feel of the soft leather could not be rivaled by something made in a chemical plant.

I put the Tamagra into a slow one-hundred-and-eighty degree turn on its Z axis. After a minute, I had the craft lined up with the docking bay, and over the next thirty seconds proceeded to back my ship until the corona section was speared by the primary guide rod. The last five-hundred feet was the easy part as the ship coasted to a stop on the thick rubber grommets.

"SON, engage locking clamps for the corona section and prepare separation."

"Confirmed."

The planet Taleon spun below, to my right. Dark gray, with swirling white streaks of clouds, it was one of the dozen planets found that would support life. That's not to say that any of them had inhabitants. Indeed, after looking at three-thousand planets, we had not found anything as simple as a native microbe, much less a plant or an animal. Eleven planets had semi-hospitable environments that enabled habitation with varying degrees of protection from the atmosphere or radiation. One planet, Fermos, had an atmosphere quite similar to Earth. Taleon, on the other hand here, had all the beauty of the underside of a gravel truck. The winds were gale force and the rain persistent. That always combined to create a white-ash mush that tried to track its way inside every building or vehicle you wanted to visit. It was, not surprisingly, what one would expect from a place that was rich in precious mineral ores.

"Separation sequence prepared," SON told me.

"Confirmed."

I chuckled at my short reply. My verbal mannerisms seemed to have adopted those of SON, and not the other way around. Two years of living with that thing can do that to a person.

"You have a recorded message, keyed to your arrival," SON advised. "Caller is Captain Burgess, Taleon Planetary Security Force."

"Play."

A fifteen-inch by ten-inch section of the clearsteel displayed an image of a bearded man in his upper forties, rounded dark eyes, dark brow and shaggy reddish hair. He smiled a perfect row of teeth. "Alexi, I heard you would be coming out to visit us. Give me a call when you've arrived."

The screen disappeared, replaced by the view of several spacecraft slowly maneuvering around one another, jockeying for docking bays.

"Disengage section locks and separate," I told SON.

There was a moment, barely imperceptible, where the massive corona drive of the main section and the miniscule corona drive of the crew craft broke their embrace. This instant always created a sickening feeling that went straight to my stomach.

"Ewwww," I murmured, feeling myself nearly retch.

"Dry heave?" SON asked, coldly, absent of a compassionate tone.

My gut settled, and I looked at my outstretched, booted feet. "Thank you for your medical diagnosis, SON. As always," I flipped a couple of dashboard switches, "you are on top of your game."

SON was a non-emotional computer system; still, was there a slight hint of sarcasm in her voice? It had been two months since I had left the artificial gravity field of a spacecraft for the real, honest-to-god gravity of a planet. Maybe, the real issue was that I needed to get away from SON as much as I needed to feel solid ground beneath my feet.

"Separation is complete. Secondary corona drive engaged," SON informed.

I eased the crew section away, slowly at first and then with increasing speed. The Tamagra's smaller component was comprised of a smaller, limited-use corona star drive. It was really incapable of making safe star-to-star jumps, but could cover, oh, the distance from New York City to Radial City on the Moon in about twenty minutes.

The body of the craft was very clean. A thin, rectangular shape, with 45-degree angled sides, a nearly featureless exterior, and a steeply raked front end, containing the cockpit, enveloped in diode-transreflective clearsteel. The body of the craft was covered with FrictionLite, an almost frictionless material painted onto the skin. FrictionLite came in a variety of vibrant colors suited to your personal style: as long as your palette consisted of gray, or the ever more popular, dark gray. Large white letters on the sides, top, and bottom of the craft read "POLICE". Smaller text indicated "C308", my district and call-sign, and then "RANGER". It was repeated in smaller letters in Dutch and Japanese, rounding out the other two primary languages used.

Protruding from the foremost edge of the Tamagra were thin instruments and two closed gun ports that sported twin 20 mm dampened automatic machine guns. Laser guns made great science fiction, but those were at least 50 years away from really being viable.

On the inside, the cockpit contained two pilot recliners and a wrapped pod-style instrumentation display on the outboard sides. I always piloted with my space suit on, and helmet within one second's reach, clamped to the left of my gun belt. The StacGun was holstered and always accessible.

A strong sliding door was in the middle of the bulkhead behind me, leading to a reasonably-sized bedroom, kitchen, dining area, exercise area, and pantry. The back third of the craft was bracketed by two engines, water and air tanks, and a narrow passageway that led to the back airlock connected, opened into the corona section.

A few pieces of art graced the walls and magnetic tabletops. Regardless of the generated gravity field, every now and then a pursuit or other maneuver would cause things to float about, so it was best that things where kept tied down or secured the old fashioned way with magnets. I was planning a four-day working cruise next year in Boston on a replica 15th Century Portugese Caravel; even the "How To" book on my desk was secured with a small magnetic bookmark.

I put my craft into a slight left-angle and dropped toward Taleon.

"Flight tracing beacon is active," SON told me.

"Received," I replied. I saw the overlay on the screen of the flight path. I gradually eased to the right and centered my craft on target.

"Hull temperature is two-hundred degrees, rapid increasing," SON told me.

"A bit warmer with this mess of thick air, isn't it?" I said aloud.

"Two-hundred thirty degrees," SON replied.

You want a better conversation, talk to a wall. It will be more entertaining.

I was able to see the landing lights' "X" pattern on the ground.

X marks the spot, I thought to myself.

"Elevation is two-thousand feet," SON told me.

"This looks like a good place to stop," I said aloud.

"One thousand feet."

"I wonder if the brakes are working." I asked SON.

"Five-hundred feet." SON ignored my question.

Then, "Minus six-thousand feet," SON said, as emotionless as the prior measurements.

I laughed aloud.

With about two feet to spare, I stopped the craft. A set of lights on the taxiway lit up, with my screen flashing in synchronized patterns. I turned slightly right, about ten degrees, and then piloted slowly across the taxiway.

Low, squat block buildings lay ahead. Dark gray, featureless walls were pierced by rectangular glowing green building number signs. Waves of light gray dust floated by, similar to sheets of rain, trying to block my view. There were a dozen other craft, large and small, moving about on the port. A section of my clearsteel screen, to the right, showed an above-view graphic with icons representing the crafts around me. One had made a sharp 120-degree turn away from me and was heading back to a hangar slightly behind my right side. When the police arrive, an action like that was always an attention-getter.

"SON, identify that craft that just turned away. The small one, headed about five o'clock."

"Commencing," SON replied.

On the screen, the graphic for the craft turned from green to red, and a yellow circle was depicted around it. Several lines of information came up. Beshrell Mark IX Personal Flier. The craft registration dates were valid.

Still, my curiosity continued as the data scrolled on the screen.

"Skip to the registered owner and port-of-call history, SON."

Another panel of information appeared.

"Frank Tellingson," I said aloud. "Registered in Bristol, United Kingdom." I watched the craft on the display.

Then I pulled my craft to a stop. I was now the only craft on the ground that was not moving.

"Let's see if he's watching us."

I made a gradual pivot to my right, slowly pointing my craft in his direction.

"SON, look at the last twenty ports of call or check-in points on the locations that this craft has been. Give me the closest location to the Taleon system."

"The closest port of call was the Branston system."

"That's not even relatively close. So... Mr. Tellingson suddenly takes a big leap of distance out here."

"The craft is not registered as stolen," SON said.

"Not yet."

"The suspect craft is slowly increasing speed," SON told me.

"I bet he really increases speed in a moment. Call planetary security and alert them."

"The suspect craft is..."

I cut SON off. "Send the alert."

I hit a control that simultaneously activated the radio broadcast, emergency pursuit lights, and recording devices. I squeezed the accelerator controls in my hands and felt my body jerked back into the leather seats as the Tamagra jumped from about five miles per hour to about fifty miles per hour in two seconds.

SON knew the routine already: all irrelevant data on the displays went gray, with only a central graphic displayed slightly to my right field of view. The clearsteel screen was free to give me an unencumbered real-life view of the space sport. A few nearby crafts had received the pursuit notice and their automatic piloting systems were bringing them to a stop.

"The suspect craft has jammed the auto-stop transmission," SON noted.

"Surprise, surprise," I said.

The suspect had increased its speed and was genuinely fleeing me now. However, I was gaining on it.

The suspect turned abruptly into a row of parked commercial crafts. Small support vehicles with small trains of supplies came to a stop as the suspect screamed past them.

This could be dangerous.

"SON, there's too much on the ground here. I'm going to back off and see if he gets up into the air." I slowed.

There was a flash ahead from the suspect as he made another hard right turn

16

down a row of buildings.

I had just started to back down, making the turn without such a hard angle.

"Suspect craft has intentionally rammed a support vehicle," SON explained the flash.

It was starting to happen very quickly, the sequence of events. I unconsciously reverted to my training and experience which fought off the temptation to get tunnel vision, a narrowed field of view and thought.

I surveyed the clearsteel information for identified stationary and moving objects and, in particular, the whereabouts of people.

The explosion was followed by after-explosions as the cargo reacted to the initial impact. I drove our craft through the ball of flame – there wasn't a way to stop or any other direction to go – save for running through one of the buildings.

The suspect craft had rammed one of the trailers, which had whipped the drive-car into a wall. The driver would probably be all right, was my guess.

Metal fragments pinged off the clearsteel of my screen.

Breaking through the smoke, I saw the suspect craft turning left.

"He knows once he gets into the air, we can shoot him down," I said aloud.

"Back-up has been dispatched," SON advised. Help was on the way.

"Activate targeting system," I said.

A triad of electronic crosshairs appeared on the screen in front of me. I knew the gun ports had been opened. A number displayed on the screen: "200 yds" to target.

The moment the suspect craft hit the support vehicle and fled, the pursuit became a felony and a whole new game.

We made another sweeping right turn between buildings. There were fewer ground vehicles here. We were approaching the edge of the space port and headed toward the semi-surfaced town.

Then we made a right. I was gaining again on him. One-hundred yards to target.

Finally, we had a short straight and unobstructed view of the craft. Fifty yards.

The targeting light turned bright red, indicating a clear shot.

I fired, softly depressing the button on my right thumb control.

Hot green tracer rounds leapt from the front of my craft. Of course, it was the bullets in between the tracers that would cause the real desired effect.

The bullets propelled out straight into the aft, right side of the suspect craft

There was a momentary series of white-hot flashes peppering the side of the craft before it turned another right.

He had made a full square – we were now headed back toward the more densely-populated part of the airport. A trail of smoke indicated the suspect craft was damaged.

"This course will return to where the suspect vehicle collided with the cargo vehicle," SON advised. "Thirty seconds ETA. There are several pedestrians there attending to the collision scene."

There was a moment where I again had direct view of the suspect vehicle's engine exhaust. We had moved closer to the craft.

The targeting system was yellow, which did not indicate a clean shot.

"Warning: you are not at a safe firing dis—" SON advised.

I fired.

And then I got on the air brakes.

The tracers bounced off the body of the flier – but a horizontal row of bright lights pinpricked the edge of the body of the craft, and then at one end, they went into the blue-white rectangular exhaust outlet.

Fortunately, automatic polarization of my craft's clearsteel activated.

I had a slight image burned into my eyes, even when squeezed shut, of the explosion.

I had barely set the equivalent of an anchor on the craft when --

The impact wave plowed into me.

The Tamagra was shaken hard. My seat straps clamped down on my body, and I felt my teeth rattle. I heard objects pelting the body of my craft.

As quickly as it had washed over us, it had passed. The clearsteel resumed a normal view and the seatbelt straps relaxed.

Things were quite a mess.

Large, smoking five-foot by five-foot chunks of metal lay on the pavement, the black swirls of smoke mixing with the light gray planet dust. There were buildings on either side, about two-hundred feet apart from one another. Fortunately, we had been going down the center of the road, so damage to the buildings was pretty much evenly distributed. But there was damage. I could see small space crafts in the building to the right, now exposed through shattered, hard-edged tears in the stone buildings.

"The crew cockpit ejected to the right, five degrees," SON said.

The swirling mess of smoke continued to obscure my view beyond; SON automatically adjusted the clearsteel display to an electronic format. Objects were now graphically displayed, in enhanced 3-D.

Yes, big chunks of space craft.

The "Stolen Vehicle Recovered" report would have an interesting foot-note.

About three-hundred yards further on, embedded into the side of a building, was an upended crew cockpit, sealed, looking fairly intact.

I would have to go up and over the damage to reach the crew cockpit. It was a narrow fit for me at ground level, but impossible with the debris ahead.

"Ranger Charlie Three Oh Eight, this is Security," SON transmitted to me.

"Checking for suspect vehicle survivors," I replied.

"We will be there in a moment," was the response.

"Medical units have been dispatched," SON advised.

Everyone is going to come to see something like this.

I put down by the cockpit. It had big dents on the body.

"Scan for decoys or explosives, SON."

"Negative. Sensors detect two life forms."

"Scan the structural integrity of the door mechanism," I ordered.

"There is an eighty-five percent reliability estimate that the door is functional," SON told me.

"Good enough for me."

Several ground police vehicles pulled up, all pointed toward the downed cockpit. A large, space-faring capable Security craft came up on my left side, setting down.

"Shall we?" I said. I unbuckled my seatbelts and headed for the doorway.

SON opened the side-exit as I grabbed a handy rifle from the now-unlocked gun rack.

Captain Burgess was coming out of one of the ground craft.

"Jesus Christ," he said, with a half-smile. "I knew you couldn't just stop by for a simple call without fucking up my place."

A thick plume of smoke blew between us as we got within a couple feet. I looked around at the smoldering pieces of metal and could taste the acidic smell of the burning synthetics and molten corona plates. Not to mention the gray dust of Taleon had a stingy, almost biting sulfuric odor. A few people described the air here as having just a touch of jalapeño in it.

Another breeze pushed more black smoke into us.

I swept the scene behind us with my hands. "What?"

"Fucker," he said, laughing. Burgess surveyed the scene and then shook his head. "Thanks."

He turned back to the cockpit. "Think they are all scrambled in there?"

"No, I think their craft's computer saw the shots coming and separated before I got them."

"Good thinking," Burgess said. "I mean, good thinking about taking them out. I had about twenty people on the ground there. This asshole would have killed all of them."

"How's the driver?"

"He's roughed-up. But, he'll be okay."

"Just want to knock on their door?" I asked.

"It may be *my* jurisdiction... but *you* started this crap," Burgess told me. "You clean it up."

A couple more planet-side Security folks appeared beside us.

"Alexi, I want you to meet Sheri Jordan, Chief of Operations," Burgess pointed to an attractive, short, black-haired woman. She clutched a heavy-caliber rifle, and her face was a bit flushed.

We shook hands. Hers were sweaty.

"Pleasure," I said.

She had a slightly tight-lipped appearance. "Hello." Then she let out a breath.

"Sheri, don't get all bent. Alexi and I go way back," Burgess said, clapping my shoulder. "He may get into the weirdest shit, but it's always legitimate." He looked at me, "She's just worried about the mess you've made here. And... she's always serious."

I looked around the craft, which was now surrounded. "Looks like your people are ready." Ourselves, we were positioned by the left front of my craft, using it as protection.

"It's your show, boy," Burgess said, finishing with a dry, Southern style "boy-ah".

It was my turn to give him a tightly-lipped, beady-eyed glare. He knew I hated to be called that.

Slinging my rifle down to my right side, I tapped my left collar communicator, "SON, start transmitting."

"Transmitting," SON replied.

"Attention inside the craft. You are under arrest. You will have thirty seconds to exit, or we will forcibly enter your craft. Injuries or death caused to the occupants will be of no concern, if we are required to use force."

It was only about five seconds before we saw the door pins spinning.

"Transmitting off," I said.

"Transmitting discontinued," SON replied.

About twenty weapons were pointed at the door as it opened. The door had been damaged, though, because instead of swinging on its hinges, it simply dropped to the ground, small pieces of metal showering down behind it.

The first suspect was a male, about thirty years old, five-foot ten, one-ninety pounds, brown hair. He wore the heavy clothing typical of ground cargo crew. He was clutching his right arm above the elbow.

"That's interesting," Jordan said.

He hopped onto the ground.

"Lay down!" I shouted.

He did as instructed, albeit slowly while favoring the right arm.

The second suspect came out: male, in his mid-twenties, five-foot eight, one-seventy or so, with black hair and a mustache. He had on jeans and a shirt.

"The getaway driver," Jordan noted aloud.

"Yep," Burgess replied.

If you're going to have an "inside" guy, you need an "outside" guy, too.

"On the ground!" I shouted.

"Wave your rifle around for emphasis," Burgess said.

"Good idea," I said, making a slight jabbing action with the rifle.

The suspect lay down.

"See? It works," Burgess told Jordan.

"Ready?" I asked.

"Go," Burgess said, his smile disappearing, all business now.

We moved out of the cover of the side of my craft and into the open. Our weapons drawn, we advanced on the two suspects, keeping a wary eye on the inside of the craft.

I heard Jordan's voice behind me. "You two worry about the guys on the ground. I'm watching the door."

Burgess wouldn't have her on his team, if she didn't know how to do her job. So I concentrated on the suspects.

As Burgess kept his gun trained on their backs, I approached and tossed handcuffs on them, one at a time. Then Burgess and I searched them quickly for weapons. I pulled out a handful of electronics and personal items and lay them on the dust-covered pavement. Burgess had a similar pile.

Another Security officer had advanced and paired up with Jordan. Crouching on their knees, they continued to position themselves between us and the door of the craft. Jordan glanced over at us.

Burgess looked at me and asked via facial expression.

I nodded.

Jordan and the other approached, splitting apart slightly, to either side of the door.

"Is there anything in there that's going to hurt anyone?" I lied, "Because that's my girlfriend, and if she gets hurt, I'm going to ram the rifle up your ass and fire the entire clip into you."

"There's nothing in there," my suspect said.

"This can't be happening, this can't be," the other said to himself, nervous and eager to say something.

"No kidding," Burgess said, "I'm missing lunch because of you idiots."

We watched as Jordan and her partner cleared the inside of the cockpit and gave us the thumbs-up sign.

"Now, what are you guys doing? Tell me."

They didn't answer me.

"See that yellow goo on the ground over there?" I pointed. There was a large area of brightly-shimmering yellowish liquid on the ground. "That's the corona oil. You know it's made out of superheated platinum extract. Anyhow, I'm going to make you stand barefoot in that stuff until you tell me the entire story. For about every two minutes you are touching that oil, you'll lose about a year of your life. And, well, my meeting doesn't start for a few hours anyhow."

Burgess looked at me, "We could move the meeting to tomorrow."

Chapter Two
Menance in our Midst

I finished dictating the report and told SON to sign it and transmit the criminal package to the Vega Melbourne system, the closest Ranger administrative station.

Jordan came over to my desk and plopped down into the chair in front of me.

The office was pretty nice, considering the distance from Earth and the regular shipping lanes. Typically, only heavy ore cruisers stopped at Taleon. A craft loaded with furniture must have been –

"Seized equipment, yes?" I asked Jordan.

She smiled. "Yes."

I recognized the sparkle in her eyes. "Your bust?"

"Yes. It was about a million and a half of office furniture, plus drugs, and other assets. All in a day's work," she said modestly.

"She's not telling you the whole story, is she?" Burgess asked, walking in.

"I did a routine inspection," Jordan told me, looking down.

"Routine, my ass." Burgess sniffed. "Alexi, it was as much 'routine' as your little 'routine' traffic stop today. Which, by the way, continues to grow." He pointed over to the window where one of his officers was leading another prisoner. "That makes five people – that makes this official as a 'conspiracy' case now. Thanks for the notoriety."

"All in a day's work," I said, giving Jordan a wink.

"Exactly," she replied.

"I'm going to remember that corona oil scam," Burgess told me.

"Amazing how many people that use that stuff as their source for transportation don't know it's harmless in that state," Jordan said, looking from her computer keyboard.

"Yes, amazing." I grinned at her.

Burgess sat in a nearby chair and rolled over beside me. "The original reason you are here?"

"Yes. Corrigan. I assume he's ready for me?"

"He's the baddest guy we've ever had here. I haven't been around someone that dangerous since the Delphi Mines."

"How did his identity get made?" I asked.

Burgess frowned. "Several of my crew let him slide by a dozen times on his trips through here. For about three months running. Someone noticed a trend and started doing a little investigating on *her* off-time." The last he added with emphasis.

"All in a day's work?" I asked Jordan.

She looked again from her keyboard, "Exactly."

I laughed. "She's making you look good."

"Someone has to do it," Burgess told me.

"So where has Corrigan been going for the last two months?"

23

Jordan shrugged, "I can't figure that out. He had irregular patterns. His craft self-destructed when we arrested him... no logs or history."

"What would a guy with a history of gun running be zipping out into the middle of nowhere?" Burgess asked aloud. "His usual stomping grounds have been in the Brehems Sector."

I leaned back and crossed my legs. "That's the scary question, isn't it? I don't see him trying to change his line of work. We have to assume he's been transporting weapons. We might have the supplier information. But we have no idea about the buyer. There's really no trouble going on here at your base, right? No revolutions or strikes going on?"

Burgess let out a hearty laugh before punching me lightly on my right shoulder. "There's a riot planned for eighteen-hundred today – but it's a secret. Don't let the cops find out."

"We were thinking about sending you to handle it," Jordan said, this time without looking up.

"It's that 'one ranger, one riot' thing we heard about you guys from Texas," Burgess said.

"Actually, we're much tougher now. We do two riots per Ranger."

Burgess stood to his feet. "It's getting deep here. Let's go see your prisoner. How long are you staying?"

"I'd like to spend the night here, and then get going in the morning."

"Then don't mess with seeing Corrigan tonight. He'll just irritate you. You're in 498-R, fourth floor."

"Awww, you kept my room for me," I said, standing.

"It took us these eight months just to get it fumigated," he said, walking to the door. "Nobody else wants to risk using it."

"Hey, Alexi," Jordan said.

I stopped and turned, "Yes?"

"All of us working people meet at eighteen-hundred in Twister's for drinks and dinner. You're invited."

"Thanks. I'll be there at about eighteen-oh-five," I said.

She frowned.

"Got to take five minutes to disperse two riots," I told her, walking out ahead of Burgess.

*****

"And then, wham! The beams flashed, and that thing blew like a mother fucker!" one of the security staff was saying, standing by the round metal table. He had his hands spread above him, chest high, expanding. "And smoke and T-dust. The Tamagra swooped in and..." He stopped after noticing me standing behind him.

Several others facing him around the table had been winking at him while he had been talking.

"Don't stop," I said. "I didn't get to see it from the outside."

Everyone laughed.

God, I felt like the old campfire chief hanging around the new recruits.

"When did you decide to shoot, sir?" one of the women officers asked.

God. Sir? Oh, jeeesh. How old did I look?

24

I looked at the name tag on the original story teller. "I decided to shoot when I knew that Officer Youst was in place as a witness. "

"Ranger Alexi Malind is a true living legend," Jordan said, walking up.

Several of the group of twenty gave her "heys" and "hellos". She was apparently quite popular.

"From all the war stories I've heard about you, I just think you need competition," I told every one.

Several of the group raised their glasses in the air to her.

"Christie, one for our real life legend here," Jordan called over to the bartender.

"Screwdriver," I said.

Jordan snorted. "Pussy drink."

"Not the way I make it," I said. "Christie, use the real stuff, hiding under the sink there."

Christie laughed and shook her head. "How do you remember that?"

There were several video monitors in the place, most with news, others with a recent rugby match, and one with an ice hockey game.

The table conversations turned into small groups, about sports, about one other guy and his attempts to find a date here among the ground maintenance staff, and others about a new wingback for the hockey team in Metroplex City.

"Ranger Malind, you're from Metroplex City, right? What do you think about Jeverson?" one of the guys asked.

"I saw him play in San Francisco about four years ago," I said. "He was really good then, in his rookie season. We'll see how he does in Texas with the trade."

"Stanley Cup this time?" another asked.

"Hell, I don't know," I admitted. "I might try to get leave and see a game or two of the series if they do. I haven't been home in two years – way overdue."

One woman jerked a finger at Jordan, "The Boss is a big fan of the Stars, also."

"Really?" I looked at her.

Jordan flashed her teeth, "I was in Houston when I was a kid. Back then, we were still hoping to get into the playoffs someday. But my older sister used to take me to Metroplex City for games. She was dating one of the support crew. So while she was hanging out with him in the sound room, I got to watch every home game for two years, sometimes from the team's box."

"No ice here," someone chipped in.

"Good thing, or the Boss would kick your ass," someone else laughed.

Jordan must have seen me scrunching my face.

"Ranger? You don't believe I know the game?" she asked.

I laughed, but told her honestly, "No, that's not what I was thinking."

She was unsatisfied. "Well?"

I looked around at the closest faces that were watching us. Then I leaned towards Jordan and whispered in her ear, loud enough for the others to hear. "I was wondering if I had seen you in the team box before and maybe had you confused with the cheerleaders."

She bit her lip. Then she said, in a normal voice, "Is that a compliment?"

"Absolutely," I replied.

"No. The cheerleaders said I was too fat, and the players said I was too skinny." Then, she smiled.

This was a good crowd of officers. I could tell they were a team that had a great amount of experience and camaraderie.

It was a different job out here at the edges of the Expansion. Earth and the Associated Central Systems had dramatically reduced crime over the last hundred years. Many people claimed that it just moved further out. Technological innovations had done a great deal to lower both crimes against persons and property theft; but not out here. Here... there was fast money, a rapidly moving population, and the people usually associated with a frontier environment.

People. And that was the key thing. I remembered reading something from the late 1800s from the old United Kingdom, before it was the leader of the United European Commonwealth. The newspaper article was touting the innovation of modern technology in the form of electric lighting – the streets would be safe for the common man to walk at all times; the bright, never-ending glow would deter even the most devious culprit. People. They commit crimes... not technology. And people like these here, they stopped crime.

There were a few grins around the table, pulling me out of my thoughts. Someone ordered more appetizers and drinks.

"Not for me." I declined the beer. "Early day ahead. I'm a little beat."

I stood and shook a few hands that were extended to me. Then I turned to Jordan, "Great crew you have here, Boss."

"Thank you, Ranger," Jordan replied.

I left the bar to several well-wishes. I headed down the hallway in search of my room.

*****

The shower here was a wonderful change from the lukewarm pencil-thin spray I usually had in my police craft. It was so decadent that it seemed like a good idea to take one before going to sleep *and* in the morning.

I wrapped a towel around my waist and stepped out of the bathroom, another towel in-hand, rubbing my hair.

The door chime sounded.

"Yes?" I asked, walking over to the desktop comm panel.

"Laundry," a female voice told me.

I had sent a half-dozen uniforms to the planet-side laundry for cleaning and minor repairs. They were supposed to be delivered in the morning, though.

I opened the door, but stood slightly behind it, with my left shoulder and my head peering out.

"The laundry department is always losing our uniforms," Jordan said, with a small hover-rack beside her. "Seemed like a good idea to make sure you –" she looked at me, and then she moved her head inside to take a good view "—have something to wear tomorrow. Or not."

She strode in, the hover-rack following, walking into the neat living room.

"Come in," I said as she sat down and then stretched out on the sofa. I pushed the door closed.

I walked behind the sofa, behind her.

Jordan had changed out of her uniform and was wearing snug dark gray leather pants, a light gray short-sleeve v-neck shirt, a wide black leather belt, and adorable black patent-leather calf-high boots topped off with three silver buckles on the outside.

"I would guess this is not a professional visit?" I asked.

She looked up at me and slowly, seductively licked her lips, painted in a light gray in the current fashion. She shook her head "no" once.

No, not a professional visit, I thought approvingly.

She stood, turned, and walked around the sofa slowly, dragging her right index finger along the couch. "It's a small duty assignment," she confided. "I can't do anything with the people I work with, of course. And almost everyone coming through here is a miner – or someone just looking for a trick."

Jordan was right. I typically was on solitary duty for two weeks up to two month's time, while she was permanently stuck with the same people that inhibited any action.

Jordan came around and put her right hand over my right hand, which had been resting on the edge of the sofa.

Then she came behind me and pressed herself against my back. I moved my left hand off of the sofa, but she put her left hand over it and slightly pressed down. Then Jordan rubbed her body against mine. It wasn't but a few seconds until my towel fell to the floor, covering our feet.

The feel of her cool leather pants against my ass was intoxicating as she continued to gyrate and softly bump my body.

She rubbed her lips against my left ear, she whispered, "Hold still."

I tried again to turn around, lifting my right hand.

She pressed harder, pushing my palm deeper into the cushion.

"No," she whispered.

She continued to rub against my body. Her left hand stroked my forearm, then the inside of my arm. Nails dragged lightly along my bicep, then down my chest, and slowed as she reached the side of my waist. Then she reached around and took me in her hand.

"Quite a handful," she whispered, her tongue darting a few times into my left ear. It was warm; her breath was moist.

Jordan moved back just for a moment; I slid my hand from under hers and grabbed her wrist, while twisting my body. The plan had been to turn around and push into her. But she instead pressed her body against mine, and I found myself off-balance, my back arching over the rear of the sofa.

She laughed and pressed herself against my erection.

"That feels good," she whispered.

With no chance of getting myself vertical again, I pulled her closer into me and together we slid down to the seat-portion of the sofa where my skin melted into her leather outfit.

"That feels good," I said, my pulse pounding in my ears.

She had straddled my legs, her boots on either side of me. Light glittered from the metal buckles.

Jordan moved lower and pressed her crotch against my erection. I slid back a bit further until my shoulders were on the edge of the sofa and my head was slightly hanging off.

She reached behind my head with both of her hands for support and then showered my mouth with several hot, wet kisses.

My hands found her belt buckle, and I snapped it open, pulling it to the side. Almost unconsciously, my hands moved inside her shirt. Her nipples were erect; her body shuddered as my fingertips massaged her.

27

"Pants," I managed to breathe out when we separated for air. There was no way that I was going to be on the bottom.

Jordan pulled up for a moment. Unsuccessfully, she tried to wiggle out of her leather pants, but they were too tight for her position. She tossed one leg over me and half-stood on the floor.

I pushed her down lengthwise on the sofa and pulled off her pants for her.

Success! I was on top.

In a half-second, Jordan had pulled her shirt away and tossed it overhead. I reached around her and was about to remove the leather bra when I realized that it looked really great on her. Her chest was heaving and she rolled her head to the side, eyes glossy.

It took another half-second to realize the bra was blocking me so it came off. I pressed my mouth around her left nipple and licked.

Jordan's right hand reached down to my hard erection. She took a firm grip, rubbing the head with her fingers as I pressed my mouth on her.

"Beeeeeep" I was jarred out of my skin as her comm chimed loudly. It beeped twice more. It wasn't the normal kind of notification tone – it was more ominous.

"Fuck!" Jordan exclaimed. She reached to the floor and dragged her belt over to the sofa. Then she unhooked her comm and pressed a button.

"Attention all units, armed robbery in progress, officer down, Section Nine, Level Fourteen, Gray Thirteen."

Jordan looked at me for a second, a totally pissed-off expression. She pulled on her shirt and saw the bra on the floor. Cussing under her breath, she pulled off the shirt, put on the bra, then the shirt, and her pants and boots. She headed to the door and flashed a smile. "Hold that pose!"

Jordan ran out the door.

I lay there, hands and knees on the couch.

I pressed my face into the seat cushion and could smell her.

And I lay there another moment.

Talk about bad timing. What? This place, with population of fifty-thousand people probably gets one armed robbery every six months!

I stayed there another moment. It seemed like I was there many moments.

A long, deep breath – perhaps it was a sigh – escaped me.

Of course, by now, all of my blood had returned to its normal, non-aroused designated locations.

Finally, I crawled off the sofa onto the floor.

Hmmmm. Think I should get involved with this local crime?

Yes, of course.

I snapped the towel from the floor.

But, I'd need to wear more than a towel...

*****

". . . are pinned down in the dock area!"

"Who has the east side entrance covered?" Jordan demanded.

"Franklin, here. I got it," a male's voice answered.

"Tamil, move over to the loading trucks as cover," Jordan instructed.

"I can't make it," Tamil replied. "Once I start moving over there, he unloads on my

28

position."

As I got closer to the dock, I lowered the volume on my comm. Two security officers were controlling the access to the area.

"I was listening, but what's the start of this thing?" I asked one of them.

"Hey, Ranger. Uh, a guy was trying to steal a craft and stabbed the pilot. A dock worker saw it and called us. Ali got shot in the leg trying to arrest the guy, but is going to be okay. The suspect is on one of the loading platforms. Those are built with steel plating. We cannot penetrate it with our guns. He's just firing down on us. We threw in gas, but he must have air, because it didn't slow him down."

"I've got armor-piercing in my craft," I said. "It will definitely poke a hole in that."

I heard a series of shots from down the hall.

"Everyone okay?" Jordan asked.

More shots.

"Tamil?" she asked.

"Okay, Boss. But I'm pinned down."

"Hang on. Don't be a hero. I'll give you a day's time off for every hour you sit there doing nothing!"

"Who's the suspect?" I asked.

"Did we get that?" one of them asked the other.

He picked up his comm and switched channels. "Fifty-eight to base. Do we have the suspect's I.D.?"

"Fifty-eight, it's Cedric Tomas."

"Roger."

"Local guy?" I asked.

"I've never heard of him," the first officer replied, fairly casual in his response.

The other one shrugged. He was dripping sweat.

"I'm going to get that gun – be back in about ten minutes. If you get a chance, tell Jordan I'm bringing something to the party." I stopped for a moment and looked at the first officer. "Things are getting busier than normal around here," I said.

"Not just the frequency – but the violence level, too," he shook his head.

*****

Jogging down the hall, I tapped my comm tag, "SON?"

"Receiving," was the reply.

"Search on 'Cedric Tomas'."

"Confirmed."

"I'm on my way to grab the Browning," I said.

"Confirmed."

After a few minutes I was inside the Tamagra and grabbed the gun from the rack. It snapped open with a click, and I connected the .50 caliber ammunition drum to it. This would be pretty effective.

"Records found," SON advised.

"Audio, condensed," I replied, running out of the craft, glancing once over my shoulder to be sure the door shut.

"Cedric Tomas, born on Netter Seven, age 48, white male. Criminal history includes felony convictions and misdemeanor convictions."

"What are the convictions?" I asked, shifting the weight of the heavy gun to my

29

other hand.

"Felony for 'Possession of Controlled Substance with Intent to Distribute', four year sentence, Carson Federal District.   Misdemeanor for 'Possession of Narcotics less than four grams', 180-day sentence, Carson Federal District. Misdemeanor for 'Possession of Narcotics', less than four grams, 180-day sentence, Hilo Federal District. Misdemeanor for 'Possession of Stolen Property', 8-month sentence, Corallis Federal Distict, Misdemeanor for 'Possession of Stolen Property', 90-day sentence, Brehems Federal District. Misdemeanor for –"

"SON, hold-on," I said. I stopped my jog. "Did you say 'Brehems'?"

"Confirmed."

"What was the stolen property?"

"Stand by."

I headed toward the scene at a brisk walk. I could hear a few gunshots in the distance, the echo cascading down the wide walkways. I passed the first intersection and check-point where civilians were being detoured by uniformed officers.

"The stolen property was computer equipment," SON told me.

"Check the other stolen property record... the one from Corallis. What was the property involved?"

SON waited just a moment, "Weapons."

"Oh, fuck!" I said aloud, making the connection.

I ran as fast as I could the last three-hundred yards of passageway and came to the original two security guards, plus another who had joined them.

"I informed the Boss that –" the first officer was saying.

"—give me your comm," I demanded.   He handed it to me, and I pressed the button.   "Alexi to Jordan. Urgent."

"Did you –" she started to ask, but I cut her off.

"— contact your holding cell. Make sure your officers are okay."

There was a pause.

The pause lengthened. Every second of delay in Jordan's response strengthened my suspicions.

Eight more shots were fired, ringing off the loading docks. Eventually, one of those would end up on a ricochet into this part of the building. I heard one zing off to the right. I turned around.

"Fuck! You," I pointed to the first officer, reading his name badge again. "Come with me!" And I ran back to my craft.

"Alexi, there's no answer," Jordan advised as we ran down the hall.

"I've got Officer Roberts with me," I huffed.   "We're heading to my craft.   The Browning is with Officer Cates, back at the scene. But I bet that Cedric is going to give up in a moment anyhow."

"What's going on?" Jordan said, her voice rising.

"Corrigan," I replied.

The series of alert beeps sounded over my comm and Roberts' radio.   The overhead public address speakers crackled as well and red "Alert" lights blinked at all of the hallway intersections.

"This is a station-wide alert. A prisoner has escaped from the Detention Center. He is armed and very dangerous. Do not attempt to interfere with this person. He is a white male, age 40, brown hair, brown eyes, six-foot three-inch, 200 pounds. He was last seen wearing a red prison jumpsuit. If you see this person, please contact the Police as soon as it is safe to do so."

"Notify your flight control to shut down all traffic," I told Roberts. I handed his comm unit back to him. I tapped my comm, "SON, pursuit mode!"

Roberts spoke into his comm, his breath puffing.

We rounded the hallway and saw the craft hanger. The landing lights on the Tamagra were already activated, normal running strobes blinking. I could hear the engines making the distinctive "pop-pop" sound as they warmed.

The door opened.

Roberts followed me into the craft. "What do you think Corrigan is going to do?"

"Corrigan is thinking five steps ahead," I said, walking into the cockpit. "Strap in."

I ran my fingers over the controls and the flight system activated. "SON, what's happening with flight traffic?"

"Flight control is advising one craft to hold position, but it has pulled out of Bay Six and is approaching the launch ramp."

Roberts was getting a near-simultaneous story on his comm. He nodded to me, "We're dispatching a craft to intercept."

Bay Six wasn't too far away from us. I started the engines and pulled forward out of the Bay. It was a left turn to Bay Six, but I waited a moment.

"Bay Six is that way," Roberts informed.

"Yes, it is."

I bit my finger. "How many crafts do you have on duty that can do an intercept?"

"One."

"Tell Flight Control that we are moving to assist your craft and that we are almost at Bay Five now."

"We're at Bay Two," he said.

"Yes. We're headed to Bay One. But don't tell anyone that."

"Roberts to Flight Control, we are headed to back-up FP-two. Tell them we're close. We're approaching Bay Five now."

"Received," Flight Control advised.

I turned toward Bay One and accelerated to approximately thirty miles per hour, staying low to the dust-covered pavement.

"Detecting launch from Bay One," SON advised after about thirty seconds.

"Let's get it," I said, pulling back on the controls and easing the engines up.

"Jordan to Roberts," Roberts called on my system.

"Go," he said.

"Cedric surrendered. Corrigan took down two of my people. He's launching from... Bay One. Goddamn it! Get that sonovabitch."

We cleared the building level and could see the twin-pinlight engines ahead of us of the true suspect craft, streaking nearly vertical toward the sky.

"SON, craft information?" I asked.

"Craft configuration is a Braker-Hughes Four-Forty," SON advised.

"That's fast," Roberts noted.

"It can outrun our present configuration," I nodded. But not when we hook up with the rest of my craft.

"SON, notify Celion base to stop all traffic. Break out the corona section and plot an intercept course for us. I want to be synchronized and back in pursuit in 60 seconds.

And keep tracking that Braker-Hughes."

"Confirmed."

"And see if anyone else is in his course... order them to turn around immediately."

"Confirmed."

"Hell, put out a general broadcast, too, all commercial channels."

"Confirmed.

"Corona section has disengaged, and we are on an intercept course." SON paused about five seconds. "One craft has been instructed to divert away from suspect course. General broadcast warning has been distributed."

"On-screen tactical," I said.

I noticed that Roberts' eyes were pretty wide.

The clearsteel display lit on the right. I could see an elevation map, with our craft in blue, arcing toward another larger blue set of numbers. On the "left" was the planet and in the middle of all of this, heading at a perpendicular angle, was the suspect ...Corrigan.

"Time to Corona intercept?" I asked SON.

"Sixty seconds."

"Roberts, hang on. This will likely be a bit rough. It's going to be as fast and as hard as the equipment can handle it – and it's not going to be done with passenger comfort as a concern. It'll feel like we're breaking apart, but it'll be okay."

"Thanks."

"The suspect craft is indicating a Corona drive signature," SON told me.

"No," I said. "In that thing?"

"Confirmed. Thirty Seconds to intercept."

The two blue arcs were getting closer.

I saw the corona section to our right, slightly below our elevation. Then the elevation was equal, and it was moving behind us – well, we were also moving ahead of it.

"Have you ever been on a wooden rollercoaster?" I asked Roberts.

"Yes, sir." He was clutching the side of his seat, fingers twitching.

"This is going to hurt much more," I said aloud. "Keep your head back against the headrest!"

The corona section disappeared from the right-side view out the clearsteel cockpit.

"The suspect craft is reaching Corona drive conditions.

"Ten seconds to Corona intercept," SON warned us.

The Tamagra was rattling. The rattling turned into jarring. I have explained this before as a ride on the worst wooden rollercoaster you could ever imagine.

"Thhh.iiissss... issssnooooor-mallll?" Roberts struggled to say.

I could hardly breathe out a reply, "Yessssss... Stttillll mooooreee."

It felt like we were about to tumble forward. We were lurching. My neck was hurting, and I struggled to keep my head pushed back against the headrest. My stomach almost turned over, and I felt bile rising. It seemed like SON read out more time, but I couldn't hear it.

In part technique and in part fear, I tried to guess the remaining time until it was over. *Five*? *Four*? My right ear popped from the pressure change. *When was this done*?

"Aaaaaaaaaaah" I heard Roberts shouting. I was unable to turn my head to look at him.

Then it stopped. The planet rapidly disappeared from view and we were pointed directly at the fleeing craft again.

"Complete," SON advised in the non-emotional tone.

I gasped for air. My teeth hurt. My jaw hurt. Actually, I felt like I had been beaten. I turned to look at Roberts. He had his eyes clinched shut, tears running down his face. I realized my cheeks were wet as well.

"Please report occupant status," SON inquired.

"Battered, but okay," I murmured.

"Run over by a truck," Roberts said. "But okay."

"The suspect craft is activating corona field," SON said.

I blinked. "Plot – analyze direction and cross-…" I took another deep breath. "And cross-reference model and pursue to overtake. And relay the information to Celion."

"Confirmed."

The suspect craft disappeared into a blue flash of light.

There was about a ten second delay, and then everything around us turned a brilliant blue. The clearsteel screen darkened and then we could see nothing.

We were in Corona Space now.

* * * * *

It had been two hours.

"Do you have anything to drink?" Roberts asked.

"Whew, yes, you're right." I unsnapped the seatbelts. "It's going to be at least another hour before we overtake Corrigan. He got a ten-second head start, but we are slightly faster than he is."

Roberts followed me back to the dinner table. "There's plenty in the refrigerator there, under the countertop," I pointed.

He opened the door, surveyed the bottles there, and pulled out a fruit drink. "Sushi?"

"I eat a lot of Asian food," I told him. "My first assignment was in Kyoto."

"Ahhhh. I've never been to Earth," he replied.

"You should get by there someday," I said, opening the lid to hot green tea.

"The suspect craft has changed course," SON announced.

Roberts looked at me quizzically, "I didn't think that was possible."

"It is *not*," I said, sitting back into my seat and pulling the straps around me. "SON, please explain."

"The suspect craft has changed course by ten degrees horizontal axis, three degrees vertical axis."

"Did it change speed?"

"Unknown."

"Can we do that?" Roberts asked.

"Course changes are not possible," SON replied.

"SON, you reported that the craft made a course change," I pointed out.

There was no reply.

"Interesting," I said aloud. SON doesn't get stumped very often. Especially since the upgrade in '88.

"SON, how soon until we reach the exact location that Corrigan's craft turned?"

"Unknown," SON replied.

"Do you have a range of locations?" I asked. This was a bit disturbing.

"The suspect craft's course change occurred over a distance of seven-hundred thousand miles."

"It's got to be a diversion," I said.

"Could he have launched something or separated a part of his craft while in Corona Space?" Roberts asked.

"That could be it. SON, have you been tracking all objects, or just the primary Corona signature?"

"Stand by."

We waited about two minutes.

"Additional echo or matter path has been detected."

"Damn," I said, looking at Roberts, "good idea. Corrigan wanted us to stop, turn, and pursue the larger craft.

"SON, maintain linear path on the echo."

"Confirmed."

"The question is," I asked aloud, "is that if he's using a smaller pod or something like that, then he has got to be expecting someone to be at his destination. SON, what's the rate of speed on the echo?"

"The smaller craft is decelerating. Estimate exit from Corona Space in ten minutes. Tracking capability of larger craft is now unavailable."

We had passed the turning radius of the craft, and we would never be able to track it now. It would disintegrate as it slowed as a result of the fatal course change.

"As soon as we drop out of Corona Space, scan for other crafts and have weapon systems ready," I instructed SON. "Calculate the new data and advise how much time behind Corrigan's craft we are."

"Four minutes."

"That is plenty of time for him to get into another craft and get going again," said Roberts.

"If he is in a hurry, but Corrigan always assumes someone is chasing him."

We waited until SON made the announcement, "Suspect craft has exited Corona Space."

"Get ready," I said.

The blue light outside flickered.

"Ten seconds," SON told us.

This countdown was uneventful.

"Disregard count," I said at "five".

The blue light disappeared and was replaced with a field of stars.

"Other crafts detected," SON noted.

"Give me a tactical," I said.

Ahead of us were two larger crafts and one very small unit. The small craft was nearly loaded inside the bay of the large craft on the right.

I turned slightly to head directly to the larger craft.

"Targeting solutions," I instructed.

The display changed to indicate optimum targets. Areas on the craft likely to cause total destruction were highlighted with red "X" and areas likely to disable were highlighted with yellow boxes.

The two crafts moved away from us. We had momentum on our side, but were still too distant to fire.

34

"Just give me red targets," I said.

The yellow boxes disappeared.

Both crafts kept abreast of one another.

The tactical display indicated that they were approaching a planet.

"SON, tell me about that planet."

"Unknown. We are in an uncharted area. Planet appears to be life-supporting, containing significant oceanic and atmospheric characteristics. No electronic signals are emanating from the planet."

"Look at that," Roberts pointed out the tightly-packed dots belted around the planet.

The planet was surrounded by a string of asteroids... or moons. There were maybe thirty of them, with the smaller ones on one side of the planet and with larger diameter moons rising as they got to the other side of the planet.

The two crafts were headed for the moon... moon belt.

The second craft broke off and started to arc to the right.

"He's going to come around," Roberts said.

"Yes, and that's not the one that we want," I admitted. It was the one sent to intercept us.

The second craft had completed its turn and was pointing toward us.

"Damn," I said, turning off the primary craft and aiming toward the secondary craft.

The tactical display lit up the entire front of the craft with red Xs.

"Strellion Mark Seven Flier," SON announced. "Limited front plating. On approach."

"Not for long," I said, firing.

We could hear the electric belts beside us feeding the guns with rounds. The tracer rounds streamed out ahead of us. I adjusted the position of the Tamagra a bit and then watched as the tracers skipped onto the front of the approaching craft.

It disintegrated, parts of metal expanding backlit by pockets of oxygen exploding into a brief flash of blue.

I banked low and left, going "under" the remains of the craft.

"Where's the primary target?" I asked.

The tactical display highlighted an object going through the moon belt. I changed our course.

"Good shot," Roberts said.

"They didn't even try to evade us," I noted.

The primary craft was doing a moon slalom, cutting through the pitted rock bodies, racing to the other side of the planet.

"We'll have him in range in just a moment," I stated, looking at our progress on the tactical display.

About twenty seconds later, I was on him, approaching from behind.

"Right about... now." I opened fire.

Tracer rounds were streaking ahead.

"Incoming fire," SON said. It almost sounded like an exclamation.

The tactical display showed something above us to our left. It must have dropped out from behind one of the moons.

We were hit.

"Hull breech in primary engine section," SON said. I heard a warning klaxon. I squeezed off another burst of fire at Corrigan before Officer Roberts and I were pushed down onto our side, aiming off-course.

"Primary suspect craft has been hit," SON stated.

I glanced to my left and saw that the first craft had changed course, also, and appeared to be alight. A pencil-thin blue streak of solidifying Corona oil left a line across the planet.

Our tactical display showed the new craft immediately behind us. Directly behind our primary engines.

"Emergency separation of corona unit!" I shouted. "Blow it backward now!"

Our lights flickered.

Then I did vomit. I heard Roberts lose it, too. We flipped, literally, the entire front section tumbling. More than once. Several times. In the dark.

Smoke.

We were on fire.

Soft red emergency lights came on.

"Collision alert," SON warned.

Somehow, I pushed the hand controls roughly to one side.

"Auto drive!" I shouted.

"Automatic Control System is not available," SON said.

"Alexi!" I heard Roberts scream – it wasn't a shout, but a scream.

We hit something.

And I passed out.

* * * * *

Screams. I kept hearing the screams... my name being called out. I was standing, trying to find who was calling me. Down the stairs, across the featureless hallway. There were stairs – but no steps. I couldn't see them, but I knew there were steps. Somewhere. I was using them, so they had to be there. If you can use it then – the scream again. My name. Who was calling me? I could not feel the step under my foot, but I knew it was there, pressing against my heel. I pressed again.

* * * * *

"Alexi!"

I shook my head.

We were tumbling. I saw the planet. Then I saw space. Then, the planet. The rotation was slowing.

"Alexi! I can't hold onto this anymore!"

I reached out with both of my hands and grabbed the controls.

"SON?"

There was no reply.

The rotation stopped, but we were still descending. Much too fast. I tried to press down on the speed controls with my feet, but there were no foot pads. Looking to my left, I found a switch to move speed control to my left hand steering device.

"I got it!" I told Roberts. He let go of his controls and fell partially back into his seat, groaning loudly.

I saw a streak of flame slightly ahead of us, on a wider arc, going down also. It

36

was Corrigan's craft.

Another streak of many pieces of brilliant blue flame was going down beneath us, on a steep arc. It was our Corona drive and the remains of the craft that had shot at us from behind.

I tried the secondary and emergency engine systems – nothing was working save for steering control. All of the electronic instrumentation was defunct.

Navigational detection was also dead. I didn't even know what I should aim for on the planet. Cabin integrity was still secure, though, according to the analog instruments.

And it looked like SON was not going to be much help.

"Can you land this?" Roberts asked between ragged gasps.

The back end of the Tamagra rattled.

"It won't be pretty, but we can only go one way – down."

"Do these have lift without the engines?"

"We have steering engines," I replied, over the increasing sound of vibration. "That's something. Are you okay?"

I couldn't make out his face with the diminished lighting. "No, not really. Think I'm hurt pretty bad."

"Where?" I could barely see him. Only a few analog instrument lights were active; all cabin lights were dark.

"My feet... legs ... can't feel them," he replied, his voice faint.

The craft was shaking harder. A few more lights flickered before dimming entirely. There was a clicking noise above my head, but it was too dark to see what was making it.

Additional instrumentation was failing.

And controls. Steering was getting sluggish.

"Actually, this is going to be a crash," I said.

Roberts did not reply.

"Hey?"

No reply.

I could not see his face now. I could barely see anything outside of the clearsteel. It was fractured, with small flows of liquid electricity leaking in a dozen spots.

"Roberts?"

We burst through the clouds. It was raining, I think. We were going very fast.

The primary deceleration controls failed.

I switched to the secondary system. Nothing. Not even a "click" when I pressed the touchpad.

"If this next switch fails, we are going to make a two-mile deep crater in about 30 seconds."

I pressed it.

Nothing.

"Detecting component failure," SON said. There was a noise I never heard before – an electrical-like hum in the audio system.

"SON! Fix it, fix it now!"

"Component transferred. Secondary braking system is routed via a non-propulsion source and is now active."

We lurched.

It could have been a decent landing – but we were too low, too fast, and too late to make it smooth.

We were coming down in a desert, in a kind of sandy depression below a mountain range. As long as I didn't hit one of those intermittent outcrops, it looked fairly flat.

The speed had slowed, and my elevation began to plane-out; but the vibrations continued.

All of the remaining ten or so instruments on the right side dimmed.

As I got closer, I could see that the "flat" sand was really closely-lined sand banks.

"SON, let's see if we can skip across the top of those!"

"Navigation is not repaired."

Then we plowed into the sand.

* * * * *

Silence.

Ticking noises. A fire? Wires?

I opened my eyes to bright light.

The right side of the craft was broken open. The clearsteel had a one-inch wide gap between the center of the window and the passenger area.

Rivulets of liquid electricity ran down the surface, creating a yellow, wax-like puddle on the right instrumentation cluster.

Bright light streamed in through the crack.

We were facing about 60-degrees upward, the left side of my craft buried down.

"SON?"

There were no instrumentation lights of any sort functioning. Everything was dead.

A few more drops of bright blue liquid electricity dropped onto the floor. I watched it glow for a moment – and then after exposure to the air it faded into a yellow solid.

Roberts was slumped in his seat.

With the light from the broken Clearsteel, I could see his feet... or where they would have been.

The entire bottom section of his area was mangled... to his knees. This didn't happen due to the final crash on the planet – he must have been struggling with the controls – even though his legs were mostly amputated by the crush of the impact in the moon belt.

It was a heroic effort on his part.

I looked at myself.

Everything seemed to be okay, mostly. My right foot was also hurt, though. The floor was buckled. I think my foot was broken... maybe it was my ankle.

There was vomit everywhere. Blood from Roberts' legs was splattered all over the cockpit. He probably bled to death.

Only a few wires hung down – most of the equipment was built into the frame of the Tamagra.

I unsnapped the belts.

Gravity seemed to be within a range I could work with – it was similar to Earth at about g. And the air – other than smelling like my breakfast, it was – distinctive, I think. I hadn't died yet, so it must be okay.

I realized I had a big cut on my right cheek. I touched my fingertips to it, and then looked at them. Okay, so all of the blood in here wasn't his blood – it was also mine. It was a deep gash.

I realized my upper teeth were sore. Sure enough, I had a very small piece of metal lodged into my gum line. It was numb. Or, I was in shock. Yes, probably both. I had to get back to the medical kit and pull this thing out, get fluid into my body, take antibiotics, and rest. But first, stop the bleeding.

With shaky hands, I lifted myself and gradually descended to the cockpit door. I had to use the manual hand crank to open it. Every turn of the crank made my jaw ache.

"Stop the bleeding," I said aloud, my voice a harsh whisper. I felt blood and saliva drool over my swollen lips.

Now the metal shrapnel was starting to hurt.

Was that a good sign that I could feel it?

The door... opened. Many turns.

Three of the battery-powered lights were working.

I was moving slowly.

Couldn't go fast.

Crawl to the medical counter.

Open lid.

Lid stuck.

Need to push latch to side.

Open lid.

Stop... the... bleeding.

Locking forceps. Grab them.

Open mouth. Do it.

Guide forceps.

Slippery. Wet blood.

Clamp on.

Pull.

Pull harder.

Pull harder!

Out now. Metal is out now.

Bleeding bad.

Mouth full of blood.

Look in mirror.

Two broken teeth. Bleeding. Pain.

Guide forceps.

Pull. Tooth shattered. Piece of tooth. Guide forceps... pull out... rest of tooth.

Tooth out.

Cotton balls.

Stuff cheek on inside. Pressure.

Medicine pads. Put on outside.

Injection, need. Find needle.

There. Needle in arm. Push.

Dizzy now.

Need to find spot to sit and –

Chapter Three
Desert Recovery

It was the shivering that woke me.

I opened my eyes and peered for a moment into the gloomy red darkness. My familiar orientation of the lighting in here was distorted because only the intermittent red emergency lights were on – and everything was pointing up.

Uncomfortable, I shifted my feet and felt a searing pain.

My right foot was broken – I had forgotten about that.

And the discomfort? Well, I was curled up on the side kitchen counter, sitting on the refrigerator unit, resting the left side of my head on the edge of the sink.

I was already mostly vertical, but I straightened my head and looked across to the cockpit. There was no light coming... it was dark outside.

There was a wind, creating a low, ominous "whirr" outside. It would be perfect for a haunted house soundtrack.

I reached under the counter and grabbed one of the two flashlights. I shined it on my right foot.

The boot was partially torn away. My heel was exposed. It was a dark purple and had a not-typically swollen area. It was very sensitive to the touch.

I reached into the medical kit, which was still opened and blood-splattered, and withdrew the hand scanner. I put it over my foot and read the illuminated display.

There was a short crack in the bone. There would be nothing to do except inject it with the proper medicine to stimulate bone growth. The hand-scanner sent data to the medical kit. A properly mixed syringe popped out of its holder. I stabbed my foot in a soft place and injected the solution before replacing the syringe into the kit.

I illuminated my face.

The bleeding was stopped. Gingerly, I removed the outer cheek patch. The medicine had stopped the bleeding and was already healing the skin.

I removed the blood and saliva-soaked mess of cotton balls and dropped them onto the floor (or, rather, the wall). Two gaping holes were on my gum line. Oh, the teeth. Gone. It was sore... and raw, but again, the medicine was healing the open wounds.

I did a quick check again, starting at my head and going down. It seemed that the head injury and foot injury were pretty much all the damage.

"SON?" I asked.

Nothing.

It was cold... about fifty degrees maybe.

I needed to change out of these clothes. They were horrible, and I wasn't warm enough.

Roberts' body. I had to get his body outside. Could I bury him in the sand?

What was outside?

I was thirsty.

The inside of the refrigerator was a wreck. Fortunately, everything was in unbreakable containers. The power source would keep it refrigerated for several months. But there were only four weeks of water and maybe three weeks of food. Once I was mobile, I'd have to start searching for shelter and food.

Moving very slowly, I pulled off my clothes and let them drop to the back wall. I was about to make my way to the restroom when I realized that the sink here was much closer anyhow.

After that, I eased onto the carpet and moved over to the sleeping section, pulling open the closet containing my clothes. I dressed slowly and put on warmer clothes and a uniform assault jacket.

It took about twenty minutes to do this complicated maneuver. Then I moved back to the kitchen and medical cabinet area.

I stood there – tears streaming down my face, jaw in pain from the missing teeth and punctured cheek.

It took another ten minutes to satisfactorily bandage my ankle, using formed plastic to make a protective hard casing around my ankle and heel. Then, I fell asleep.

* * * * *

Medicine, food, clothing, rest. What was on my list? *Roberts' body.*

Something else came to the top, though. I moved over to a computer system monitor and reached under the cabinet, removing a cylindrical, bright red device about two feet in length.

Bold block letters were on the side "DISTRESS BEACON." It would transmit for as long as ten years before the internal power unit failed. It was nearly indestructible under normal crash conditions.

Were Corrigan and his band here by accident? This planet was likely a rendezvous point; would activating the beacon attract the wrong kind of help?

Fighting them again would at least give me an opportunity to attempt taking their craft; otherwise I would never be rescued without the beacon.

It was a calculated risk. I pressed a button on it and slid the lock-catch "on" so it would be difficult to deactivate.

Besides, it was a good bet that the automatic distress signal had already been triggered – but since I could not check the computer systems to confirm that fact, this would add extra insurance.

Not that I had any idea where I was.

SON did not have this system on his charts.

And, with a sinking feeling, I realized that "help" would be looking in the wrong direction. They would trace the path of the larger decoy ship!

"Oh, damn."

I got over to the primary door. Of course the automatic systems were dead, but it did appear the hand crank would let it go. With several spins of the control, I opened the door just enough to peek out.

There was nothing to see.

I was down in the valley of a sand dune. There were not nearly as many stars in the night sky as I expected. There was a light being cast from my right, because it left a bit of a shadow on my craft. I looked up and observed that the nose of the Tamagra was slightly illuminated.

Reaching to my lower left, I pressed a switch.

The outside lights came on, flooding the entire area with imitation daylight.

I pulled my handgun out of its holster – you never know.

After making sure I could reach back into the door, I pulled myself through it and carefully put my feet down onto the sand. Then I let all of my weight down, but still held onto the side of the Tamagra's hand-grips.

Just because the sand was holding the weight of a space ship did not assure me that I wouldn't sink like a rock in water.

But it seemed to be okay. My booted (and bandaged) foot sank about a half-inch into the sand. I reached out and picked a handful. It was cold and of a fine grain. It reminded me of the sand that I saw in Basra about eight years ago on vacation.

"That's enough for a night trip," I said. I crawled back into the Tamagra and shut the door. Then I worked my way to the cockpit and started the gruesome task of cutting Roberts' legs from the twisted floor panels.

* * * * *

Two hours later, I was back outside, digging with a shovel. The grave was only about three feet deep – endless sand had continued to flow back into the hole. Finally, I dragged Roberts' plastic-wrapped and sealed body to the hole, pushed him inside, and covered the area with more sand.

There was light to one direction. I decided that would be designated as "east" for the time being. I had a compass inside, but had not looked at it yet.

I checked out the mound of sand. It seemed unlikely that his body would remain covered – but it couldn't stay inside the Tamagra with me.

"You will be missed," I said. It sounded insufficient. I did not know the guy well enough to comment about him. I knew his name, Ken Roberts, and I knew that he had never been to Earth. His identification documents were sparse. No photographs of anyone. He had one Identicard. His wristwatch had an engraving on the underside: *To Ken, Love Dianne.* Was Dianne his mother? His wife? Lover? Daughter?

Another moment, and I got back inside the Tamagra. I could feel the warmth of the morning sun headed this way.

* * * * *

I tossed the medical scanner out of the doorway, dangling it with a length of nylon cord. I left it outside the door for a minute before I retrieved it.

I reviewed the display and smiled. It was nice to have good news.

The ultraviolet light wasn't going to kill me. It was less intense than what Earth had these days.

But the air temperature was hot. The medical scanner identified one-hundred degrees. The Tamagra was heating a bit. It had great insulation – but there was still the crack in the front clearsteel to deal with.

I spent about an hour repairing and sealing the clearsteel.

Then I turned to the inside of the Tamagra. It took another two hours to track down the power lines to the interior lighting and then another two hours to repair them. The core power system seemed to be fairly intact. But the primary and backup computer systems were down.

After a snack, I investigated the primary computer system. It only took about one minute before my conclusion was reached.

"Totally dead."

It was physically damaged. The core unit was wedged between the living quarters and the corona drive. Several super-heated metal bullets had burrowed through the length of the computer hardware. It was so bad that any repair was impossible under the best conditions. It was a replacement situation.

I went over to the backup system.

Thinking with their heads, the design crews had put the backup hardware system in another section of the craft, the left side, mid-ship. But that part of the Tamagra was now buried in sand and it was the part of the craft that had received the hardest impact from the crash.

It took about ten minutes to cut through the twisted, buckled metal under the cabinets. The typical entry panels had been smashed.

I laughed. This was how SON was functioning until the crash. At least the backup system got me to the ground. If it hadn't been for the backup system, I would have been a melted pile of goo fifty feet down into the sand.

Speaking of goo, I wondered if Corrigan made it down in one piece. He was on an easier trajectory than I was, but his craft was tumbling. For just a moment, I had seen another explosion on the side of the second craft – it was falling apart as it hit the atmosphere. Hard to believe anyone could have survived that.

I looked around at the wrecked and object-strewn interior of my craft. My hand probed the skin sealant over my cheek as I picked up objects from the carpet.

"Hard to believe anyone could have survived this."

* * * * *

Adjusting the magnification of the binoculars a bit, I could see shrubbery around trees.

I was standing on the top of my neighborly sand dune. The sun was directly overhead and would have been cooking me if it weren't for my uniform cowboy-style hat.

To the east and north was a vast desert. It went to the horizon... maybe hundreds of miles... maybe only fifty miles. It was too difficult to tell without a vertical object to measure against.

Fortunately, to the west was the uprising of a rock wall with green vegetation along the top. In fact, I was in a canyon of sorts. It appeared to curve as it went south toward the east slightly until it disappeared at the horizon.

I activated the range finder in the binoculars. Ten miles to the cliff face.

That wasn't too bad.

But ten miles in this sand was a bit deceptive. The sand would make it slow-going. Those ten miles were as the crow flies. Since I would be going down, then up, then down... *hell*. The frequency of these sand dunes was going to be a bitch. They were about five-hundred feet apart with thirty-foot elevation changes. And that was assuming the characteristics of these four or five closest dunes were the same during the entire trek.

I used to think that walking in sand was no big deal. Then a colleague took me out on sand dunes near Kirkut. After about ten minutes of that crap, I saw his point.

But, I knew that in a day or two, I'd have to evacuate here and find a reliable source of food and water. My foot was healing nicely and should be ready for walking in another day.

I headed back to the Tamagra and to figure out what to pack for the first excursion. Assuming I found a good place to make camp, there would be several trips back and forth to my craft to get supplies and equipment.

* * * * *

It was the third day. There was one backpack. And two bags I had packed on top of a sled made of the plastic runners from my bed. At least many of the pieces of the Tamagra were light-weight.

I took half of the dry emergency rations and packed them with me. The bulk of my supplies consisted of liquids. And ammunition. If I needed to survive on the land, I might have to play "hunter" man. Assuming there was food.

I checked my hand-held computer. It was able to zero-in on the location of the Tamagra from pretty much anywhere on the planet by tracking the distress beacon. Provided it did not get too covered in sand...

But, it did not appear the sand shifted that much. The grave was still covered. There was a dust-line on the body of the Tamagra from the sand. Who knew if a storm ever came out here.

I looked into the sky. I had not seen any clouds yet.

Or birds. Maybe they did not fly over this way. If this desert was as expansive as it appeared from space, birds might not be able to make it across the thing.

But, with vegetation ahead, it seemed a good bet there would be animal life.

I hooked the sled to my belt and then slung a rifle into my hands.

With one glance back at my battered Tamagra – my only way home – I walked up the dune.

And I kept my eyes open for giant sand worms.

I tried to assure myself... *It was just from an old movie.*

* * * * *

It was a clear example of how conditioning and exercise can make a difference.

But it had still been a hard day.

As I neared the edge of the canyon, the sound of water gradually became louder. This was good news.

The dunes became more flat and longer in frequency. Finally, I crossed the top of one sand dune and was able to see a fast-moving stream below the sloping sand.

The stream was narrow, perhaps fifty feet wide, straight ahead. The low, desert-side had an irregular line of low carpet-line vine running along the bank. The other bank had been cut into the rock, eroding it for countless years.

Paranoia comes with my line of work; so suffice it to say that I didn't rush to the stream.

I looked upstream and down. Nothing was moving.

There was a chance that other creatures stopped by here. But I didn't see anything that --

A bird swooped on me.

I dived to the sand, and whipped my rifle upward as the bird headed back to the rock cliff.

In a second, it was already two-hundred feet up and over the top of the ledge, beyond sight.

Two-hundred feet.

That was a long way to climb without any gear.

I looked back at the water. That could mean that there would be fish to catch – and eat.

Birds might mean other animals. Otherwise...

I've never been much for eating duck or other birds, but I might be the author of a new cookbook soon.

It took me another two minutes to get to the water's edge. The consistency of the sand changed somewhat, but it still remained solid. The ground vegetation became thick.

I put the medical probe into the water, and then I looked at the display.

It was pretty clean. There were limited unknown bacteria, but the scanner indicated they were probably harmless. It recommended a medical precaution for me.

I sat down on the grass, unhooked the sled and located the larger medical kit. After a moment I had dialed-in the settings for a solution and then gave myself the immunization.

The medical scanner recommended that I wait 48 hours before consuming the water; after that it should be fine to ingest. That was okay – I had five days' worth of fluids with me now.

It occurred to me that I was not keeping a log or diary. Maybe later. Who would want to read about a crazy bird chasing me, anyhow?

There was a nice breeze coming off the water, too. My back was warm; my face was cool.

Under different circumstances, this place would be a tremendous discovery. Right now, it was good to be off the sand. I could pitch a tent here for awhile and rest. The order of survival was shelter, water, food.

The water current looked gentle and the depth not too deep. There was nothing swimming around. From time to time, occasional pieces of plant-life floated past.

I changed my gaze from looking at the water and turned my eyes toward a sound behind me.

Someone was standing there –

Chapter Four
Problematic Introductions at KoVer

I was knocked down to the ground, my right shoulder exploding in pain. Instinctively, I rolled left several times, ending in a prone position. My left hand automatically reached across my body during the roll and had reverse-drawn my handgun, leveling it in front of me.

A human-shaped person wearing a hood and cloak moved toward me, a club in hand.

"Stop!" I warned.

He, or possibly *she*, was of very slight build, only about five-foot tall, wearing light brown garments. There was a hesitation, and then he waved the stick at me; but did not move in.

"Drop the weapon!" I shouted, much louder this time. What I couldn't accomplish with comprehensible language, I could encourage with the increased volume.

"Shri-egho," replied a young male's or female's voice. It was said nearly tone-neutral. I could not guess the emotion behind it.

"Drop... the... weapon," I repeated, trying to contort my face into as menacing an appearance as possible. I jabbed my handgun once in the person's direction.

At that point, he seemed to notice the gun. He looked at it for moment, and then backed up a step. Then another step. One more. "Ee-tah. Ee-tah anjek!" he cried and turned to run.

I holstered my gun and gave pursuit. He was not going to be permitted to call for reinforcements.

My long stride and experience running had me overtaking the person in just about thirty yards. I knocked his feet out with a kick to the back of his right calf, while I grabbed the club from his left hand.

Into a pile of sand he crashed, with me right on top, reaching for his hands.

Overpowering him was quite easy. I pulled his hands behind his back, and I swept off the hood.

It was a human-like young adult or teenager, probably a male. Short, straight blonde hair over gray eyes, smallish lips, a curvy face, not too dissimilar from an Asian variant. The combination made me think of a Swedish-Japanese genetic similarity.

"Ooommmmfff" he tried to shout, but my left hand stopped that.

"I do not want to hurt you," I said softly. "Calm down."

Still he continued to struggle.

The attempted call for help signaled something else to me; there were probably other persons nearby.

What to do? Killing him was out of the question. Letting him go was risky. If I did that, and tried to run away, I might be forced into a fight with others. Of course, whatever way he ran to, I could run in the near-opposing direction... on foot.

Maybe they were actually a friendly people. I probably looked very frightening. I was still dressed in my uniform with all of the accoutrements. Plus, there was a good coating of blood on my clothes, which were torn in a couple of spots. Hell, looking like this I would probably frighten my boss.

"I know you do not understand me," I said. "But I'm going to let you go now. Okay?"

He struggled a bit more.

I slowly let my hand away from his mouth.

He did not make a sound, but looked wildly at me over his shoulder.

Then I let go of his hands, pointed ahead and said, "Shooo."

He again looked surprised.

Then he took off running again. North.

That was fine.

I turned and jogged back to my gear, gathered my items, and then moved east. After twenty minutes, I turned due-north again, trying to parallel the river.

The terrain was becoming green, with low weeds breaking through the sand. Soon there were small shrubs and sparse patches of sand. After another thirty minutes of walking, the sand was replaced by outcroppings of rock ledges. It was a geographical escarpment; everything north of it was full of vegetation. Normal-sized trees were growing and small insects flittered about from plant to plant.

I was walking through a narrow valley of sorts and came to a small rise. There I stopped, looking down.

I was on the south edge of a village.

Perhaps a hundred simple-looking structures were scattered about, several of them larger, lodge-type buildings. It looked much like a ski resort in the summer. People moved around, going about their business. I dropped to the ground, resting on my elbows.

I reached into my pocket and put on my glasses which sensed the presence of my body and activated. A photodigital image was transmitted to my eyes; moving objects were highlighted, as were living creatures as they sat and walked inside their homes. There were no indicators of energy signatures. I took the glasses off and put them back into my pocket; these were much more fragile than others, but easier to wear. However, I did not need to frighten anyone here given the trouble I'd already stirred up.

I guessed that I could retreat southward a bit, then move east another half hour before heading north again, to circle around the village.

And, exactly, where was I going?

My goal was to find a place to live for awhile. At some point, I would have to encounter the locals again.

But I was tired. My ankle, though treated and healing quickly, was still in slight pain from having walked on it. The heat of the day was wearing down my energy level. I had been walking for almost an entire day.

Being social right now was not on the top of the plan of action.

"Fre fre oh loe fre she!" I heard shouted from behind.

I rolled over, pulling out my handgun.

There were six robe-wearing persons a bit below me, spread out slightly.

"Fre fre!" I heard shouted from the distance of the village, just over the hill.

I peeked and saw another six persons approaching.

On this slight hill I had a great viewpoint of the surrounding area. So I could see three persons riding from the south; they were on an animal that looked... well, it looked like a camel, sort of. It was without a hump, but it was gangly with ridiculously long limbs.

My finely-honed police instinct told me that I was in deep shit.

"Hello!" I said loudly to those on the south. The riders were getting closer. Then I repeated my greeting in Dutch and Japanese... *couldn't hurt to try.*

Shouting was coming from the west now. I couldn't tell what they were saying, but I had little doubt it was concerning me.

Tactically, this was a terrible position. I suspected I had superior firepower, however.

One of the three riders raised a hand, and they all slowed to a stop, about fifty feet away.

To the north, two more riders arrived and stopped, also about fifty feet away. I saw several shiny metal items strapped across the backs of the riders' waists. They had to be swords.

Yes, this was a bad situation.

I studied the three riders to the south. All wore robes and hats. Their animals had impressive equestrian-style equipment which glittered in the bright sun.

The riders in the group on the north were also wearing the same robes, but in patterns of beige and brown. The riders were each about 5'10" or so. I noticed that six pedestrians of the group had gone to a kneeling position when they stopped.

"Iz-ta, soorel," stated the apparent leader to the south. With a wave of an arm, the person pushed back his robe.

I was visibly shaken.

She was human and strikingly beautiful.

Well, mostly human, like the younger one. Very similar to human form, with minor... differences. It was hard to grasp all of the details at the moment.

But "beautiful" struck me again as the right description.

Black hair fell from the hat, which she still wore, draping down between her breasts. She wore a light-gray snug-fitting shirt or blouse that was belted to either a skirt or pants – it was hard to tell from my position.

"Soorel Brieneia!" she said with a decided intensity.

"Yes, I will accept your surrender," I replied.

She started to move my way, but I aimed my gun squarely at her head, "Stop!"

She was able to detect my intent and held her position.

"Ee-tah, fre, oh mit yun derel vendraal," she replied.

I noticed that one of the kneeling persons stood and removed the robes and hat.

It was a male. He had a strong build and looked young. He was wearing only a loose wrap of cloth around his waist, drawn between his legs. A thick metal collar encircled his neck.

One of the others standing near him said something. He looked afraid, but then walked toward me.

"Stop!" I ordered, swinging my gun around to him.

He stopped, obviously in fear.

"Derel! Ee-tah fis" the leader ordered.

The near-naked man walked again toward me.

I fired a shot into the air, just over his shoulder.

He stopped again, crouching low.

I heard a rustling around me. And then I recognized that every rider had an arrow drawn on a bow – pointed directly at me.

Tactical superiority had just given way to negative probability.

"Oh, oh," I said. I was outnumbered on two sides, six-to-one. The odds were almost in my favor. Slowly, I put my gun into its holster.

The man who had been walking toward me had a relieved expression on his face.

"Frey!" the woman said, but it sounded more like an inquiry.

"I have no idea," I said, shaking my head.

I slowly made a drawn bow movement with my hands and then pointed at the woman.

"She ka chi," she said and all of them lowered their bows – except for her.

"Frey?" she said again.

I pointed at myself. "Alexi."

"Ahh leee hee?" she asked.

"Alexi."

"Ahhlexee."

I nodded, smiling slightly. "Yes,"

"Sovee." She nodded.

"Ahhlexee, mit yun derel vendraal," she said with a bit of menace in her voice.

I did not move.

The riders trained their arrows on me.

There would be no way I could get all six of them. Three on one side, yes, but not the other three behind me. If all their shots hit my clothing, I'd be fine. But if one arrow went to my neck or head, I'd be mortally wounded.

"Ahhlexee, mit yun derel vendraal," she said again, this time unmistakably a threat.

I could see one of the riders next to her, a smaller version, having difficulty holding the arrow. Once one of them let them fly, the other five would be instantaneous.

"Koh loe ev!" Another figure approached from the south. It was female, dressed in similar attire, but wearing shoes instead of boots. She was followed by three males. She approached the leader.

I believe the leader noticed my continued and concerned gaze at her younger, nervous associate. She said something softly, and the rider aimed the bow at the ground, letting the arrow move slightly forward.

The leader and the newest person talked for a moment. Then the leader rode her *horse* over to one of the three males. He was the one I had encountered earlier.

She spoke rapidly and firmly, and he cowered. She pulled out a whip and let it fly, wrapping his bare thighs with it. It cracked as he howled for a moment.

She rode back over to the other two riders.

"Shemana, aarl aarl frey!" she shouted.

"Tie die, aarl arl!" I heard a female voice on the north side reply.

"Ahhlexee, soo des see vedvon," she told me. She took her right hand and made a "gun" with it, pointing to the sky and said, "Raaaa!"

"Gun," I said.

"Gun," she replied. She pointed to the ground.

I had a backup gun in my boot, plus the rifle over my shoulder. This seemed the only way out of this situation alive. Plus, I needed to develop relations with these people.

Without a sound, I set the handgun on the gravel-covered footpath.

The leader made a gesture for me to move away. I obeyed.

"Tharka. Drella," said the leader.

The two figures next to her dismounted from their horses and approached me, cautiously, their bows near their sides. The hood on the smaller one slipped off – it was another female. She kept her bow pointed at the ground.

When they were within teen feet of me, the other dismounted rider put her bow over her left shoulder and reached over her right shoulder to cross-draw a short, shiny sword. Looking into the hood, I could detect what I thought was also a feminine face.

At that moment, I stepped back another foot, not so much out of graciousness about the handgun, but because I was hit with a realization that every female was armed and mounted on horseback while all the males appeared to be servants or slaves.

I heard others approaching from behind, close.

Even though it was a very different position than I usually found myself in, I slowly went down to a kneeling position and lifted my hands into the air. I did not want to get shot.

Hands pushed me down to the ground. I barely got my hands out to catch my fall. Then, with complete skill borne from her experience, my hands were pulled up and behind my back and snugly bound by something that felt like wide leather bands. A band was wrapped around my neck, snugly. I felt it tied or connected behind me. Then my wrists were connected to my neck, pulled uncomfortably. If I pulled my hands too low on my back, the bands tightened around my neck.

They rolled me over.

The leader touched my shirt and fingered my badge for a moment. Then she tried to pull it off with a tug, but my uniform material would not tear. She looked over the side and saw the pins. She released the catch, and the badge came off into her hands.

Hands grabbed under my armpits and lifted me to my knees.

"Iz-ta, brieneia!" the leader ordered.

"We might need to try this all over again," I said.

She slapped me, hard.

I blinked and shook my head.

"Iz-ta, brieneia," she said.

"I have no idea what you are saying," I protested.

"Leil, Iz-ta ufanta ufanta hi-ri-tovv," she explained.

Two hands grabbed my hair and pushed my face down to her boots.

The hands held my head there.

Then they pushed my lips hard onto her boots for the count of thirty seconds. My teeth mashed into my lips.

Oh. I get it.

"Brieneia," someone said. Then I was let up for air, still on my knees.

"Brieneia," I said.

Someone hit me across the back of my head, and I fell over.

It seemed best to lay there on the dirt for a moment. I looked at the women's boots.

The leader had an animated conversation with the other women. Then there was a question.

One of them knelt down and searched my clothing, removing my belt, holster, equipment, and gun.

I remained still as another pulled off my boots.

There was a bit of an exclamation when the backup gun fell out of the boot.

Then they performed a very thorough search.

One knife.

Another knife.

Utility tool.

Then the handheld computer.

Flashlight.

One woman made a sound, and a couple of them opened my packs.

The leader told them something that sounded like "Keep the hell out," and they shut the packs.

The leader said something else, perhaps to me.

I continued to lay there.

"Brieneia," she said.

I struggled to get to my knees.

She was standing right next to me.

Okay... I kissed her closest boot. I had to forcibly push my wrists higher up my back to prevent the leather strap from choking me.

I did not receive a blow to the head, so I assumed that we were making inroads on the language barrier.

"Any chance you'll let me go?" I asked.

There was silence.

I looked at the leader. Her five female friends were now all un-hooded and displayed a range of ages. Four of them had a not-too-friendly expression. But the leader and another woman appeared amused.

"Alayhee," the leader said. Then she pointed at herself, "Sklera kre-tah-la."

"Sklera kretahla," I replied, trying to nod my head a bit in her direction.

Being insolent wouldn't gain me anything at the moment. Perhaps if they recognized that I was not a threat, they would let me go.

I noticed that all of the males remained in a kneeling position, eyes downcast.

This was, I hoped, only an isolated situation.

"Alayhee, koo ret sa doh-la?" Sklera asked.

"What?" I asked.

Sklera waved her hands around her, expansively, "Koo ret sa doh-la?"

"Oh," I said. I was not able to point with my hands, so I looked at the sky.

"Sa doh-la?" Sklera asked again. A couple of the women looked at each other with quizzical expressions.

"Way up there, Sklera," I said, looking straight up.

"Defal!" one of the younger women exclaimed, about to slap me in the face with her open hand.

I was trying to move as Sklera blocked her.

"Alayhee," Sklera said, taking my chin in her left hand. She pointed at me with her right finger, "Frey Alayhee." Then she pointed at herself, "Sklera kretahla."

Alexi, the man? Sklera, the woman?

The woman whom I believed was named Tharka, who seemed to be more temperamental also, chuckled. She snapped her fingers. One of the young males crawled to her and kissed her boots. She reached down to his neck and pulled him slightly up, displaying a black metal collar that encircled his neck. "Frey," she said.

My wide eyes must have been quite amusing. All of the women laughed.

"Frey," Tharka said, pointing at me.

"Aleckshe," Sklera said, still holding my chin. She pointed to the sky, "Koo ret sa doh-la erhloo?" She pointed again upward, "Erhloo?"

"Erloo, Sklera Kretahla," I replied. "Big Erloo."

Sklera let go of my face. She reached into her pants and pulled out my badge. She ran her fingers on it, looking closely at the polished metal. She looked at Tharka, who came close to her.

I noticed that Tharka's male stayed in his kneeling position. None of the males were apparently watching what was going on.

Sklera handed Tharka the badge. They spoke rapidly – too fast for me to catch much, except that the words "Alexi" and "Erloo" were mentioned a few times. Tharka asked Sklera a question, to which Sklera nodded. Tharka reached over and felt my uniform shirt, which was a pull-over polo-type shirt made out of a modern material that was soft, water repelling and bullet and knife resistant.

From nowhere, Tharka had a knife at my neck. She held the leather strap around my neck with her right hand, and with her left hand pushed the point of the knife into the loose collar of my shirt, expecting to gently cut it. She pushed a bit harder. The knife would not penetrate the material.

The women spoke among themselves for a moment. I noticed that one of the males sneaked a glance.

Tharka said something to Sklera. Sklera nodded.

Without a word, two of the women came to my back and fastened leather bands around my ankles and tied them together with a thick leather line. My ankles were only two feet apart – enough to let me walk slowly, but prevent me from running.

Tharka said something else to Sklera.

Sklera flashed a set of even, perfect teeth and came over to hold my chin again with her right hand. She covered my right ear with her left hand for a moment, feeling me. Then she slowly dragged a row of fingernails along my left cheek, stopping under my chin. She smiled again and looked back at Tharka, nodding.

Sklera let go of me and walked over to her horse. Before she reached it, one of the males got to his feet and held her horse steady, exposing his bent-over back so she could use him as a platform to mount the saddle.

"Drahhl," said one of the women behind me.

"What?" I asked.

Two strong hands yanked me to my feet, thankfully by lifting under my arms, or I would have been gagging.

"Drahhl," one of the women ordered, pointing to Sklera.

I slowly walked over in her direction, stopping a few feet away.

The other women mounted their *horses* (I still did not know what they were called) and the males filed in behind them.

Sklera began to ride, and I had no choice but to follow her on foot.

* * * * *

53

Fortunately, it wasn't a long distance before we got to the edge of the village. After about two miles of changing terrain, we approached what appeared to be the village I had attempted to circumvent earlier in the day – only this time we came in from the east.

The narrow path had widened into a dirt-and-gravel-mix road, about fifteen feet wide. Hand-painted signs on posts were written in a foreign script, composed mostly of single curved lines with dots.

We passed two women riding the opposite direction. They each had similar horses, but the saddles and personal clothing seemed, well, of less stature than what my captors had. Also, the other women gave way to our group.

It appeared that the robes and hoods of the women and men served only one purpose – to keep the sun from bearing down on them. I was starting to feel the effects of the mid-day sunlight. Again, thank god, the village was close.

Most of the one-hundred structures were made of a shale-colored stone, layered in brick-like fashion. The structures were typically one-story high with slightly angled flat roofs made of timber. There was about a two-foot high gap between the ground and the bottom floor of all of the buildings. It was either to allow high water to pass-by or to provide airflow for these hot days.

The village streets were made of a dense amount of gravel and crushed stone. Sidewalks of flat shale ran on both sides. I envisioned a cross between an American Old West town and an Oxford village.

There were trees and shrubs and many lush vines racing along fences and sides of residences, meticulously steered along the corners of the buildings. Okay, maybe American Old West meets Oxford meets Japanese Garden.

And people. Many people were moving about. I was jarred again by the observation that the males all appeared to be subservient to the females. There were even a few women who pulled males along by a leash attached to the metal collar!

Finally, I saw a few male children, about ages six or eight. They were uncollared. But there was an older girl, perhaps ten years old, playing a game with a large round ball. As we went by, there was a momentary dispute, but she said something, and everyone went back to the game.

When we got close to a few of the village people, they stopped what they were doing and looked at me. What happened, actually, was that everyone would look, and then the female would order any males present to look down to the ground.

It was a guess on my part, but it seemed that the more people we passed by, the higher in the saddle Sklera rode.

I had been taking in so much of the village that it took me another moment to recognize something. I had found a new race of people! Intelligent people.

And, just how are you going to tell someone about this great discovery of yours?

Sklera said something, and we stopped abruptly.

It appeared we had reached our destination at a heavy wood, open gate. It was a series of buildings, on a slight elevation from the rest of the village. There was a two-foot wide, ten-foot high shale wall encompassing a wide compound that ran at least a thousand feet to my left and right.

Two women stood on either side of the twenty-foot wide entrance, bearing heavy swords. They were protected from the heat by a fabric canopy that covered the gate. One of them made a hand gesture to Sklera. It involved taking her right hand, holding it horizontally, palm down, and basically saluting from her left shoulder – instead of bringing the hand to the forehead as we did on Earth.

Sklera returned the salute, and we entered.

The compound was fairly large – open grounds to the left that were about a thousand feet by a thousand feet. At the end it turned into low-ceiling structures, all very uniform in appearance. A gravel path continued at the gate here and ran perfectly straight at least two-thousand feet ahead. On the right side of the path were several one- and two-story structures, solidly built of shale. I could see holes in the walls at regular intervals – either for viewing an enemy but, more likely, as archer holes for defense. The roof of each of these buildings had a low shale wall with wooden poles exposed from the top at regular intervals as well.

Our group moved over to the large structure that appeared to be the main or central building. Several colorful banners hung from the ceiling beams. A heavy wooden door opened, and two women exited. They had the same plain robes draped over their left arms.

Each wore a short skirt of brown leather and light, tan leather, sleeveless vest, buckled with several straps across the breasts and at the midriff. They were both very slender, from a human-perspective, and very... well, very sexy looking. They wore dark brown, almost chocolate-colored calf-high boots with short heels. A wide brown leather belt had several shiny metal items hooked on with a variety of rings.

"A troes!"

I realized they were both looking at me looking at them.

One moved toward me, closing half the twenty-foot distance before Sklera said something. She stopped and asked Sklera a question.

They conversed for a moment, with the woman on foot asking a few questions. Finally she smiled and put both of her hands on her curvaceous hips. Then she laughed. It was a funny sound because it wasn't our "ha ha ha" kind of laugh but more like a "oy oy oy" sound.

She slowly approached me. I held my ground, but was more than a little nervous. Something about her countenance suggested that she could be trouble. Call it my finely trained police instinct... it was sending me warning signals.

She stopped, about a half-inch away from my face, looking directly into my eyes.

Her eye brows were either sculpted or naturally razor-thin. I could not detect any makeup on her face, which was, like the others, beautifully shaped. Her lips were full, and she had a half-smile that exposed a small view of perfectly-white, flat teeth. She had two earrings, pierced, from which hung a small silver metal ball with tiny spikes.

I noticed that she had a scar on her left side, below her ear that ran down along her neck to under the vest on the top of her shoulder. It looked as if she had taken a nasty cut.

"Oh to do, Alexi," Sklera said.

"Aleshi?" said the woman. "Alexi."

I nodded. And then I added, "Frey Alexi." And I asked, "Kretahla?"

There was laughter.

The woman pointed at Tharka, "Kretahla Tharka." She pointed to herself. "Drohnin Aluta... Aluta."

Aluta pointed to the other woman who dressed like her. "Drohnin Leral."

Then Aluta pointed to Sklera. "Sklera Kretahla."

"Thank you," I nodded. "Drohnin Aluta."

Aluta put her hand on my sweaty forehead. She noticed my pulling a bit, unconsciously, on my arms to keep them up. They had been aching over the last fifteen minutes.

She looked at Sklera, who nodded.

Aluta came behind me, and something jingled on her belt. Leral pulled out a short knife, which she instantly placed at my throat. "Ree daal," Leral told me.

I assumed that meant "don't move".

Aluta cut the leather straps from my neck to my wrists.

"Oh," I said softly, letting my arms slowly drop to my side – except that Aluta grabbed my right wrist. She cut off the leather straps and instantly wrapped a three-inch wide leather cuff onto it. It had a metal band running through the middle and a metal D-ring. She pulled the D-ring through another part of the cuff and then produced a formidable padlock on which she put onto the D-ring. She lifted my wrist and put the palm of my hand on the top of my head.

Then she repeated the steps on my left wrist, except she pulled my right arm down and secured both of them together behind my back. It was a massive improvement in the comfort factor. My fingers stung as blood rushed back into my extremities.

"Thank you," I said as she came back around, facing me again.

"Juu Loh?" she asked.

"Brieneia?" I said, a half-question.

They laughed again.

Aluta said something and then grabbed my hair and shoved me down to the ground.

I tried to put my hands out to my left side, but I still crashed to my knees. She held my hair and kept me from falling flat on the ground. Expertly she steered my face to her foot.

I kissed her right boot for a moment; then she pulled my head to her other boot and made me kiss it. Then she let me go.

I started to get to my feet – but I was met by a great many expressions of displeasure; I slowly moved back into a kneeling position.

Aluta nodded and approached Sklera.

They talked again, rapidly.

During this conversation, a column of women, armed with swords and bows, passed by. There were about twenty of them, cloaked and hooded. Three men followed at their heels, one pulling a wooden cart while the other two carried light packs. They marched by us, turning right after the main building.

"Alexi!" Aluta said.

"Juu Loh?" I asked, thinking that meant "What?"

"Defal," Aluta said.

I had heard that word before...

Aluta pointed to her eyes, and then to the ground.

Oh.

I looked down at the grass.

After another minute or two, Aluta's boots appeared in front of me. She reached down and put her fingers on my lips. They were dry and nearly cracked.

She tugged on my hair, and I got to my feet, straining without the use of my hands.

She wrapped a thin metal chain around my neck, loosely, and tied it with a strip of leather. Then she pulled gently on the leash.

"Draal," she said, walking.

I followed.

I looked over at Sklera and the others – they were engaged in their own conversations and didn't appear to even notice I was being led away.

* * * * *

I followed Aluta down the road past several buildings.

Aluta wore metal arm bands on her biceps and wrists. They had different-colored patterns of dots and curved lines.

We came to a one-floor structure that appeared to be solidly built like the main, a primary structure near the entrance. Two women guarded the double-wood entry doors. They were dressed similarly to Aluta, but with less gear, and fewer decorations on their arms.

We went in, and I could tell immediately that it was a jail or prison. There was an intake area to my left, office area to my right, and then a single heavy-looking metal-barred door. Peering through the dimly-lit area past the cell door, I could only detect burning torches and a long hallway. I stiffened a bit, reflexively.

Aluta gave me a soft jerk on the leash and led me over to the intake area, where two more guards sat, chatting until we came in. They made several excitable comments until Aluta flashed a stern expression.

The front area had a stone floor, wood-beamed ceiling, and stone walls. Furniture was quite ornate, made of wood and fabric. Lighting was provided by brilliant burning lamps with a mantle-design... kerosene-like without the smell. The torches in the hallway behind the cell appeared to be the same lighting with the intensity adjusted to be dim.

There was an overhead winch, about eight feet above me, which was lowered a bit. It was connected to a metal bar, a little more than shoulder-width apart, with heavy metal rings fastened on the bottom. Welded, most likely.

My wrists were hooked by metal locks to the winch. It was raised until I was stretched out to being on the balls of my feet. I swallowed my fear.

Aluta studied my uniform shirt. She figured out how to pull down the zipper and slowly zipped down my shirt. She made a sound and then lowered me slightly before she unhooked my right wrist, making sure to indicate that I was to keep it still. Awkwardly, she fed my right arm through the shirt. Then she hooked it back to the bar. She repeated the process with my other arm until my shirt was off, which she set on the table. She said something to one of the guards, and they produced a cloth bag into which the folded shirt disappeared.

Aluta then unbuckled my belt, which took her a moment. In any other situation, I might have complained. But this was a no-win environment at the moment, and I suspected that saying anything would just cause more problems.

She stopped, and then pulled off my boots.

Then she came back and finally got my pants loosened. She pulled them off and exposed my usual black thong.

She said something that sounded like "Jeratal" to the guards again, and they repeated the word back, smiling.

Aluta looked at me and rattled off something in her language.

I shrugged.

She shook her head disapprovingly and promptly pulled off the thong.

And there I was... totally naked, in an alien land, helpless in a prison, without any weapons, equipment, or, actually, immediate hope for escape. It didn't seem like things could be much worse.

Aluta went over to a shelf of items and returned with a metal band. It was about one inch high, one-eighth inch thick, and hinged. She reached around my neck and it encircled me. She closed it, and it was fairly snug, but not too tight. She nodded approvingly, and then produced another padlock. It made a loud click as she locked the collar onto me.

I reflexively pulled on my wrists a bit. Struggling seemed completely useless here, but I couldn't help testing the bonds.

She said something to one of the guards. The guard rang a bell, and a male appeared in a side entrance. He looked older than anyone I had seen so far; he was about five-foot two inches tall, with thinning, sandy hair. He wore a metal collar without lock that appeared to be welded on. He sported silver metal nipple rings and wore only a belt made of fabric that supported loin-cloth-type shorts. He was shoeless.

The guard talked to him, and he disappeared for about thirty seconds. He returned with a clay pitcher and two cups.

Aluta waited for him to pour water into one of the cups. She then approached me. I licked my lips involuntarily.

"Frey Alexi," she whispered, taking a sip herself. I could almost smell the water. I could see her throat move as the water passed into her.

She stuck out her tongue for a moment, and then she pointed at me.

I did the same, holding it out. She took the cup and dropped the water onto my tongue.

It was cool and wonderful, and slightly carbonated. It had a high mineral content.

Then she stopped.

I strained a bit at my bonds to chase the water.

Then she did something that completely shocked me. Aluta pressed her body against me, putting her left hand around my buttocks and pushed me against her.

Her breasts were firm. Against my heated and sweaty body, the feel of her leather was cool and inviting. I involuntarily pushed a bit against her.

She produced the cup of water with her left hand. I stuck my tongue out again, and she poured a steady stream of water for a moment.

Aluta stopped and slowly pushed against me with her hips. I swayed just a bit, still partially suspended. My wrists were aching again, because they were holding nearly all of my body weight.

Aluta again pushed against me with her hips.

I felt myself becoming aroused.

I shook my head slightly, letting a soft "no" escape my lips.

Aluta stepped away.

"No?" she asked, laughing. Then she said something in her language to the other guards. They laughed, with one of them mimicking me saying "no" herself. They all laughed.

I rocked back to my feet.

Aluta looked down at my cock, which was starting to thicken.

Then she moved closer again, holding the cup of water near my lips.

"Kay-ee" she said, pressing the side of the cup against my lips.

I knew what they were doing to me. This was a psychological game. But, I was so thirsty. I had been getting cooked in the sun for almost two hours without anything to drink, forced to march beside them on the hot, dusty road. The momentary taste of water merely made me crave more.

Now was not the time to resist or try to escape. I would need to intelligently find a time and means to get away and get back to my craft.

"Kay-ee," I nodded.

Aluta pressed against me again, lining the center of her body with mine. I could feel my cock getting harder. She continued to gyrate against me, slowly, rhythmically, while pouring water into my mouth. After another moment, I was fully erect, pushing into her skirt, slightly spreading her legs.

Suddenly, she backed away.

I swayed, getting on my feet again.

All three of them were silent. The male slave was on his knees in the corner of the room, looking down.

The expression on Aluta's face was one of surprise. Then she flashed a grin. And then Aluta slapped my cock with her open hand.

I yelped, trying to pull back.

She hit me again.

"Agggghhh!" I shouted.

She hit me again. Then again. I tried to turn away, and she reached out for my chest, making a grab in the air. She seemed surprised for a moment, but then grabbed onto my hair with her left hand.

She hit my cock again.

The pain and surprise caused me to get flaccid pretty quickly.

She hit me one last time, and that was it. I was soft.

Aluta held onto my hair to keep me from turning away from her. Then she moved around me to my back. With the fingers of her right hand, she traced my spine from my neck, running down to my buttocks. She reached between my buttocks, not too far, pushing my skin apart. Then she reached around my right hip and grabbed firmly onto my limp cock.

She made a sound, a purring sound of sorts, and pressed against my back. The leather was cool again.

I realized that I was panting. And I was sweating again.

She asked something of the other guards.

I noticed that they were on the edge of their seats, looking directly at me.

One replied. The other repeated the same series of words.

Then one of the guards said something to the slave; he quickly exited through the main door.

The first guard walked to a shelf and returned with a length of rope. It had a natural, hemp-type appearance. The rope was wrapped expertly around my left ankle, and then it was pulled along the floor to my left and secured to an eyebolt hammered into the base of the wall.

For the first time, I noticed that there were similar eyebolts scattered throughout the place: walls, ceilings, baseboards, tables. Most of the walls had heavy-duty metal rings, like large door knockers, affixed into the stone. Frighteningly and totally unbreakable.

Aluta rubbed my cock with her right hand. She let go of my hair with her left hand and put it around the left side of my hip, meeting both of her hands.

She said something to one of the guards, who appeared with a small flask. She removed the wood screw-on cap and poured a small amount of a liquid into Aluta's left hand and then retreated to the chair by her fellow guard.

I struggled, trying to pull away from Aluta. But with that strange purr, she rubbed her hands together for a moment and then slowly rubbed the tip of my cock.

I was fully erect in a matter of seconds.

Aluta encircled my cock in her fist. She slowly pulled it toward me.

I tried to move away from her hand, but she met my resistance from the back by pushing her leather-covered body against me.

"No," I said.

"Kay-ee," she told me.

I shook my head.

"Kay-ee," she whispered into my left ear.

I guess she noticed that I reacted to her whisper.

I felt her bite my ear, softly at first.

In frustrated agony, I felt her slick hand finally reached the base of my cock.

She let completely go of me and then put her hand on the head of my cock, and slowly slid it down again.

This time, I did not pull back so much.

And she bit my ear somewhat harder.

"Kay-ee," she whispered.

"No," I said, less emphatically. This... this wasn't happening. I had to fight it. I couldn't let them feel they could control me. I had to –

"Kay-ee, Frey Alexi," Aluta whispered.

Her hand slowly moved down along my cock. I felt myself holding fast, unable to pull away from her.

Finally, she reached the base again. Then Aluta quickly put her hand on the head again and slid. This time, I thrusted slightly into her hand.

"No," I said.

Aluta licked at my left ear. It was warm and wet and –

Aluta moved her hand along me again... but this time, instead of letting go, she stroked me up.

I could not prevent the moan from escaping my lips.

With her left hand, Aluta reached under my cock, grabbed onto my balls and pulled down.

I didn't think my cock could get much harder, but it did.

With her right hand, she stroked me. My hips thrust into her. She pushed my buttocks with her body. Just when I thought she would stop, she did it again. She pulled her hand up and then stroked again toward me, thrusting her body as I thrust into her hand.

The leather on my wrists creaked; the ceiling bar pulled against the chains above them. My feet were almost completely off the ground; my toes straining to touch the stone. I didn't care.

With every move of her hips, she timed her down thrust with her hand and I thrust my hips and cock harder into her tight, wet hand.

I was panting. I needed release.

Then she stopped.

I thrust into her hand as she held it still.

She stopped pushing into my body.

I thrust again into her hand, but it was difficult because, I had nothing behind me to push off of.

I thrust again.

As I was about to sway my hips, she let go of me entirely and stepped away.

I thrust my hips into the open air. Once more, then again.

I listened to my own pathetic desperation.

Then I swayed back onto the balls of my feet. Nothing. I demanded, "What?"

I felt my back light up in flames as Aluta dragged all of her fingernails down my shoulder blades and to my buttocks. I tried to pull away from her, but she raked me a second time. Then a third.

My erection died as I swore at her.

She raked my back again. I was sure she was breaking my skin. I could feel my sweat stinging the scratches.

Aluta said something to me and then she reached around and frantically stroked my cock again. It became hard again in a moment.

And she raked my back again with her left hand.

I struggled, not knowing which way to move. I couldn't move away from her.

She let go of my cock and then raked my back again with both of her hands.

I shouted. I cussed. I was on fire. And, finally, I begged, "Please, please, stop!"

Aluta purred and stroked me again. My cock surrendered to her, and she stroked me fast for about ten seconds, before letting go again.

I whimpered. This couldn't be happening.

She said something, but I couldn't catch it. I was panting. Completely unable to support the weight of my body, I was hanging limp on the wrist cuffs. I couldn't feel my hands anymore.

My cock was fully hard, pointing away from my body. I looked down at it. *Traitor.* Conflicting thoughts ran rip shod through my mind. I was disgusted with myself for getting aroused... thrusting into her hand... letting her "use" me. I willed my cock to go limp.

Aluta laughed. She came around to my front side, flashed her teeth at me, and laughed again.

One of the guards lowered the bar a few inches. Aluta took my wrists and hooked them together behind my back.

"Brieneia," ordered Aluta.

With difficulty, I got to my knees and kissed both of her boots.

She snapped a chain metal leash onto my collar and tugged. I got to my feet.

One of the guards unlocked the cell door.

I was naked, mostly erect, and shivering when Aluta led me into the hallway.

I followed her past three cell doors on the left and right, and waited while she unlocked the fourth cell door on the right. She unhooked the leash and pushed me to my knees. Then she locked a long length of chain to my collar. The other end was welded to a center eye bolt in the middle of the stone floor.

I kissed her feet again and remained motionless for what seemed like forever.

She said something, then walked out and shut the cell door. It clanked with a heavy metal, solid sound. I heard her booted feet walk back to the main cell. Then it shut.

I rotated on my knees to look around. There was only the light coming in from the cell door, from the lamp affixed on the opposite-side hallway.

My cell was stone on all walls, floor and ceiling. It was about ten-feet by ten-feet square and high. Several rings hung from the walls. There was a fabric bag against one wall that looked like it was stuffed with something. There was a single folded sheet next to it.

A small clay cup sat on the floor. I crawled to it. Getting to my feet seemed like a tremendous effort – and I was already on the same elevation as the cup was. It held a clear liquid. There was also a piece of bread, about three-inches wide, next to the cup. Maneuvering my hands to my sides, and trying to get the cup to my lips took a combination of luck and skill. I had to strain, observing the right wrist cuff moving slightly along my forearm and then digging into my skin. But I was successful.

The water was tasty. It had a soft texture, almost fruity, and I recognized it as the cool, mineral water. I drank the whole cup. Then I finished the bread, mostly by stuffing large pieces into my mouth.

There was a chamber pot in the corner. I crawled to it and, best I could without the use of my hands, urinated.

Well, that seemed to explain something, too.

Here I was, in this fortress-like prison, in a cell, naked with a metal collar around my throat, chained to the floor, and they left my hands locked behind my wrists. Why? Escape seemed very unlikely. It would appear they have done this before and knew exactly how to hold someone here. Why the cuffs?

Probably to keep me from finishing what Aluta had started.

The cell was, fortunately, cool and dry. I could detect a slight breeze of air at floor-level. I moved over to the bag, and I was able to press it down mostly-flat. Then, with effort, I got the blanket over most of my body. No matter how I twisted around, I was unable to get my torso covered with the blanket.

The prison was quiet – I heard no other noises except my own breathing.

Finally, exhausted, I fell into a deep sleep.

Chapter Five
Conformity of Frey

The metal sound of the cell door unlocking woke me with a start. For a moment, I forgot where I was and what had happened. My back hurt.

Two guards, different from the ones I had seen earlier, came in. They stood near me, looking down at me.

Shaking the fog from my head, I rolled to my side and got to my knees, kneeling in front of them.

The metal chain clinked as it moved across the stone floor, snaking over to the center ring.

I waited.

I could hear their breathing.

What else was I supposed to do?

"Frey," said the one on the left.

I looked up.

She stuck out her index finger and rotated it.

I moved myself around a half-circle and waited again.

My neck was pulled back by the collar as one of them tugged on the chain. Then it was unlocked. I felt something else hooked on and heard a "click". My wrist cuffs were unlocked, and I was allowed to put them on the ground in front of me, doggy-style.

She said something, and I understood it to be an order. I turned around, and she walked, leading me by a chain metal leash.

I crawled along the stone floor, the metal not quite touching the stone.

It was, though, a good view. The first guard was superior to the one holding my leash, opening cell doors and shutting them behind us. Keeping pace with the second guard was not too difficult at first, but as we went passed another ten pair of cell doors, my knees became sore. I slowed down. The first guard waited for us to pass.

"*Crack*!" I heard it, before I felt the burn on my ass.

She held a stick in her hand that she lifted again to strike me. I hustled along, no longer thinking about my sore knees.

Well, the "good view" I mentioned before getting hit: They were wearing the standard guard uniform of pleated brown leather skirts and vests with artfully-crafted boots. Quite attractive. In fact, even though there were obvious differences in their genetics from humans, these people were good looking.

The scent of her clothing wafted to me as I crawled behind, listening to boots clap on the stone. She had a nice ass under that skirt, I noted.

Then I noticed that there was one person here who did not smell good. Me.

We stopped when the first guard unlocked a cell door. The leashed tugged. I crawled inside.

It was a large, fifty-foot by thirty-foot room, all stone, with several bright lamps in the corners and hanging from the ceiling. And it was, undoubtedly, a torture chamber.

I froze.

Another whack on my ass had me moving again.

Reality took over. If I was to try to resist these armed women, I wouldn't get far. This was not the time for an escape. Yet.

I was led to the farthest wall. There were several medieval-looking manacles on the wall, hanging by solid chain. My leash was locked onto a separate wall ring. The floor area was recessed a few inches, and there was a small metal grate in the stone.

"Frey," said the first guard. I looked at her, and she motioned for me to stand.

Stiffly, I stood up.

The second guard tossed a rag to me, which I easily caught. Then she tossed a small sliver of soap. I was wondering where the water valve was when I was hit with a blast of cold water from the first guard. She held a metal tube in her hand that gradually snaked to the ceiling. The water pressure was even and strong. After about ten seconds of spraying me, she stopped.

Cue taken, I used the soap and the rag to clean. I washed my hair and then turned slightly away from them to hide my groin area.

"Ta Na Ta," the first guard said.

I turned to expose myself to them while I cleaned. Then I sat the bar of soap and the rag on the stone floor. I was extending myself again when I was hit by the cold water.

After about a minute of rinsing, I was clean, dripping wet, and somewhat shivering.

I brushed off as much water as I could, and hoped these two appreciated my cooperation.

The first guard pointed to the ground, and I dropped to my knees. The leash was unlocked. I was led in the general direction of the cell door and fervently hoped we would not stop.

Seeing the torture chamber had another chilling effect on me. As I passed through it a second time, particular pieces of the equipment jumped out at me. There was a long stretch-rack type table, maybe fifteen feet long, with an oversized ratchet wheel on one side. I could see rows of eyebolts and several chains on the ends of the table.

Another piece that caught my attention was the stocks partially affixed to a wall. It had holes for the neck and wrists. There was also a horizontal, two-piece wooden stock at groin-height with another hole, obviously for securing a male. Finally, there was a wooden baseboard that had holes for ankles.

The last thing I noticed were several sets of chains hanging from the ceiling, all connected in an intricate design to winches.

There were more items, but I did not get a good view. There were dark, hulking pieces of wooden and metal furniture. A metal cage. I looked away.

Finally, I followed them out of the room and back down to my cell.

The first guard led me to the spot where a new cup of water and two pieces of bread were. *Two?* This was an improvement.

She held the leash.

I nodded and grasped the bread, eating it quickly and finishing with the water.

She pulled on my leash, and I crawled out again.

We went to the front area, the intake room. Two other guards were there, talking.

One handed a small amount of cloth to the second guard, who tossed it to the floor in front of me.

Staying on my knees, I unfolded the clothes. One was the cloth belt, which I tied around my waist. Then I stuffed and pulled the other part of the loin cloth around me.

"Frey Alexi," the first guard said, pointing over to a kind of chalkboard in the room. Someone had drawn pictures.

The first frame had a stick figure with a penis and a ring around his neck standing, with a woman, more artfully drawn, leading him.

The second frame showed him running away from her, the leash dangling.

The third frame showed four women with bows drawn.

The final frame showed him face-down on the ground, with four arrows stuck in his back.

I nodded.

The second guard picked up a small round dark red object from a basket on a desk. It looked like a fruit. She walked down the hallway, to about the fourth row of cell doors, and put the fruit on the stone floor.

As she walked back into the intake room, she went over to a rack of weapons, swords and bows, and withdrew a bow and an arrow.

She looked at me for a moment, then she spun around and let fly the arrow.

The arrow speared the fruit and they rolled down the hallway about thirty feet before coming to a rest next to one of the cell doors.

To make the point, she took another fruit out of the basket and tried to hand it to me.

I shook my head in refusal.

She pointed at the fruit, and then me, and then the apple.

I nodded.

She put the fruit back.

The first guard tugged on my leash, and we went outside.

I crawled down the steps.

It was morning. The sun was still low on the horizon, casting long shadows on the grounds. The grass had a great smell to it. Other scents wafting by me were those of morning cooking fires. I could smell... meat, perhaps. Several people, female and male, moved about, most without hoods or robes. Apparently, full nudity outside was not proper decorum, even for a prisoner.

There was only one male crawling, though.

And it was getting rough on my knees.

After about fifty feet of pain, she changed her course a bit and walked along the gravel pathway. This allowed me to crawl alongside on the grass. It was damp and sticky, but gave much relief to my knees. I felt grateful.

After passing several buildings, we turned and went up a few steps to a nondescript building that sported written signs and a banner.

I followed her past unguarded doors and found myself in an apparent classroom. There was no one else there yet. It appeared to have four open-air classes with rows of chairs and tables pointing toward each corner. Each corner had large chalkboards and a teacher's desk. Shelves with books, charts, and small signs adorned all of the walls.

I was led to the front row and made to kneel, sitting back on my heels. The guard sat next to me in the closest chair, to my left, just slightly behind me.

We waited for a few minutes.

She adjusted the leash, moving it from her right hand to her left hand. The metal chain clinked a bit, as I felt the collar shift its weight. It was uncomfortable... a constant reminder that I was their prisoner.

Despite knowing better, I looked around for a moment, trying to identify possible avenues of escape. Still, I might get outside, and then I'd get the target-practice-dummy treatment.

I jerked when the guard put her right hand on the back of my neck. I felt her fingers rubbing along the metal collar. She played with it for a moment, and then lifted her hand away.

At least she had not done anything to torment me. So far.

Heavy footsteps entered and stopped. I resisted the automatic urge to look up.

Two pair of light tan boots, ankle-height, appeared before me. A long light tan-leather skirt, with a single side slit on the left side, was as far up as I could see.

Several words were exchanged, most of them decidedly unfriendly. The new arrival seemed to be displeased about something. Finally, she made a sighing sound.

"Drop no?" she asked.

"Frey Alexi," the first guard said.

"Frey Alexi?" the new woman asked.

I looked at her, slowly, not sure what she wanted me to do.

She had a white, sleeveless fabric shirt, sort of pull-over with a high collar. Anywhere else, it wouldn't have worked. But on her, it seemed to do well. I could also detect that she wasn't wearing any kind of undergarment; her nipples on smallish breasts poked against the grainy fabric of her shirt. She had jet-black hair, falling to the middle of her back, but tied in a single long braid wrapped with black leather straps.

She tried to force a slight smile and pointed to herself. "Ohh-tah Hula... Hula."

"Ohh-tah Hula." I nodded.

She walked over to the desk and opened a drawer, pulling out something that looked exactly like a stick of chalk. She went over to the blackboard and drew a few characters. She looked back at me.

I shook my head.

Hula frowned at me and said something.

The guard used several of the same words and shook her head.

Hula looked at the guard, "Koo ret sa doh-la?"

"Alexi, breen sa doh-la."

Hula chuckled. "Sa Doh-la?"

The guard nodded. She opened a pouch on her belt and withdrew my wrist watch. She handed it to Hula.

Hula's eyes widened and exploded into an animated conversation with the guard that lasted about two minutes. The guard mostly answered with one or two words.

Holding the watch, Hula went back to the chalkboard. She drew a single straight line, then another, and then made a horizontal line to the right.

I lifted my right hand and showed her two fingers.

She then made eleven marks on the board, horizontally, evenly spaced. The first one was obviously a zero. She pointed at me to come over.

I looked at the guard for permission. She stuck the leather handle of the metal leash into my mouth and told me something. I bit onto it and then stood and approached the chalkboard.

Hula handed the chalk to me and pointed to the board.

Below the row of numbers she wrote, I drew a zero, then a *1, 2*, and so on, until getting to *10*.

Hula took the chalk back and, moving to the right, she drew her language equivalent for a *10* and a *5* with a line between them. She then drew a *2* to the right of a new symbol.

Okay, ten divided by five equals two.

She handed the chalk back to me.

I drew, in her letters, a *49* then a *7* in her letters and what had to be a square root symbol.

She erased the square root symbol and replaced it with symbol of hers. Then she drew a row of other symbols.

After a moment, I drew my equivalent of a *+, -, /* and *x*.

Who knew the Rosetta Stone here would be mathematics?

Hula pointed to the ground, and I got back on my knees. My respite was over.

She reached out slowly to touch my cheek and feel where the skin sealant had been working to regenerate the tissue. Her fingers ran along the edge of my lips.

Then, to my surprise, she sat down on my back.

I shifted my hands a bit, to adjust for the unexpected weight.

Her leather skirt was soft, supple, and cool as it draped over my skin. She had another conversation with the guard, this time with excitement in her voice. There were several times when the guard would utter words of a cautious tone, but otherwise, there seemed to be an agreement.

The guard removed a couple of coins and offered them to Hula. Hula politely refused.

Then, given the tones, it appeared they changed the subject. It sounded like a social chat.

Foremost, these people were not as heavy as humans. I doubt that I could have held a typical human woman on my flat back for this much time. It was probably a combination of muscle mass, body fat, and bone weight. I was larger and, likely, stronger than anyone on the planet. I had not seen very many males without robes, but they seemed of more slight stature than the females. Regardless, I had to shift my hands a bit.

Hula swatted my left buttock with an open palm, not even making a pause in her conversation. Then, after a moment, she changed her tone and asked a question.

The guard affirmed.

I felt Hula's left hand go straight under the left side of my cloth belt and tightly grab onto my cock and balls. A breath of surprise leapt from my mouth. She let go and said something. The guard laughed, walked to the chalkboard and called my name.

I looked up. Hula shifted her weight on my back, rotating a bit to see the board.

The guard drew a stick figure, laying flat. Then she stabbed at the board with four short lines, each terminating into the stick figure.

I nodded. *No arrows for my body, please.*

Hula stood up, thankfully, and escorted the guard to the door.

After a moment, Hula returned. She said something, and pulled the leash to the side.

I got onto my knees.

She shook her head and crossed her arms.

I sat on my butt, crossed my legs, and crossed my arms for good measure.
She erased the board and then wrote two characters. "Hula."
I repeated, "Hula."
She wrote six characters and said, "Alexi."
And thus my first day of lessons began.

*****

My head was swimming with new symbols and small phrases. After what seemed to be about two hours, Hula stopped. I had learned the word for "stop" and she used it. Then she walked over to another part of the room, near the front door. She rang a bell and then returned to sit at her desk. I realized that she had been standing on her feet during all of this time.

A young male, perhaps around ten or eleven years old, entered. He was dressed in the usual belt and cloth, -- and collar – but carried a basket that he brought to Hula. He stopped at her feet, knelt, and kissed her right boot.

"Up," she said.

He got back on his feet and presented the basket to her. She waved him off, and he left, hustling out in bare feet.

Hula reached inside and removed a flask, two cups, two napkins, and two cloth-wrapped bundles.

"Alexi," she said, pointing at the table.

I got to my hands and knees and crawled over the few feet to her desk. Then I stopped, not knowing what to do.

She pointed at the flask.

I retrieved the flask. Call it intuition, but I knew that pouring myself a cup of the drink would be the wrong thing to do. As Mom used to say, "I was born at night, but not last night."

One of the cups was a bit taller than the other. I poured the liquid into it and sat it down, closer to Hula.

"No," she said, extending her open hand.

I lifted the cup and put it into her hand.

She took a sip and handed the cup to me.

She pointed to the bundles.

While both bundles were wrapped in the same cloth, one was slightly larger than the other and had a bright red string used to tie it together; the smaller bundle had a plain brown tie.

I fumbled with the red string for a moment. I did not know the word for "knife" but it seemed a fat chance that Hula would provide one to me.

I opened the cloth and exposed a sandwich made of meat between sprouts and layers of yellow sauce.

Now, was I supposed to stick this in her mouth?

Hula could detect my indecision. She reached over, picked up the sandwich and took a bite.

Again, it seemed like a safe bet to just wait about getting myself something to drink. After a few minutes, Hula looked at the cup resting on the table. I placed it on her open palm.

Was this intuition and instinct? Or just being chivalrous? Either way, I did not see any option except to comply – for now.

I noticed that of all the writing Hula had done on the chalkboard, she had noticeably avoided erasing the arrow-pierced stick man.

Hula looked at the board. She looked down at me and shook her head. "Alexi, no."

But, she did go over to the board and erase selected letters. She wrote new letters, and we exchanged the same word game for a moment that had allowed me to learn. "Mo kee sha," she said.

Dead.

Hula tapped the dead stick man. "Mo kee sha, pravera," which meant "Escape and you are dead."

"Yes." I nodded.

Hula sat down again, crossing her legs in front of me. I could smell the leather of her skirt.

And the food... I could smell the food. It was real food. Not just bread.

Hula nearly finished her sandwich, leaving just a couple of bites.

"Now, you," she told me.

"Thank you."

I opened the cloth and found plain bread again. But it would have to do. I tried not to eat it like a famished dog, but it was still rapidly disappearing. Finally, I poured the last of the drink. It was, fortunately, something other than plain water. It had a light, taste that somewhat reminded me of saffron, but sweeter.

I finished and folded my cloth.

Hula stretched her feet in front of me and pointed to her boots.

I kissed both of her boots and then she said, "More."

I started to kiss her right boot again, but she interrupted me. "Off."

Oh.

Slowly, my hands moved into the slit of her skirt and found the top of her right ankle-high boot. There was a simple bow to untie, and then the laces were easily loosened. Removing the boot exposed ankle-high socks which also came off easily.

Hula offered her other foot. After a moment, it was also bare.

She said something unknown to me, and I replied as taught, "Please pardon my misunderstanding."

She clasped my hands in hers, and then she wrapped them around her right bare foot.

So that word meant "massage".

Her foot was much softer than I had expected.

Hula laughed. She asked something, and we went through a regular routine of trying to figure out the word. She reached over to the chalkboard and wrote additional letters.

"Yes, Hula. New," I told her.

"Alexi needs training," she said, a phrase she used several times today.

I rubbed her feet, admittedly quite clumsily.

"Stop," she ordered. "Hands up."

I lifted my hands up, palms down.

She slapped them. She slapped them hard. The sting was not so bad – but it was a surprise.

"Alexi needs training," she said again. "Boots on."

As I put on her boots and laced them, I noticed the backs of my hands had a red imprint from her impact.

No one had slapped me in... well, maybe in twenty years. I couldn't remember ever being slapped, actually. Mom must have given me a slap on my hands once or twice when I was a kid. Maybe not.

"Sit," Hula instructed when I finished kissing her boots.

It took me a moment of adjusting my legs back into a sitting, cross-legged position. Hula stood, walked over to the board and wrote.

"Arm," I said in the native language, as she pointed out words. "Hand. Foot. Leg. Sit. Run. Stop. Start. Boot." There was one I could not recall. I shrugged.

Hula pointed at it again with her chalk.

I mean, for three hours of class, I thought that learning about fifty words was pretty good. Yes, I already knew English, Japanese, and Dutch, which helped, but this language had many sounds that were completely foreign to me. Even Japanese, with all the millions of little squiggly marks, had sounds that were familiar. This...

"Alexi!" she said, louder.

I shrugged.

She walked over. "Hands at back," she said.

I put my hands behind me, waiting for her to secure them.

She reached around and crossed my wrists. Then she stood in front of me.

Hula raised her right hand, in open palm fashion.

I knew what was coming, and I flinched, but no more than a half-inch.

This seemed to make her angry. "No move!"

I held still.

She reared her hand back.

I flinched, but maybe only an eighth of an inch... almost unnoticeable. But she saw it.

She struck my right cheek.

My eyes blinked, and I pulled myself toward her when she hit me again from the same side and direction.

I tried to look back again, but she hit me again. And it was starting to piss me off.

She looked over my shoulder and saw that my fists were clenched.

"No, no," she said.

I opened my hands.

She was about to strike again, but stopped.

"No," she said again, looking away from me.

She reached over to the couple of bites of food, wrapped them in the cloth, and tossed them into a trash bin.

Then she said the word, which meant "Bow or bend".

She erased everything (except the dead stick man), and then wrote out a whole new set of letters and words.

Their language was somewhat similar to Japanese, with short, simple phonetic letters. It was constructed, however, of about forty characters and a few extra punctuation symbols that I had not completely figured out. I had learned about a hundred words and two dozen phrases that I could not yet write or read because of their complexity. It seemed that the most important words a prisoner needed were being taught to me first.

I had been trying to figure out additional words for food. However, I did not have

70

any relation to the items Hula was writing because the food items were unknown.

The first guard appeared through the main door and, upon seeing her, Hula left the board and greeted her.

I kept my head down as they discussed something, just barely out of earshot.

They walked closer, different cadences announced by their heels.

"Bad Alexi." The guard pointed to herself after a moment. "O-tra."

"Khatrana Otra," I said, as taught.

That word was used in most titles to address the females. It dawned on me that it might be the same as using the English word "Mistress".

Otra hooked a leather leash onto my collar and walked out. I turned quickly, moving on my hands and knees behind her. We went out into the afternoon sun and turned on the road toward the main entrance. The heat was already high; the sun's rays intense.

Along the road we turned again and came to a rectangular-shaped grassy area, slightly more elevated than the road. There were four massive wooden posts in the ground. These had to have been made from the trees I had seen two days ago. There were chains and manacles hanging from each post.

This did not bode well.

Four new guards approached from the direction of the prison. A few other people, women and men, all wearing cloaks and hoods, stopped and looked curiously in our general direction.

"Kneel," Otra said.

I got on my knees and crossed my arms behind my back, wrists touching.

Two of the new guards flanked my sides. The third one was near my back, her right hand resting on the hilt of a sword. The fourth guard floated slightly behind me somewhere.

Otra slapped me, the blow knocking me to the grass. My left ear rang. I lay there on the grass for a moment until Otra shouted, "Alexi, kneel!"

I pushed myself upright and assumed the kneeling position.

Otra slapped again, before I could flinch.

The hot grass on my right cheek smelled like it was burning.

The warm, salty taste of blood was in my mouth.

Again, I assumed the kneeling position.

Again Otra slapped, but much lighter this time. I turned my head, and she hit me on my right cheek next, lightly. Then my left cheek. Then my right.

My nose was bleeding.

She wouldn't stop.

That's just about enough, my body told my brain.

My brain wasn't so sure.

I was slapped again. Again. Again.

Teeth gritted, I held back,

My fists clenched, and I rose slightly off my knees when Otra slapped twice more.

I refused to hold my head still, and I looked sharply to my right. She hit me again, and I cursed her, wildly and in English.

They were trying to provoke me.

My hands were tightly clenched and balled into fists.

Still, she would not stop.

I wasn't trained to be hit repeatedly. My entire professional life was to react offensively – and this was the...

My right hand whipped upward and blocked Otra's strike, simultaneously catching her wrist. In response to years of police training, I spun her wrist around, stepped into her, and pulled her body in a half-circle and had her arm up behind her back. I was standing, and she was half-cocked before me.

It had been fast – I'm sure I had moved far quicker than anyone there thought possible.

Nobody moved.

I was positive, now, that I was much stronger than the people here. It would have taken just a simple action to break Otra's arm and then snap her neck. Maybe that's why nobody rushed me.

There were no bows nearby, either. Everyone was armed with a sword strapped to their back or, I saw for the first time, a whip.

"My apologies, Khatrana Otran," I said, letting her go and dropping to my knees, arms crossed behind me.

Everyone remained still. I honestly thought I could hear the breeze brush across the grassy field.

Though – I knew I was in very real danger.

Otra turned, wiped my blood from her shoulders, and looked down at me. She asked something about me that I could not quite understand.

Hula intervened. "Alexi, what is your life?"

"Pardon my misunderstanding,"

"What is your life before? Before this place."

Not knowing the vocabulary, I pointed at Otra.

There were words among most of the women.

Otra spoke a rapid string of words to Hula, who nodded several times. Then Otra glared at me. She started to walk off, but turned back on her heels and said something else to Hula.

"Alexi, undress," Hula said. "Otra wants you to see."

I untied my cloth belt and held my clothes together, my nakedness partially hidden by my closed knees.

"There, push," Hula pointed a few feet to my right.

With easy effort, I tossed the small pieces of clothing about three feet to my right.

"Ka chi!" Otra shouted.

A whistling sound and an immediate "thunk" to my right: there was an arrow now sticking into my clothes, an absolute dead center hit. I looked over my right shoulder to see an archer on top of one of the buildings, perhaps one-hundred-and-fifty yards away, thirty-feet high.

Otra approached slowly and put both of her hands around my neck. She squeezed and pushed me back off my kneeling position. I put my hands behind me, but she pushed me further.

I fell backward and intentionally landed on my hands, making sure they were pinned behind me.

Otra continued to squeeze.

"Alexi," she said, before saying a few more things I could not yet understand. Then she said a phrase I knew, "Mo kee sha, pravera." It was the warning about escaping and being killed.

I was unable to breathe.

72

She rattled off a few more words and then shoved me back into the grass before storming away, accompanied by most of the other women.

Two guards remained, along with Hula.

"Clothes, on," Hula said.

I gathered myself, tried to breathe without gasping, and walked over to the clothes.

I started to reach to the arrow and, thinking better of it, waited until one of the guards approached and removed it.

My loin cloth and belt were both torn, but still belted on.

I knelt again and put my wrists behind me.

One of the guards snapped a lock on my wrist cuffs and jerked me to my feet. She took the leash from Hula and locked it to my neck. As she was about to walk, Hula stepped closer.

"Alexi, you bad. But we know you are new. You do not know our life."

I looked at her, because I was sure there was more.

"You will be punished," she said.

"Yes, Mistress," I replied.

"Letters and words tomorrow," she told me, as I followed the guards to the prison.

I thought about her words all the way back to the prison cell. I'd be punished, but not so much that I couldn't learn. I could handle that.

Two days ago, I would have thought very little of that small prison cell; now, with the fear of the unknown, I had to resist an urge to drop to my feet and hang onto the cell bars. They weren't taking me to my cell.

As we got closer to the last cell door, I slowed, involuntarily.

But that was not allowed; a hefty jerk on my leash, and I kept up again.

As the lead guard unlocked the cell door, the other two took positions on either side of my arms and put their hands around my biceps as if they had done it a million times.

I was being helped inside the dungeon, because my feet refused to move forward.

"Come," the leader said, pulling on the leash and taking most of the slack so that her gloved hand was about four inches away from my metal collar.

I was led to the center of the stone-walled dungeon where there were four heavy duty eyebolts in the stone at equal distance, perhaps four feet away from a center fifth eyebolt. Ugly, three-inch wide metal manacles were connected with heavy chains to the eyebolts.

As the leader held tight to my leash, the other two guards each took one of the manacles, opposing each other, and locked them around my ankles. There was considerable slack in the chain, which made a clinking sound against the stone floor.

Two chains were lowered on a pulley, each from about the same vertical point as the two eyebolts that secured my ankle manacles.

My wrists were unlocked and then hooked to the chains from above.

Then the chains were ratcheted up.

The leader let go of my leash and then unhooked it.

I watched her walk over to a table that had many objects on it, mostly black, but a few with shiny metal parts. She had her back to me for a moment, but returned with a bag. It was a leather hood.

She reached over my head and pulled it down over my face.

There were small air holes near the bottom, but it was sightless. And it was heavy. It had a powerful leather odor. She tightened something around my neck securing the collar. It felt like a wide, thick leather strap or band.

The chains continued to go up, finally taking my weight almost off the ground.

It was uncomfortable, with my arms spread wide and wrists being pulled.

My heels came off the ground.

Up further, straining my shoulders, my toes were finally above the stone floor; the chains between my ankles and the floor pulling tightly against me.

I really didn't know how long I could take that. It was already hurting.

I hung there for at least a moment, barely able to move. I tried to rock myself a bit, but the most I could manage was about a half-inch of body movement. All of the chains were perfectly adjusted to prevent significant movement.

Was I going to be hanging here for a long time? Was that my punishment? How long until my shoulders were dislocated? Would I be like this overnight?

The three women were quiet. Or, was it that the leather hood was so thick it also muffled sound?

Fire!

I was on fire.

There was a burn all around my body and a loud, ear-piercing pop.

I had been hit with a whip!

It had wrapped around my chest, under my arms, and around my back.

After a moment, I realized I had screamed.

I took a deep breath and –

Fire, pain.

I tried to jerk away, but I was immobile.

I screamed. The leather hood muffled my pleas. I was taking in another breath when she hit me again, this time around my waist. There was a burn all around my body, ending with a piercing hot sting on my right buttock.

I felt the whip moving in the air, and I tried to jerk my body away – it was a useless attempt.

I was still screaming when the whip struck again. This time it was lower, around my thighs. I barely caught my breath before my chest exploded again.

Tears flowed down my cheeks, soaking into the leather.

My body was sweating profusely, with the salt getting into the whip burns and stinging even more. I lost track of the times she whipped me. Back. Thighs. Chest. Ass. Then it happened all over again.

I could not move.

"Noooo, please!" I begged, knowing they could not understand me through the hood.

Back. Thighs.

I was unable to make a sound, my screams hurting only my own ears.

Chest. No, not my chest.

I did not even know where it hit me. I hurt so bad, I could not tell what was going on now.

My body jerked against the strike, but my mind was numb. I don't know when I passed out.

*****

The chains from above rattled.

I collapsed on the stone, still chained at four points.

Locks were unhooked, and I was lifted by my arms to my feet. They partially carried me and then made me kneel on a blanket or padded cushion.

I couldn't stop from silently sobbing. The hood was black and damp and musty with the smell of my tears, and I hurt and I was lost and I wanted to stop hurting.

While four hands steadied me, another pair of hands wiped my body with something cool and damp. Then something else was rubbed onto my burns – it stung a bit, but also had a cooling feeling... like rubbing alcohol.

My wrists were locked to the wide collar around my neck. Then I was gently pushed down onto my left side. It was a thickly padded, leather cushion or mattress.

Shaking in pain and fear, I felt my teeth chattering and my breath labored.

Then something happened that was...   It was unexpected.

I felt the guard lay down behind me. Her leather outfit was cool, but comforting because in a moment it warmed my naked body.

She pressed tightly against me, almost spooning my shivering form. I could feel her breath on my neck, rustling against the damp, fine hairs on my skin. A gloved hand stroked my right bicep. She ran her leather-covered fingertips along my arm and to my wrist collar.

I could feel her leather vest and her breasts pushing into my shoulders.

Something like a sheet was pulled over my body.

She continued to stroke my arm, and then she went to the side of my body and softly stroked my side to my waist and back again.

I tried to tell myself that I should be hateful and wanting to do everything possible to kill this woman for what she had done to me.

Involuntarily, nearly imperceptible, I moved my body back to push against her.

She took her arm and wrapped it around my ribcage, holding tightly.

I think I softly cried for another few minutes before falling asleep.

*****

I awoke after my foot was shaken.

With an unconstrained groan, I opened my eyes and saw it was still pitch black. The hood.

My arms were sore.

Everything was sore.

"Kneel," a female voice told me.

There was no one sleeping next to me. Perhaps it had been a dream.

I got to my knees.

"Close eyes," she said.

My wrists were unlocked and allowed to drop to my sides. The collar around my neck was removed.

Then the hood was slowly lifted.

It would be a good thing if this place was like what I expected a dungeon to be – that is, dimly lit. However, not here. There was ample lighting. I looked down, squinting.

75

After a full minute, I was able to see through the cracked eyelids, caked with dried tears.

I looked at my chest and legs. Red stripes lined my body. Several welts marked my skin in an angry blue-black color. There were a few scabs where, I presume, the end of the bullwhip had dug into and opened the skin.

I turned behind me suddenly, trying to see who had been lying next to me while I slept. But there were only the two guards. Where had the third leader guard with the whip gone? Maybe after hitting me, she decided to hold onto me. Why did she go away? When did she go away? I had a feeling, deep in the back of my mind that she had stayed next to me for many hours.

I was led over to the morning shower for the cleaning ritual.

This time I was given a small wad of spongy material and gray lotion. When I held them in my hand with a dumbfounded look, one of the guards pointed to her mouth, "Teeth."

I brushed my teeth with it and cupped the water from the hose to rinse.

This was all much more slow moving than yesterday. The whipping was still affecting my body with every movement. It did not hurt tremendously, but was still there. A few years ago, I had a crash on hyperskates and slid along a concrete retaining wall, catching my right thigh. That friction burn was intense when it happened, and it had a lasting burning effect until a few hours later when I received treatment. This felt a bit like that burn did a week later. It was there, and it kind of hurt, but not too bad. Like a healing bruise would hurt to the touch.

Naked, I crawled back to my cell for breakfast and a new, clean loin cloth and belt.

Otra was nowhere to be seen. In fact, all of the guards were new. Was it a shift change? Day off from work?

Two guards had me crawl to the school and into the classrooms.

Hula was already at her desk, opening a bag of items and putting them on her desk.

Unleashed and kneeling, I waited for her to finish. The two guards walked out.

"Alexi, you punished?" she asked, not looking up from her sorting of desktop items.

"Yes, Mistress," I replied, looking down, mostly.

She was wearing nearly the same outfit as yesterday. It was a more pale leather skirt. Black boots instead of brown, flashed through the slit in her skirt as she stood and walked over to the chalkboard.

As she wrote, Hula spoke, "Face... teeth... slap... bite."

And so we had another lesson.

Before lunch time, Hula made me review. This time I matched all of the words properly.

I opened her lunch and served her. When she was done, she allowed me to drink of the sweet water and eat my bread. Then she picked up a small amount of meat from her leftover sandwich.

I knew that it would not be a matter of just handing it to me.

Hula stood up, and walked over to one of the rows of chairs. She took a small pinch of meat and put it on the floor.

Then, skirt swaying while she walked, she took another pinch of meat and put it on the floor a few feet away.

76

After four more stops, her hands were empty. I had mapped her path so I could repeat it.

"You may crawl. No hands to eat."

On my hands and knees, I crawled to the first piece of meat and grasped it in my teeth. It was slightly salty and oh-so-tasty.

There was no point in being self-conscious. I knew she was trying to humiliate me by making me eat like an animal. It did not matter. The meat was the first real food I had eaten in three days.

I crawled to her feet after I finished.

"Kiss?" I asked.

"You may kiss," she replied.

I kissed her boots and added, "Thank you, Mistress."

Hula abruptly stood and walked over to the chalkboard.

"Alexi home is?" Hula asked.

"Mistress, may I write?" I asked.

"Yes."

"Thank you, Mistress." I picked up a piece of chalk and drew a round ball, shading part of it at the lower right. Then I drew a multiple-point star to the left of it. Then a circle to represent the planet.

I recalled from a computer image during the crash that this continent was about one-fourth of the planet's surface. There was one northern polar ice cap, an arid southern hemisphere, and three major land masses.

I pointed to a small square I drew on the planet KoVer.

Then I looked at a chalkboard in the other wallless classroom.

"Please, may I write?" I asked again, pointing.

"Yes."

I walked over to the other classroom's chalkboard and sketched another planet, a star, and then drew a small square. Another big circle around the planet and I wrote, in English "Earth".

I walked back over to Hula and knelt in the usual position.

"How get here?" she asked, pointing to the chalkboard.

Carefully drawing a native bird first, I then made it more rectangular and made a chair, finally, depicting a stick person inside of it. As a little bit of humor, I added a penis to the stick figure.

Hula laughed. She pointed at the stick man and then took her own piece of chalk. With a grin, she lengthened the white phallus. "Now, is Alexi."

I chuckled. It felt strange for me to laugh here.

There seemed to be little prospects for escape. They had mastered the techniques of keeping prisoners – but there would be a time and a place.

And then….what? Could I live as a hermit, always at risk of being caught and executed?

A rescue craft was a remote possibility.

And they were conditioning me. There was no doubt about that.

Was I being coerced into falling prey to Stockholm Syndrome? It was a centuries-old psychological term used to describe what happened when victims begin to associate positively to a kidnapper.

Kidnapping was a crime. In this place, it appeared that this was a cultural norm. Was it like this everywhere on the planet?

"May I ask question, Mistress?"

She nodded.

"What is name of place?" I emphasized her whole planet.

"Aervanta," she told me. It sounded like "Air-Vahn-Ta".

"What is here?" I pointed to the northern half of her continent.

She indicated the lower half and pointed to herself at the same time, "Erska". She pointed to the north and shrugged.

I took the chalk and outlined the other large continent.

She shrugged again.

"Have Erska people go there?" I asked.

"Water," she pointed at the coast.

I drew a simple boat. And she replied with a word.

"Erska people have boat to go here?" I asked, drawing a dashed line in the water to the other continent.

"Erska die on boat. Not come home," she said. For a moment, she looked sad.

"You know Erska people that die on boat?" I asked.

"Yes."

"My apologies, Mistress."

"Yes." Then she looked at me seriously. "Hula will ask more questions. You need more letters and words for talking."

I assumed the kneeling position and learned more words, not to please her, but to survive.

At the end of the day, Hula administered another review. It was not easy, but I mastered every word she had taught to me. By this time, I was starting to learn other words and getting a feel for the patterns.

Two guards, one from the first day in my prison, returned. They locked my wrists and led me out on a leash to my cell.

It was, thankfully, uneventful.

There was bread and water again, but of a lesser quantity than previously.

I did not complain about the food, nor that they left me stripped of clothing and locked by my collar to the center floor chain.

After about ten minutes I savored the bit of bread and drink. It seemed like a good opportunity to stretch my legs and check the cell. Escape was, again, on my mind.

If I could get enough weaponry to the top of the cliff I could fortify a camp overlooking the river. It made sense that the birds lived there, safe from the deadly grasp of the large cats below.

The cell bars were welded. The Erskans knew metal-working technology. They were accomplished builders. Mostly what I saw were heavy iron, some bronze. The collar on my neck was, unmistakably, steel. The chain was iron, but was thick and evenly forged.

The stone walls and floors were put together with a minimal amount of grout between the pieces. All ends were cleanly cut and fit perfectly.

On each of three walls there hung a ring. I guess it could be called a "slave ring". It was a thick, half-inch diameter iron ring that was on a large metal pin that was recessed deep into the stone, about five feet from the floor. I ran my hands on one, pulling it like a simple door knocker, and let it rock for a moment. From the polished surface inside the joint it was easy to see it had been worn through much use.

But the prison seemed quite empty – there was only one prisoner here.

78

I walked to the cell door. There was just enough slack in the chain to allow me to get my hands onto the bars and get my forehead to just touch the bars. This made escape a two-obstacle problem: picking the lock on the cell door, and picking the padlock on my neck collar. It was a padlock I could not see but, like everything else here, would likely be perfectly crafted.

There had been little time to think since being captured. Perhaps it was their way of socializing the prisoners... of socializing the males. Were the Erskans the only female dominant culture on Aervanta? No, that did not fit. They were not dominant; they were female supremacists. *I think.*

So, for the last three days they had kept me either moving at top speed or exhausted.

The welts from the whipping had disappeared, but my body was still crisscrossed with scores of angry, bruised stripes.

I had been hurt too much since coming to Aervanta. Crashed, tortured by the Erskan women, slapped, and whipped. Well, maybe "torture" on the first night here was not entirely correct. That was... torture of a sort.

The real torture was not being allowed to orgasm.

I realized that they had left my hands free.

Why?

The main cell block door was unlocked and I heard boots approaching.

Without being asked, I stepped away from the door and knelt.

Two guards entered.

Without a word, they locked a leash onto me, released the floor chain and led me out, crawling. No clothing was offered this time.

The sun was going down, but it remained warm outside, perhaps around ninety-five degrees. They led me along back gravel roads, all the while allowing me to crawl on the grass, until we came to a small, square "lawn".

There were about thirty women, dressed in a variety of attire, a few accompanied by male slaves wearing the usual loin cloth. I, however, had been brought in naked.

The sun cast shadows from the buildings as a few more women approached the area, each leading slaves.

Everyone formed a line around the grassy lawn, which was about thirty feet square. I waited on my hands and knees.

Then I felt weight on my horizontal back and a soft, warm leather skirt. I recognized her scent.

"Alexi, stay," Otra said.

A couple of women descended on her speaking too quickly for me to comprehend. It seemed they were discussing a meeting.

During this time, Otra's right hand drew circles on the small of my back and buttocks, her nails sometimes scratching lightly. I hoped she would not stop.

"Alexi," she said.

"Yes, Mistress?"

"You know word 'fight'?"

"Yes, Mistress."

"You can fight and not kill?"

"Yes, Mistress."

"Yes, Noomala," she said to one of the women.

The woman turned and walked over to three women who had a male slave on his knees. One of her women pulled the loin cloth off of the male and told him to stand.

He appeared to be slightly under my age, assuming that visual impression actually meant anything. He had black hair, was about five-foot ten, around one-hundred-sixty pounds, with the native long slender arms and legs, a curvy face, rounded nose, and wide round eyes. Compared to the other males I had seen closely, which were only four or five, he was muscular.

And he appeared quite nervous.

I smiled.

It could have been that he did not want to fight this strange, rather large alien. Or maybe that he did not want to fight anyone, anywhere, no matter who it was.

After making a long, light scratch of her nails that ran from my buttocks to my neck, Otra stood and whispered, "Fight."

I got to my feet and looked at him again, trying to guess what his first move would be. My years of training and experience had my eyes looking at his wrists, hands, and feet, making estimates on what would be easy to grab or, equally, the most dangerous.

Strength did not seem to be the greatest attribute of the natives; perhaps they compensated for it in speed. It would be foolish to assume they were physically my junior in all measure. Those legs... maybe they could kick fast or jump far.

Would this be a hitting fight or a wrestling fight, or both?

My adversary did not move.

I looked at Otra who cocked her head a bit and then made a subtle nod toward him. She practically wrinkled her nose at me.

We were twenty-five feet apart, completely in the shade. Slowly, he balled his fists at positioned them at chest height. It looked nearly comical, like the way my friend's little sisters would get ready to fight.

I walked towards him about five feet, and then unexpectedly stepped left, maintaining the same distance, but getting on his right side. He rotated his hips first, then his feet as an apparently afterthought, to turn my direction. He also retreated about a half-foot.

A thought occurred to me then. This compound had seemed somewhat like a military outpost – but what if it was a training ground for fighters? Did I want to get myself involved as a barbarian slave fighting for the Romans here?

If one change of direction was unsettling to my adversary, then another one seemed like a good idea.

I moved fight feet closer, then to the right, side-stepping past my original approach by a few feet.

He was more responsive this time, but still appeared to have difficulty with the strategy.

We were about fifteen feet apart now; it was time to engage.

I moved towards him, also moving slightly left again, until I was within striking range, keeping my right side facing him, ready to block any kicks or sudden strikes.

He opened his left hand to me into a "halt" gesture, which made an easy target. I grabbed onto his hand, rotated his thumb down, locked his wrist, and was behind him in a heartbeat, his arm pulled high behind his back. With a kick of my left leg I cut his feet out from under him, and he went down to the grass with an audible thud.

I put my knee in his back and held his arm.

"Stop," Otra said.

Conversation erupted among the women, primarily exclaims of surprise and consternation.

I stood and stepped back, turning toward Otra. I wasn't sure whether I should kneel at that location, or walk to her, or keep standing. So I bowed, holding it for a few seconds, before straightening.

She had a perplexed expression for a moment.

Then I turned to the man who continued to lie face down on the ground. He glanced over his shoulder, saw that I was a distance away, and he got to his hands and knees.

"Noomala," Otra said to the woman that had brought the fighter. Then Otra said a few more words most of which I did not comprehend.

Noomala approached the man and talked softly to him.

Otra pointed to her feet. I walked over and fell to my knees before her. "Alexi. Noomala has frey Gharla. Frey Gharla not fight in... big time. Frey here not fight. They are frey. Veslay fight, but no veslay here."

"Mistress, what is 'veslay'?"

"Veslay is frey and no Mistress... until time."

A free man. So there were free men here.

"Where is veslay?" I asked.

Otra shook her head. "Alexi no veslay."

We'll see about that.

Noomala walked over to Otra and spoke again, politely. It sounded as though there would be a rematch.

Otra looked at me and started to point to the man, but I nodded and rose to fight.

A lightning-fast strike hit below my buttocks, high on my right thigh.

She held a brown leather strap, about two feet long, with a short, thin leather lanyard on the end.

I looked down at my leg, no longer surprised at the effect of the strap. It stung. I got back to my knees and wished Hula was handling me this time. I could understand her better.

"No," she said.

I waited.

"Fight," she instructed.

I kissed her boots and then stood, walking over to the man.

He was ready, standing in the same location.

I tried the off-center approach again, which worked nearly as well. He had learned and was turning his whole body toward me, instead of rotating his hip and putting his body off-balance.

My approach was swifter this time, trying to diminish whatever muscle memory he could recall. My hand reached his left wrist, but this time, I pulled him toward me when I noticed he had not "set" his footing. As he came in, going lower, I bent his elbow and pulled.

He was coming down hard, maneuvering his right hand to break his fall. As he did so, he swung his right foot around in a lazy circle, attempting to kick out at me. The attempt was futile, because he was already so close to the ground. He landed hard.

I noticed, however, that he had managed to get his right leg around half the distance. That was something. His joints were more flexible than mine – an attempt like that on my part would have rendered me with a noticeable groin pull.

He tried to roll away, but I went over the top of him and pounded my body onto his, spinning and putting him into a head lock.

Then I jumped up, released him and backed away.

He made heavy breathing noises for a moment before getting to his hands and knees.

I walked over to Otra and was about to kneel again when she held her hand for me to stop.

"Alexi, you bend again?"

"Pardon me, Mistress?"

Otra shook her head, as if trying to think of a word. "I ask Hula," she said after a moment. "Down."

I got on my knees. The grass was now cool to the touch. There were approximately fifty women and twenty males there now. Most had removed their cloaks and hoods, with the males holding onto them or, often, watching over the garments in a folded pile from their kneeling positions.

"Alexi, you know 'two'?" Otra asked, holding her thumb and pointer finger.

"Yes, Mistress, I know 'two'."

She pointed at the man on the ground and another one standing by a different woman. This second woman wore the first garment that I could call a 'dress'. It was a one-piece leather outfit, light tan in color. It was shoulderless, with a v-neck front and back. Snug, it fell to above her knees in a skirt-style bottom. It was amazingly sexy, and she filled it nicely. Dark brown hair to the center of her back was tied in a single six-inch long leather band decorated with a dozen metal studs. Her face became one of concern.

Otra addressed this woman as Devra and told her she wanted her male to fight. Devra sounded polite, but was clearly reticent about the idea.

I looked up to the roof of one of the closest buildings. There were two archers there. Why would Devra be worried? If I seriously hurt anyone, I'd end up with a couple of sticks in my intestines.

As Otra attempted to persuade Devra change her mind, we heard a small commotion behind us near the buildings.

Everyone turned to look.

Three female riders, wearing their warrior leather uniforms, charged around the corner, their animals kicking dust and small gravel from the road. They slowed down as they approached the grassy fighting area.

Otra immediately dropped her conversation with Devra and approached the riders.

There was an animated conversation, voices rising. It did not seem confrontational, but more concerned.

A couple of other women arrived on foot from one of the nearby buildings. They appeared to be of a senior rank, but still subordinate to Otra. Otra gave one of them an order, and she jogged back into the building.

Something had happened that was definitely stirring them up.

Three women, all dressed in lightweight clothing, emerged from the building, two with slaves following carrying items of clothing. The group approached Otra and listened to her bark orders. The slaves silently and expertly dressed two of the women in their warrior uniforms as the instructions were delivered.

The third woman had been carrying two swords that she handed to the other two, who were apparently replacements for the dismounting warriors. It reminded me of the

82

pony express riders.

Parting comments were brief, and then they turned and rode away at full speed.

Otra spoke to the women a moment before she looked over at me, almost as an afterthought.

"Brezha, take Alexi."

A woman from the crowd of onlookers approached, reached down and hooked a leash around my collar. Then she stuffed a cloth into my mouth before tugging on the leash to follow her, again crawling on all fours.

As we turned onto the main camp road headed to the prison, I could see a small cordon of female warriors standing beside horses, getting ready to mount. Several slaves supplied them with gear and packs.

As we passed, I heard a word that Otra used when riders approached, "tree-slock". I would ask her about it if the opportunity arose.

The warriors rode off in a straight column through the guard gate as we continued the walk to the prison.

I was put into my cell, secured to the floor chain by my metal collar, had my hands locked behind me, and was given additional water and bread.

Before Brezha walked away, I nodded my head at her and spoke. "Mistress, may I ask a question?"

She swung the cell door shut with a loud metal 'clang' that echoed in my stone cell. She frowned at me. "Yes, you may ask, frey."

"What is the word 'tree-slock'?"

Her frown deepened. "You know 'Aervanta'?"

"Yes, Mistress."

"Treaslok is Aervanta, but not Erska."

"Not good?" I asked.

She turned her back to me and walked away. "Not good."

*****

I spent the next two weeks following a regular routine. The instruction with Hula intensified. She seemed to be in a hurry or under increased pressure. There were fewer people around the compound. I did not see Otra since the first word of the Treaslok.

Hula would not answer any questions I had about it, nor would she talk about the history of her people. This was a one-way instruction, with my learning only what she wanted me to know.

The morning following the fight, I did pushups and other simple exercises in my cell. I also felt the slight touch of hair growing on my face again; it was nearly time for my annual injection of depilatrone that prevented a beard.

For that matter, there were other concerns. My birth control injection would likewise be expiring in a few months.

All of that was on my Tamagra.

Safe. But it seemed like it was years ago that I had crashed.

It had only been fifteen or sixteen days.

My vocabulary was getting better. I could listen and talk without sounding stunted and child-like. It was now a matter of increasing my vocabulary.

On this late morning, Hula was giving instruction on conjugating verbs and of the special pronunciation changes that occurred with certain nouns. One such peculiarity was how they did not seem to distinguish a priority of taking sequential actions.

"Mistress, when the slave is kissing his owner's boots, and she starts to walk away, what does he do?"

"That depends on how fast she is walking. If he can kiss each boot, or only one, that is what he should try to do. Then when she stops, he can finish."

A guard, one that I had seen several times before, came in, shutting the door behind her. She walked over to us, her boots clicking on the wood floor. She handed a small piece of cloth to Hula, which Hula opened and read.

"Yes, I agree," Hula replied, handing the cloth back. The guard walked out.

Hula smiled at me.

It was a friendly smile. But, I had seen it before. It was as though she were happy about the prospect of pulling the wings off a butterfly.

"You are to be rewarded, Alexi," she said.

"Yes, Mistress?"

"Hula is to give the reward," she flashed teeth at me. Did she make a soft growl? She looked at me as I knelt, sitting back on my heels. "Stand."

I got to my feet as she whisked my leash from her desk and swiftly locked it on my metal collar. She headed out the door, pulling me along quickly.

We crossed the compound and headed for the prison.

She stopped at the intake desk and asked Tural, one of the guards, for an escort. Tural left Jasalin at the desk, and then had to keep up with Hula as she led us down the hall to the torture chamber.

"Mistress?" I said.

"Silence," she told me.

Tural unlocked the door and let us in before exiting.

Hula surveyed the room settling her gaze on a big wooden x-shaped cross that was leaning against the wall. It had oversized metal rings along all of the edges with short chains securing it to the floor and wall.

Next, she looked lovingly at the long, leather-padded stretch rack with its big metal wheel and axle. In one decisive motion, she pulled my leash over to the stretch rack.

"Lie down," she ordered.

I was slowly easing back when she placed a hand on my chest and shoved me down. The leather was cool to the touch. It was well-oiled and appeared to have slight indentations from being used many times.

She grabbed my wrists and lifted them above my head.

The right wrist was locked onto the chain. Then my left wrist was locked.

She gave a turn on the metal wheel until both chains had the slack taken out. Then she went down to my ankles and snapped them each to an anchored chain.

She yanked off the loin cloth and cloth belt, tossing them to the ground, exposing me. I had gotten so used to being naked that it barely registered a concern. But this was different.

From behind me, she turned the wheel again and there were two clicks as the ratchet engaged. My arms were straightened. She turned the wheel once more, and my torso pulled upward, stretching my legs. Three more clicks, and I was solidly stretched.

I surrendered a soft gasp.

She walked to my left side and flashed that wing-pulling look again before reaching

84

under the rack and producing a five-inch wide leather strap, or belt. She pulled it from the table on either side and connected it at my stomach, pulling one end through the buckle and giving it a hard jerk to pin my back and hips to the table.

I could not stifle my protest.

Hula licked her lips, and then put a finger into her mouth.

She took her finger out, glistening with dampness, and placed it on my lower lip.

My tongue licked out at her finger, but she pulled it away, making another soft growl.

I could feel my cock begin to stir.

Hula noticed also, and she took her left hand and reached under the table. I was barely able to lift my head, but strained to see.

That did not seem to be what she wanted. She dropped something on the table and then moved near my head. Another buckled leather strap appeared at neck-level. It was about three inches wide, and she fastened it snugly against my throat.

Then I felt her hands on my cock. She reached around my scrotum and penis and I knew she was concealing something. There was a momentary jerk, and I realized she had put a leather strap around my genitals.

Blood filled my cock – in a matter of seconds it was engorged. There was nothing I could do to stop it. The more swollen it became, the more blood became trapped, and the more excited I was.

She pushed her skirt to one side, and then hopped onto the rack, straddling me at the ribcage.

Her skirt fell mostly to the right, with the left slit exposing her left leg and little ankle boot.

"Alexi, do you see Erskans as lovely?" she asked, looking down at me.

"Yes, Mistress." It was an honest answer.

"Do you want to escape?"

"What do you mean, Mistress?"

Hula laughed, "We know you look for ways to escape. It is in your eyes. You can not hide your desire."

Hula had her hands straight down, straddling my upper torso, just under my armpits. Then she slowly moved her hips downward and barely guided her pelvis against my stomach. I could tell she was naked and... warm. And damp.

"Do you want to escape?" she asked again.

My cock was fully erect. It had been almost a month since I was allowed an orgasm. And it was showing. I tried to thrust my hips upward, to touch her with my cock, but there was no possibility of movement.

"At the moment, no, Mistress, I do not want to escape."

Hula moved her head down and licked my left ear. "Good slave."

Slowly, agonizingly, Hula slid her moist tongue along my neck. Then, to my shoulder. Then she lapped at my left nipple. I lost track of time as my head was swimming. I kept trying to look at her, but the neck strap prevented it.

Her hair was also falling into my face; it was softly scented with a nice odor I did not recognize.

When she bit into my nipple and latched on, I screamed. I tried to twist, but she continued to bite, harder. And deeper. As her teeth cut into my tender skin, I could feel her tongue licking at me.

I begged her to stop.

She stopped. "Earth people do not bite?"

"Not like that, Mistress," I said.

"Too bad, slave."

I could just barely see her dive for the right side of my chest before I felt her bite.

My screams echoed off the walls, as she ground her teeth on my flesh. As abruptly as she started, Hula stopped.

I panted. I drooled.

Hula growled and ran a finger across my lip.

She turned around, flipping a leg over me.

Then I felt her rub the head of my cock with her finger and my wet saliva.

"Oh," I moaned. I could smell something familiar. It was the scent of oil.

Warm hands enveloped by cock, holding the full length of it.

She rested back, allowing her body to sit on my chest.

Her leather skirt enveloped my torso, making a small pile in front of my chin.

Hula moved her hands up, stroking my cock. Then she moved them down again. I moaned and tried to thrust.

She took one of her hands and brushed her skirt wider, lifting it over my head. I was covered in unlined leather, which had a warm, damp, musky odor. I could barely see her naked ass and... then she moved back and smothered my face.

She was damp... wet. Hula did not have any pubic hair.

This was something I hadn't done. I wasn't sure what to do, exactly, except that I knew extending my tongue would be a good start. Before I could do that, though, she pressed fully down against my nose and mouth.

As I tried to gasp for hair, she stroked my cock harder and faster. It responded. It seemed so full – I would explode into a million pieces if it got any larger.

My face struggled, trying to turn. No air.

Couldn't breathe.

Finally she raised just enough.

I gasped for air, taking in deep breaths.

She stopped stroking my cock and let go. Hula then dropped onto me again, completely smothering me. Her hands worked on my cock, each one stroking in a hand-over-hand manner.

Air!

I tried to shout at her, but it only came out as a muffled cry.

Air! Air!

I could feel an orgasm approaching.

When Hula rose to let me breathe, she dropped my cock.

I'd have sworn if I had any oxygen for it. The name of the game was clear: I get pleasure only when she is controlling my breathing.

Hula said I would not have something unless she said I could. I knew what the word meant.

I had just exhaled when she smothered me again and stroked.

The oil was slick and her hands tight. She moved both hands rapidly, sliding them the entire length of my shaft. My hips hurt – I strained to thrust into her.

Air. There was no air.

If I could hold out just a moment.

I could orgasm. If I could just hold.

Air!

I struggled.

She pushed harder into my face.

My body jerked, determined to push her off.

I was dying.

She changed tactics, lifting off of my face and frantically stroking. "Beg."

I did my best.

"Beg!" she repeated.

"Please, Mistress Hula, please!"

She lowered herself a few inches but did not push onto me.

My tongue leapt out, reaching for her.

She continued to stroke. I could feel my legs shiver. It was close.

She moved down until I could touch her. I could taste her. I licked her. She made a low, long, deep growl that I could hear over the noise of her oil-slicked hands and my rapid breathing.

I licked and licked and licked.

Something told me, "Don't give in." But I would not listen. I could not listen.

She stroked.

My cock surrendered to her, ready to obey.

My neck tensed.

Chains rattled.

My arms almost pulled from my sockets.

I strained as my whole body tried to lift.

And I came! Loudly and gratefully, I came.

She slapped at my cock as it exploded.

The cum sprayed upwards, raining down on my legs. She slapped again at me as I continued to ejaculate, warm cum spurting.

I screamed, a combination of sheer and unbridled ecstasy and pain.

She took my cock in a firm hold and slowly stroked it, milking the last drops. The leather strap around my genitals was let loose.

Then Hula moved back down onto my mouth and I licked upwards, frantically trying to pleasure her.

She let me explore her for a few minutes, never allowing me to penetrate. She slowly moved off of me, another long, deep growl emanating from her.

She slid off the table and rubbed her left hand around my thigh and cock.

"Open mouth," she ordered.

I had never taste my own cum before, but I did as instructed.

She rubbed her hand around my mouth, inside and out, pushing the warm, salty fluid into me. I almost gagged on the unfamiliarity, but she pinched my nose and rubbed the leather neck strap for a moment. I swallowed.

"Good slave," she said. Her face appeared above me for a moment, smiling wickedly. Then she disappeared to release the rack's tension.

I continued to breathe heavily, even when she gave me several inches of slack and re-locked the wheel.

She unbuckled the neck and waist straps.

"No class tomorrow," she said.

Wing-pulling accomplished, Hula walked away.

I heard the cell door being opened before she got to it. I rolled my head to the right just in time to see several women step aside to let Hula pass into the hall.

The cell door was shut and locked.
I was able to twist my body somewhat, rolling onto my right side.
That was... incredible and devastating.
 Almost a dream.
I was looking down on the planet. Into the clouds. Through the sky.
I closed my eyes, only planning to float in the air for a few minutes...

Chapter Six
Traversing the Yiminee Plains

One of the regular guards, Jasalin, had come in the next morning to release my chains and help me from the stretch rack to the shower. My cell had more of the usual food, but included vegetables and a small portion of meat.

Then I had been left in my cell, alone, for several hours. It was the first day in weeks that there was no classroom instruction. It gave me time to reflect on the situation that was, all-in-all, not too horrible.

I wasn't being mistreated... well, not too badly. They treated me like an animal, of sorts, but never seemed to strike or hurt me just for the sake of doing so.

I jerked on the neck chain once, rattling it. It was beginning to feel normal.

I needed to get out of here!

After walking in a circle a few times, I sat back down, and then decided it was a perfect opportunity for a nap.

*****

It had been a nice dream. I don't recall what it was about, but it was worth trying to linger for a moment in that kind of headspace.

"Alexi," the voice called again.

"Yes, Mistress," I replied, getting to my knees and looking to see who was at the cell door. It was Jasalin. She had a serious expression on her face.

"You will be going with us this evening to Erskana. The Torino has called assembly."

"What is the 'Torino'?" I asked.

"The Torino is our leader."

"Is that one person or many people?" I asked.

"She is the Torino." Jasalin looked at me, running her eyes from my feet to my waist, and then to my face. "You will travel with us. You cannot be without a keeper."

"Who is my keeper, Mistress?"

"You belong to the warrior caste. Now we can talk to you. Soon, you will teach us about your gifts."

"Gifts" wasn't exactly the right word, but I had not found their noun for "stuff" yet.

"Come closer," Jasalin said.

I crawled over to the cell door. The chain stretched out behind my back and fell slightly to my right.

"Stand."

I got to my feet and stood closer, my hands loosely locked behind my back.

Jasalin reached out with her left hand and grabbed onto my flaccid penis. I

89

involuntarily tried to step back; however, she tightened her grasp and pulled me toward the cell.

"I watched you and Hula," Jasalin said.

With her right hand, she gripped the padlock on my collar, and pulled me a bit to my left and toward the cell door.

I tried again to back away, but she held firm.

"Hula was allowed to pleasure with you because she has been teaching you. And you are not like us. You are stronger than our frey." She pulled on my hardening cock. "You are bigger than our frey."

Her left hand persuaded me to gradually move forward, until my stomach was pressing against the cell door.

Jasalin let go of my collar, inserted her hand beneath her leather skirt and rubbed her sweet juices on my fully erect cock. It was warm and slippery. She then took her index finger and dampened my lips.

I closed my eyes as the sweet taste and aroma of her permeated my lips and senses.

She stroked my cock with both hands. I pushed against the metal bars.

"Do you want to?"

"Yes, Mistress."

"Beg, slave." Her right hand held my collar.

"Mistress, please give me permission."

"You have not earned the right," she said, suddenly squeezing down on my cock with her left hand.

I tried to pull away, but she had a firm hold on my cock and balls almost, pulling them through the bars on the cell door. With a long, thin leather strap, she encircled them several times, finally tying them off on the bars.

Then she let go of my collar.

I was stuck.

My cock and balls were tied to the cell door in front of me; my wrists were tied behind my back, and there was a heavy chain holding my neck.

"Do not fall, slave," she said.

How long could I stand like this? What if I slipped? Would I rip off my genitals?

"No, Mistress, I do not want to fall."

Jasalin took my erect cock in her left hand and held it up. It jumped around slightly. "Bigger than our frey here," she said, wrinkling her nose. "We have other frey in Erskana. Few are almost like Alexi. Here in KoVar, the frey are small."

"Mistress, may I ask a question?"

"You may, slave." She stroked me again.

"Why do you ... why do you... do this to me?" Masturbating me was making concentration difficult.

"We own you. We own your body. We own your will. You are a slave, and we will do anything we want with you. And," she reached her right hand into her skirt again, "I want you here in this way." She lifted her finger to my lips, "Suck."

She pushed her finger into my mouth. I gently sucked on her finger. It was even sweeter than before, as it was soaked in her juices.

I could feel my legs shudder as the orgasm was beginning to build.

Jasalin stopped stroking me, but kept probing my mouth with her finger. "You will no longer be allowed to have your pleasure until you have pleased your keepers. Do you understand?"

I nodded slightly.

"We will do many things to you. Understand?"

She masturbated me again.

I nodded.

"And you will accept what we do. Because you will want to have your pleasure."

I did not move or answer.

Jasalin continued to stroke my cock. I found myself trying to thrust my hips into her hand.

"You will accept what we do to your body, so that you may have your pleasure."

I nodded.

"That was not so hard."

She stopped stroking my cock and she took her finger out of my mouth.

Then she slapped my cock five times.

I howled, trying to retreat; but I was completely secured.

She untied the leather strap, and then pulled me down to the ground by my collar. She removed a short amount of chain from her belt and ran it around a couple of bars and locked it to my collar with a kind of snap.

And then she left.

I heard the main cell door shut.

I sat there on the floor, locked to the floor chain and cell door, wrists locked behind me.

My cock throbbed. I groaned. This was so hard! My tongue licked my lips, savoring every bit of her. I whimpered as my hips thrust once. Futile.

*****

Tural released me and ordered, "You may stand."

I rose to my feet, stretching. Cramps had hit my left thigh a couple of times while I had been restrained. Something had changed.

Tural was wearing a different kind of uniform. Instead of the leather skirt and vest combination, she had on light tan-colored leather pants, calf-high boots, and a white thin fabric blouse, tucked in, that had almost billowing long sleeves with wide cuffs.

"Go," she said, indicating I should walk in front of her.

It was the first time I had been allowed to walk anywhere without a leash. And, after several weeks of being here, it felt – unusual.

I stopped at the main cell door. Jasalin came from the other side and unlocked it.

I looked down at the floor. My cheeks were warm.

She made the Erskan growl that I had heard several times here, and as I walked into the room, past her, she reached out her left hand and squeezed deep into my right buttock.

"Stay," Tural ordered, right hand fingers tapping her hip.

Jasalin released her grasp and opened a cabinet.

She turned to face me with a pair of brown leather pants – no, actually, they were more like chaps. She belted the leather around my waist, with both legs hanging down. Then she wrapped the leather around my right leg and ran a leather lace through the inner thigh, pulling it together. Next she dressed my left leg. She appeared with another piece of leather that she laced to the chaps – this securely fit around from my back, through the legs, and to the front. It was the first time, also, that I had worn anything significant.

Jasalin leaned over to the counter and returned with a length of chain, which she wrapped around my waist and locked with a padlock. It had two short lengths of chain, on the right and left, which she let dangle beside my outer thighs for a moment.

Finally, Tural unfolded a cloak and pulled it over my head. "Go."

I preceded her outside.

It was, as usual, a typically warm late afternoon. The sun was starting to dip, with shadows stretching across the gaps between buildings. I noticed a great deal of activity.

Many people were walking, male and female alike, between buildings and along the paths. Men shouldered small wood crates or carried bags.

Tural pointed to the left, and I walked along the road until we came to the stables.

Outside were nearly forty women, all dressed like Tural, in various stages of mounting the "horses". Men fastened packs onto saddles; women held weapons, mostly swords and pikes, each one deadly. Every horse had lightweight leather armor covering all but the head.

It was an efficiently-run operation; everyone knew what they were supposed to do and was moving quickly. The horses were spread out in a loose column of threes along the side of the stable road.

At the rear, six horses were being loaded with supplies. There was one empty horse, about mid-column, that had no one around it.

"Slave, can you ride?" Tural asked.

"Yes, Mistress." It had been a few years, but, yes, it seemed likely.

Tural guided me to my horse.

As we walked through the women preparing to ride, several stopped their conversations to glance at me for a moment. I could not decipher their expressions.

The stirrups were a bit short, but I managed to pull myself onto the horse. Tural adjusted the length of the straps, and my bare feet fit into the stirrups – which were unique in that they were more like boots – my feet went entirely into them. Tural then produced a leather cover that went around the back of my foot. She laced it until my feet were secured inside. There was no skin below my waist that was not covered in leather.

"Mistress? Why do we have this armor?"

Tural finished securing my left foot.

"Hands." She took my wrist cuffs and locked them to the belt chain. Then she pulled the cloak around my waist and tied a simple leather belt around it. Tural stepped back, assessing her work.

"You will see," she said, before going to the horse on my right and starting to prepare herself.

A male who had been standing a few feet away attended to her. I didn't know how I felt about that.

I felt a nudge from behind.

Turning around, there was a mounted warrior I had not seen before, holding a long pike. She had poked me with the dull, handle-end of her weapon, which was apparently for combat among mounted troops.

"Slave, if you try to escape, you will die."

"Yes, Mistress." What I wanted to tell her was, *yeah, I've heard that a million times here*. I looked at my feet. If this horse loses its footing and falls, I'm dead when the fifty-thousand pounds of this thing crushes every bone below my waist.

Tural mounted to my right and settled herself into her saddle,

"Mistress, where is Otra?"

"Otra is the fort commander. She will stay."

"Why are we wearing the armor, Mistress?"

"Slave, you ask many questions. It is not your time to ask questions. The Torino will decide what you can know." Tural was silent for a moment, looking off to the distance. Apparently, she was thinking it over. "There are things you must know. We will be riding where the yimeenee are. Do you know this word?"

"No, Mistress."

She held her left hand up, and pinched her fingers closely, then moved them apart about an inch. "They are small animals. They live in the versa. They will try to bite you."

"Oh." I looked down at my legs to make sure there was no skin showing.

Tural grabbed onto my right arm, pinched my bicep, and grinned. "Only we can bite our slaves."

One of the warriors I had seen before approached the column on foot. A warrior and a slave helped her onto her horse, which was lightly supplied. She had on the same uniform, but she had wrist bands that indicated her rank.

"Erika," Tural said. "Her rank is jurina."

I grinned.

Tural looked at me, "Speak, slave."

"'Erica' is an Earth name of my people."

Jurina Erika talked to a few of the women at the head of the column. Then she brought her horse along the right flank, moving slowly. She stopped by Tural.

Tural saluted.

"Tural, you know your duty?"

"Yes, Jurina." Tural took the lead lines from my horse and tossed them to the warrior directly ahead of me.

Jurina Erika looked at the mounted woman behind me, probably for acknowledgement that it was she who was guarding me. The woman jabbed at the air with her pike.

Another warrior mounted beside me. She was taller than most of the women, stocky in comparison. She'd be what I'd call an Earth woman size 10, which was significant here.

The jurina disapproved.

"Bow your head," Tural instructed.

I complied.

The jurina rode ahead.

I looked up again. From behind me I heard the jurina order, "Gat ta chim!"

We rode. The horses took off, slightly staggered, from the front rows in close groups of three abreast.

The jurina resumed position at the front, on the right of the column, with two riders to her left. There were two rows of three riders behind her. It appeared their formation was a group of nine.

Behind her were two more groups of nine, and then the group of nine in which I was in the center. Another group followed mine. The first row was warriors, pulling along six riderless horses, all carrying saddlebags and various packs. The unit was forty-five persons in all, including the only male, myself. At least I got a horse.

I called them "horses" but their real name was ahn-la-stock. They were similar to a humpless camel and a horse, averaging about sixteen hands-high; their chest area was massive. Hula told me that they had two hearts and a triple lung that enabled them to run great distances. As we rode out of the fort, the tongue of my horse lolled out of the side of its mouth, panting.

I felt the underside of the light leather armor and found the soft thin fur of the animal to be cool and dry. So, maybe these were also like a dog?

We turned to the left, northward, going through the village at an uncomfortably fast gallop. People moved out of the way. Sometimes the occasional observant child was pulled to the side of the road as the column went past.

The sun began its dip to the west; my cloak was billowing in the wind.

It was not freedom, but it felt good to ride. Regardless of what this was called. It had been a few years since I had a chance to ride a horse.

Tural had a big smile on her face as we left the outskirts of the village. Ahead, the terrain had gradual, sloping hills, with a dense variety of low trees and brush.

It was hard to guess, but it seemed as though we were going perhaps thirty miles per hour. While that was not, in itself, a shabby speed, it was far from an effort for these animals. This appeared to be an endurance ride more than a race.

The road appeared to be well-traveled, though we did not encounter anyone coming from the other direction for almost a half-hour when the jurina raised her left hand and we slowed.

The warrior in front of me looked over her shoulder, assuring herself that my horse was instinctively slowing as well. She continued to hold the long leather lead in her gloved right hand.

Admittedly, my ass was glad we slowed down. The saddles were top quality and comfortable – but it was not a perfect fit for me.

The column slowed to a light trot as the road made a gradual climb. The density of the vegetation had increased, with the road narrowing and appearing less used. As the road curved slightly up, to the right, I could see other warriors standing, looking down on us from about a rise of fifty feet.

There was a structure there, as well.

We continued the ascent for about another five minutes until we approached the warriors.

Four low, heavily-fortified one-floor stone buildings covered a small flat clearing in the vegetation. There were six warriors and two slaves; the warriors approached the column, while the slaves appeared to be washing clothes.

We were strung out enough that I could not hear the conversation between the jurina and the warriors at the station.

The road continued to wind another twenty feet or so, and then there was nothing to see except blue sky. What was over the ridge?

The six warriors stepped back, one saluting the jurina. She looked at the sky, toward the sun, and then she whirled her horse around to look at us. There was unmistakable tension among the warriors in the column.

"Ride!" the jurina shouted and headed up the ridge.

As the horses ahead began to move, Tural advised, "Do not stop, slave. If you stop, you will die."

94

"What? What the hell does that mean?" It was a demand, the kind that did not go unpunished. But, no one was listening. And that scared me.

We topped the ridge. Below was a massive, flat, brown-colored plain, stretching as far as the eyes could see, right, left, and ahead. The road continued downward for about one-hundred feet, gradually making easy turns and allowing for a gentle elevation.

We had to be going close to thirty miles per hour. Our speed picked up a bit more... maybe closer to forty. Wind was billowing in my cloak and I had to squint.

Suddenly, we reached the brown surface, and all of the vegetation was gone. I glanced over my right shoulder and saw the ridge behind us, a looming giant band of green trees and plants.

The plain was composed of hard, dried mud. It was cracked in a few areas, but was mostly unbroken.

Now, fifty miles per hour.

I clutched onto the edges of the saddle, trying to roll them into the leather straps holding the leather armor to the sides of the horse.

They gradually changed our riding formation. The jurina and her group of eight riders kept position, but the other columns separated, with the second group moving slightly left. The third group moved to the right. My group moved right, of both the lead group and the group ahead. The group behind us moved left. We were riding in a v-formation, like birds.

And we were still picking up speed.

There was a little bit of dust being kicked from the lead horses, but I had a feeling that wasn't the reason to change formation. Maybe our speed was the reason. We needed to get distance between us.

We were now two miles away from the south ridge. The horses increased speed, their padded hoofs creating a loud staccato as they glided over the dried mud.

Tural was not smiling now, looking directly ahead and then, occasionally, over in my direction.

Sixty miles per hour. At least. There was nothing ahead of us, but more of the same flat surface.

The gait of the horse had changed, taking unbelievably long strides. And we continued to accelerate.

Finally, the horse seemed to relax and settled into a rhythm, its tongue hanging out the right side of its mouth. Saliva streamed out of its mouth, some of it hitting my leather-covered leg.

I was positive: we were screaming along the plain at over seventy miles per hour. The ground was a blur.

But, there was something different ahead. It was a small vertical white line, rising off the surface, about a hundred yards to our right. We got closer, and then passed it. It appeared to be where a large crack in the surface was allowing steam to rise.

Was there geothermal activity below?

These increased in frequency, with one appearing every couple of minutes. Then there was one every minute.

We rode right over one of them, but I could not smell or feel anything.

Well, that's not true. There was a light odor in the air. Sulphuric? Were we trying to run so fast we did not get poisoned? That made sense, in a dangerous sort of way.

Ahead, there was a thin horizontal line, forming along the horizon... well, no, it was closer than the horizon. We continued to fly across the dried mud, with steam vents appearing frequently now.

I kept my eye on the line ahead. Distances were hard to guess without a reference object behind, but it was... what was that?

"Do not stop! Tural shouted.

What the hell was that ahead? It was a gradient of brown color, darker close to the dried mud and lighter at about four feet high.

We were two hundred yards away from it.

Then one-hundred.

It was not a single "thing"... it was a massive amount of small things. All moving.

Then fifty yards.

I shuddered. "Oh, Hell!"

Millions of insects were flying toward us. They filled my vision from the right to the left, and as far as I could see ahead of us.

They were dense near the ground – sparse above four feet.

My horse sped up slightly. It could sense the coming impact.

It was everything I could do to keep my head facing forward and my eyes open.

I was, frankly, terrified.

The wave of insects hit the first group of warriors, thin at first, then solid insects. They blew away, being forced to the sides as the armored horses deflected them.

But thousands and thousands of them flew past the lead horses.

The unit in front of my group took the brunt of the swarm also, with even more of the insects dispersing to the right and left.

Then they hit us. Me.

The horse ahead of me shuddered, and the warrior raised her right hand, holding the lead line.

An amazingly loud hum filled the air that was high-pitched and deafening all at the same time.

We slowed as the swarm of yimeenee hit us. We couldn't help it.

My legs were being hit by thousands of the bugs. It was not painful, but the sensation was creepy.

I looked on my right leg and saw it was splattered with a light-colored green goo.

A handful of the insects at my thigh-level were trying to latch onto my leather, but kept sliding off.

Our column rode on.

Ahead the swarm thinned; we had apparently broken through the largest part of it.

Behind us, the swarm turned and pursued.

Sting! An insect just above my wrist cuff. Brushed it off. Looked like a wasp. Blood on my hand.

I noticed one of those little bastards on the left side of my horse's neck, below the ear. I leaned forward and brushed it off.

We continued to ride.

Behind us the swarm had gradually fallen behind... but it was a matter of us moving at about seventy-five miles per hour, and the swarm managing only seventy-three; it was that close.

There were fewer insects ahead, until we were riding with only an occasional straggler intersecting our trajectory.

My conjecture about poison air was dead wrong. I shook my head. My legs were caked with dead insects.

And I felt a sudden love of this horse. I hoped he was young and had many miles left on his odometer.

The swarm continued to chase us. It had fallen to about a mile behind.

We had been riding full-speed for at least an hour. The horse showed no signs of duress.

"Slave!" Tural shouted. "Half the way!"

Hell. This was... wow.

That would mean, give or take a few, we were going to cover about one-hundred and forty miles.

We charged on for another half hour, increasing the distance behind us. The swarm continued to pursue, but was no longer a horizon-encompassing mass.

My hands were getting sore. I looked over to the right and wondered how far the barren plains stretched. Surely it had been a dead sea.

Something in my peripheral vision pulled me out of my thoughts.

In the group in front of us... the warrior on the right rear, suddenly slowed, and her horse turned to the left abruptly.

We were about forty feet behind them. I managed to see just enough of the blur to see her frantically trying to control the horse. As we stormed by, I saw her horse make an erratic move to the left; and then it tossed her.

They both tumbled; she was thrown clear, cart-wheeling across the dried mud. The horse flipped, its massive legs flailing in the air.

All of the horses in our group had slowed a moment, looking left as we rode past them.

Perhaps the warriors had done something to keep their horses going onward. But for me, it was a combination of my horse's reaction and my instant decision. Moving as one, the horse and I side-stepped slightly to the left and slowed. The lead line from the warrior ahead snapped out of her hand.

The warrior behind me looked like she was contemplating grabbing her javelin, but she went by too quickly.

My horse flipped its head from side to side – the lead line was in the air, and I reached forward and grasped it. I flipped the lead line over the horse's head and pulled him slightly to the left.

My horse and I were slowing and arcing to the left, making a gradual turn. The capability of the horse to turn at fifty miles per hour was stunning – he turned more sharply than I had expected.

We circled quickly, but were hundreds of feet away from the fallen horse and crumpled warrior.

To my right, I saw that Tural and another rider were also breaking formation, making a similar arc to the left. The rest rode on.

I made a straight line for the fallen warrior.

She staggered to her feet, but could not regain her balance.

The horse couldn't survive this; its legs grotesquely probing the sky. The warrior got to her feet again, and looked behind her.

The swarm was gathering. It was getting darker, creating a massive wide brown shadow as it approached its prey.

The warrior got her bearings. She understood and ran toward me. She stumbled.

"Get up!" I shouted in English.

She staggered on her hands and knees, obviously injured.

I screamed to the horse, kicking it in the sides.

"Get up! Get up!"

It was going to be close.

I had to start slowing down.

The swarm filled my view.

Crawling frantically, the warrior almost got to her feet before falling again, face-down.

I would not be able to get down and lift her – my feet were still secured to the stirrups. Besides, there would be no time. If I stopped, I would be eaten alive.

I was still fifty feet away. I heard her.

She begged. She got a knee under her. One chance, that's all we had.

I pulled the horse to approach on her right, and reached down. The chain! It prevented full extension of my hand.

She straightened, and we locked left arms, colliding at about ten miles per hour. The impact almost jerked me out of the saddle.

She swung up behind me, tossing her right leg over the butt of the horse.

"Hee-yah!" I shouted, veering left.

The swarm piled into us as the warrior let go of my left arm and reached around my waist to hold on.

The millions of yimeenee buffeted the right side of the horse as we continued to turn, picking up speed again.

The horse made a deep, guttural grunt as the insects pushed against him.

"Faster!" I shouted. "Yahhhh, boy!"

I saw a part of the swarm break off and attack the wounded horse. In a matter of ten seconds, it was a horrible picture of blood and skin and torn leather. The screams were terrible.

Tural and the other rider came around us, approaching from the rear, at their top speed. They came so close that they brushed the back of my horse, crossing behind.

The resulting draft and interference disrupted the swarm for a moment.

It was just the help we needed to get my horse back to cruising speed.

Not long after, the swarm fell back.

Tural and the other rider flanked us, ready to assist, if necessary.

I felt the warrior's grasp on my waist begin to falter; I took the lead line and moved it to my left hand. Then I took the warrior's hands in my right and held her tight against my waist. Her head bouncing against my back told me that she was unconscious.

The rest of the column had slowed.

In another ten minutes, I guided my horse back into formation, easing into my assigned slot.

Tural assumed her position. She looked directly at me and smiled, shaking her head once.

We rode without further incident.

After thirty minutes we could see a ridge ahead, rising from the desert. Though we were a few miles distant, the direction to the path up the ridge was indicated by several flashes of sunlight. We made a gradual deceleration until reaching a fast trot at the bottom of the path where the reflections had directed us. Two warriors flanked the top of the path, each carrying a hand-sized square mirror.

The warrior behind me was lucid and moving slightly; she was still out of it.

Our column climbed the path to the top of the ridge.

The jurina was already dismounted when my group arrived at the station. She and the other dismounted warriors from the first group approached on foot.

"She is hurt, Jurina," I said, bowing, extending the lead line to the leader.

She held the line while Tural reached over and helped the wounded woman down to the waiting arms of her comrades.

She was a mess, alright. Broken right arm above the wrist. Nasty cuts and scrapes on the right side of her head. Blood, caked in dirt, covered the entire right side of her head. Chunks of her hair were gone, probably abrasion from the crash. Her right foot also appeared to be twisted inward; it was broken at the ankle.

Having seen hundreds of injuries like this before, albeit from a different kind of collision, I thought that she would be okay.

"Look up, slave," said the jurina, handing the lead line to Tural.

I looked at her.

"Riko is grateful for you," she said, looking at the warrior that was being carried to one of the buildings. "I thank you."

"Thank you, Mistress... Jurina," I replied.

The jurina surveyed her soldiers. "Tural, have one of the station slaves attend to his injuries. We will rest here tonight."

The jurina walked over to a building, a couple of warriors following.

Injuries? I looked at my left arm. It had a dozen small dried blood spots on me. I had never noticed.

"Close, much close for your life to die," Tural said.

"Yes, Mistress," I said.

Tural dismounted. She brushed away layers of dead insects and their fluids from my legs. Then she untied my stirrups. She unlocked my wrists, and helped me dismount.

I was grateful.

"I am not happy with you, slave." Tural scowled, tapping her right hip. "You did not obey my command – only warriors are permitted to bite you."

Chapter Seven
Antrana's Grandeur

The room appeared to double for both dining and medical treatment. It was in the second-closest of the four buildings and was about seventy feet by fifty-feet. An angled, low ceiling was supported by heavy wood beams.

There were a handful of the warriors from the ride already sitting at two of the tables on the far side of the room; lying on a closer, sheet-covered table, was Riko. She was partially stripped of clothing, lying on her left side, facing away from the doorway and myself. One of the warriors on the ride was tending to her, as were three slaves.

The *crack* I heard coming in was undoubtedly something they had done to re-set her broken ankle because she was uttering a low, incredibly long curse.

"Sit," Tural said to me.

I looked at the chair for a moment.

"You have permission. Sit."

How long had it been since I was allowed to sit in a chair – a chair that was not in a classroom? Seven weeks?

I sat at the table, three tables away from where they were mending Riko.

Tural sat on my right side, turning her chair at an angle so as to keep watch over me.

One of the warriors threaded a needle and began to sew the open wound on Riko's left forearm. She remained silent, her body stiffening.

"Erskans are a strong people," I said.

"Are Earth women stronger than you?" Tural asked.

"Some. Life has changed on my world for the last three-hundred years... uh... one-hundred and sixty chanas... where Earth women and Earth men are closer. But in the past, men were stronger than women."

"Who are the slaves?"

"We have no slaves. Every person is free."

Tural gave me a skeptical look.

One of the men walked over, carrying a small leather bag.

"Do you feel ill?" he asked.

"No." I examined my left arm. "These do not hurt much."

It was the first time I could recall a man engaging in any sort of conversation. He was taller than the other men at the fort. He was of slightly thicker build, but was still what appeared to be a native Erskan man, wearing the typical loin-cloth. However, he wore a belt and sandals.

"They will. Unless..." He smiled and then removed a small glass flask of a clear blue liquid. He poured an ounce out onto a cloth and then pressed it onto my arm. There was a minor sting over each wound as he wiped off the blood and applied the medicine, dipping into it several times.

"Mistress Tural," he asked, looking up from his work, "is everyone well at KoVer?"

"No one has become ill," she replied. Then she looked directly at me.

"We were afraid that you had brought illness," he said, drying my arm with another cloth.

In the course of human history, we had brought deadly viruses and bacteria to the native people of other lands. It's likely that the Expansion and need for immunizations for so many different worlds had resulted in my body being safe enough to not contaminate and subsequently decimate the population here. One-hundred years ago, someone from Earth might have wiped out this planet by accident.

"That is enough," Tural said. "Frey Alexi is not to talk much to anyone until seeing the Torino."

"Yes, Mistress." He put the flask into his bag and gathered the soiled cloths. "Until next time, Alexi."

"Is he different from the other frey?"

"There is a caste system for slaves," Tural said, standing.

I got to my feet.

"You have seen only the... not in culture... of our world. Now you will see the culture part." Tural locked a leash to my collar. "Come."

I followed her to one of the other buildings, a barracks. There were enough bunk-beds to quarter one-hundred persons. There were also cages. Ten cages, five stacked two-high. Which one was I going to be put in?

There were no other people inside the room yet. Several packs had been tossed on to the beds in a random fashion; warriors claiming territory.

The cages were in the center of the room. As we walked toward them, I could see that they were not quite long enough for me to stretch out; and they were not high enough for me to sit upright. They were made of welded metal bars. A flat piece of metal covered the bottom of each cage. There was a blanket and pillow rolled inside each one.

I slowed as we reached the cages, but Tural jerked on my leash. We went down another couple of rows. She took the handle end of my leash and threaded a padlock through the chain part, and then hooked it to a metal ring at the bottom of the solid-looking wooden post of the lowest bed.

"Can you undress, slave?" Tural inquired.

"Yes, Mistress."

"Do so. Kneel when you are done. I will return in my time."

I removed all of the clothes, folded them into a pile, and then knelt on the hard stone floor.

After almost a half-hour of that, I more-or-less flattened out, laying on my stomach, hands ready to push up should anyone come.

After another half-hour, I was annoyed.

The door knob moved. I got to my knees and waited.

A different warrior, one from the second group of nine riders, approached. "You!"

"Yes, Mistress?"

She stomped her boots heavily on the stone floor until she reached me. "Tural wants you now."

Whew! It did not seem that she was mad at me.

She unlocked my leash from the bed and pulled me along, stomping away again at a quick pace.

We went outside into the dusk to another building. Lights shone from inside the thin-glassed windows. And there was laughter.

The warrior thrust the door open, and I stood there, blinking for a moment until she jerked on my leash. The steel collar choked me, but I resisted the temptation to protest.

It was a dining room. All of the warriors were there. Only five slaves. Good-sized portions of food were piled onto the tables, mostly eaten. It smelled wonderful.

The warrior pulled me over to the large group of women.

I saw women standing while others sat on chairs or tables. One man walked around wearing only a light leather apron, sandals and a blue flower stuck in his hair. He was putting empty metal drinking glasses onto a wooden tray.

Another man had the hapless duty of being a chair for a warrior, although he didn't seem to mind. He was on all fours while she sat on him. He was completely naked except for the collar.

Another man was lying flat on his back on a table. There were smears of colors on his naked body. Food stains! A human napkin. I resisted the urge to smile.

The fourth man was kneeling by the crowd of women. Naked, but wearing sandals, he was the slave who had treated my bite wounds. He was silent as the women carried on about something to do with a sword maker.

In a cage at the end of one of the tables, was the fifth man. He was on his hands and knees, naked and gagged with a wide leather strap that was locked behind his head with a padlock. I noticed his wrists and ankles were locked with manacles and chains to the bottom of the cage.

This was some party I had missed. The food scraps did look enticing.

The warrior pulled me to the large group of warriors. All conversations died.

I had the distinct feeling that I was a little piece of meat being waved over a pond of piranhas that hadn't eaten – in several decades.

The jurina was sitting there. As best I could determine, her rank was similar to a colonel. I guessed at protocol and took to my knees.

She reached out and put a hand under my chin, lifting my eyes to see her. She took my leash in her other hand. "You are well-trained. Who has trained you?"

"Mistress Hula and Mistress Otra, Jurina."

"In such a short time?" Her voice was commanding, dusty, but quite sexy. She stroked the side of my neck once, dragging her fingertips from my left ear to my left collarbone. "Training can not teach all of this. You are a slave in your heart."

I resisted the impulse to laugh.

"Hula is not happy with KoVer. She wants to be home. But we have our duties," the jurina said. She reached lower to my left nipple and pinched me lightly. "I will be there when the Torino interrogates you."

I heard, but did not flinch.

She squeezed my nipple harder, letting her finger nails mark my skin. "I do wish you will not answer easy – give her time to make you suffer."

I gritted my teeth, looking down away from her.

She licked my right ear and then let go, chuckling. Her lips grazed my cheek. Then she pinched even harder.

"Tonight, slave Alexi, you will not suffer. My duties are to bring you to the Torino without much injury, so the warriors will use the house slaves for now."

Warrior who had been stripping me with their eyes, turned away, obviously as disappointed as I was relieved.

The jurina handed my leash to Tural. "It would be best to keep him over there for now. When he has finished eating, take him to the barracks. You can return."

"Yes, Jurina," Tural replied and guided me to a table in the far corner.

Conversation resumed as warriors laughed and drank a frothy beverage.

"Frey Mak!" Tural ordered to the one wearing the apron.

He hustled over to her.

"Feed him – be quick!"

Mak disappeared into a side room.

Tural gently slapped the side of her thigh with the leather end of the leash.

I was interfering with her play time.

Mak reappeared with a bowl which he presented to Tural. She pointed to the floor.

Mak put the bowl on the stone floor and shuffled off to clean another table.

The bowl contained a piping hot mixture of meat chunks and vegetables, covered with a light gravy. My stomach growled. It smelled so good. I started to stick my fingers into the bowl.

Tural lightly slapped at my hand. "No hands."

"Mistress, forgive me, but I could eat faster with my hands."

It took her about one ten-thousandth of a second to realize that. "Use hands. Eat."

It was, without a doubt, the first time since being captured that I had a satisfying meal. The meat was grilled and tasty. The gravy was watery, but very strong in flavor. The vegetables were of a consistency like baked potatoes, but taste more like an edaname bean.

"Mistress, I am done."

"Good, slave," she said.

I looked up and saw that all five of the men were now being tortured. Well, maybe that was too strong of a word. One of them was tied to a bench, face down, legs on either side. Two of the warriors were pouring hot candle wax on his back, and then scraping it off with a wickedly sharp blade. He would make noises when the wax was poured on him. I realized one of the warriors was rubbing something around his anus, but I couldn't see what it was.

This was not the time for me to get hard.

The caged slave had been released, partially, and was on his back, head out of the cage. He was licking the bare foot of one of the warriors.

One slave was on all fours while two warriors struck his buttocks with a long stick. He whimpered as they alternated sides.

The last two slaves were giving foot rubs to the warriors.

"Come," Tural said, pulling on my leash.

I obeyed.

When one of the higher ranking warriors called to her, Tural stopped and greeted a warrior holding a metal drinking tankard.

Automatically, I knelt at Tural's feet and gazed downward.

Without warning, the new warrior pushed the tankard to my lips and poured.

I drank. It was beer! Of sorts. A dark rich ale. More like a Bass ale from England. It was warm, but...

She paused for me to get my breath, and then she poured.

"That is for the jurina's mulasto," the warrior said, before walking back over to the group of women.

"Thank you, Mistress," I called to her, still unsure why I'd been rewarded.

As we walked back to the barracks, I licked my lips, savoring the last bit of foamy ale. God, that was good!

Tural increased the flame on a lamp, and then she led me to a lower cage and opened the door.

I had to bend over slightly to fit.

She locked my leash to a metal slave ring attached to the floor outside my cage. Then she put a padlock around the cage door.

"Mistress, what is a 'mulasto'?"

"Riko," she said as she exited the barracks. "You saved the child of the jurina's sister."

*****

They returned to the barracks in small groups, most not-too-steady on their feet. It was no wonder. The ale was strong. My half-tankard had given me a buzz equivalent to three regular beers.

It was the first time I had heard the natives singing. The words were slurred, the accent hard to make out, but three warriors had come in singing rounds of a song that was about the Nerosks and how they had defeated them in battle. Still, with the slight language barrier and intoxicated singers, I could tell that while their forte may be in combat, it certainly wasn't in lyrical arts.

The slaves were brought in with the last few warriors. Initially, I thought they were drunk, but they did not smell of ale. Marks, bruises, welts and sated expressions of lust. All of them. Mellow and content, they had glassy eyes and were not the least bit talkative.

So. After being tortured, the slaves had been allowed to cum. I frowned and stifled what could only be described as envy.

The warrior that had locked the slave above me now looked down at me. Her hand disappeared inside her leather pants for a moment. Then she pushed her fingers to my face, "Lick, slave."

I suckled her fingers and moaned, almost crying out when she left me to find her bunk.

Tural came in last. She adjusted the lamp to a soft glow, gazed at me for a moment, and then retired.

I was in a room full of half-naked, leather-clad and drunk women. I was probably the only person, including the males, who had not had a satisfying sexual experience. The taste of the unknown warrior lingered on my lips, taunting me.

I pulled on the chains for a moment, letting them cut into my wrists. A prisoner is supposed to want to escape, not long for the attention of his snoring captors.

Sleep was a long time coming.

*****

We awoke at sunrise. I was probably the only person who was able to look at the watery scrambled eggs without feeling nauseous. They were delicious, really, and I was fortunate enough to be the recipient of several unwanted servings. Milk arrived, cold and none-too-sweet. I did not know what animals provided milk and eggs on this planet and decided I really did not need to know.

Suddenly, one of the warriors fled her table, running outside. She would not be the first, or the last.

The remaining forty-four women laughed. Even the slaves, three of them kneeling on the floor beside me and two serving breakfast, chuckled.

The three slaves nearest me kept a personal space that was a bit larger than what they gave one another. There were no smiles given my way or attempt to communicate. They had probably received orders prohibiting talking to me.

The jurina looked at one of her lieutenants, who then relayed the order to get in formation.

Everyone, including myself, was dressed in the same clothes as yesterday; though I noted that several of the warrior's uniforms had even wet stains on them. It looked like they had been cleaned with water.

That's one good thing about leather – easy to wipe off the stains from the night. In addition to the leather uniforms, the warriors had their hair pulled back into the standard leather-wrapped ponytail. It was yet another way to disguise one's appearance from how hard she had partied the night before.

The armor for the horses were rolled into bundles and placed in saddle bags. That was a good sign.

I was helped onto my horse, which turned its head and whinnied. Tural locked my wrists to my belt chain and checked the fit of my bare feet into the stirrups.

The last few women approached, Riko among them. She was assisted by a warrior and slave up onto a horse. I noticed that one of the former riderless horses was now Riko's mount.

Riko's left sleeve was cut away, revealing several bandages. Her right boot was laced with pieces of leather where it had been cut open.

Abruptly, she turned and looked directly into my eyes.

We locked for about ten seconds.

She made a single nod, and then turned back to answer a question.

Not quite a reward, but it was enough.

A half-hour later we turned due east at an intersection. The new road was wide and heavily traveled. Over the next hours of riding we overtook several wagons and dozens of riders, a few civilian but mostly military. Wagon traffic traveled in all directions as we crossed other intersections.

The road changed from gravel to a paved stone, equipped with unlit torches on poles every hundred yards. Pedestrians, both women and men, appeared more frequently.

At first, we saw small, simple buildings along on the roadside; then, as the road widened yet again, the monotony was broken by two-story and three-story structures.

And all the while, people would slow down a bit to look at our column, and then they would focus on me as we rode by. I resisted the urge to return the stare.

Ahead, two warriors waited for us. As we approached, they fell in beside the jurina, matching the speed of their mounts to that of our column. I realized we had slowed to about thirty miles per hour with all the traffic. Everyone did get out of our way, though, especially when one of the lieutenants barked an order.

Civilians dressed differently than our warriors. Women wore a variety of cloth and leather ensembles, mostly of vivid colors and patterns. An outfit, similar to a kimono, was becoming prevalent. It was, though, usually made of layers of light leather in reds, yellows, whites, and greens.

The men wore different clothing, as well. A few were the loin cloths, but most wore a thin fabric kimono of solid colors void of design. There were significantly fewer men than women visible – perhaps on a ratio of twenty-five to one; all of the men were collared.

I found myself turning frequently in my saddle to see everything unfolding before my eyes. It was amazing. I imagined myself going back through time to 50 A.D., taking a trip through Rome or Athens.

Stone buildings rose ten stories high.

By now we had seen thousands of citizens, all going about their business. There were open air markets, with people haggling over prices of baskets of fruit and other plants.

We approached an intersection managed by a woman on a pedestal wearing light gray leather pants and a crisp white fabric shirt adorned with bright yellow armbands. As our column approached, the traffic cop blew her whistle and waved us through, forcing the other riders and pedestrians to wait.

I stared at her as we went by; and she stared back at me. I suppose neither of us had ever seen the likes of the other.

The road widened and our column moved to the center where we picked up speed. An express lane. We galloped along at about fifty miles per hour while slower moving pedestrians and horses got caught in a traffic jam.

Other traffic cops riding horses worked their way through the people, trying to get traffic moving again.

The buildings were impressive. They were in a column style that I had seen in my last visit to Greece on Earth. They were stone, often supported by metalwork, and were just as impressive as their Grecian counterparts.

The odors were tantalizing. The scent of unknown foods, horses, people, and who know what else, bombarded my senses. Still, I noticed, fewer males were present. Were they being locked up elsewhere?

Had we remained in KoVer, the day would have been turning warm. The temperature here was staying around the mid seventy-degree range. Nobody appeared to be prepared for heat by carrying cloaks or additional water.

I could see our destination. It was, in all practical description, a castle. The road had very slight curves so far, but now made distinguishable turns. At those points were formidable looking buildings, creating choke-points in the road. Archers were on duty atop the fortifications, surveying all below.

A twenty-foot high, two-foot wide stone wall appeared at the back of the fortified buildings, running left and right. It was my guess that the wall encircled the entire castle.

We rode another fifteen minutes past more buildings and homes and markets until we reached the main gate of the castle.

The castle complex was immense. There were about fifteen buildings or towers, rising twenty stories high. I could not see the base of the complex because my view was blocked by another wall and opened gate.

The wall was armed with archers at every fifty yards. Colorful banners with Erskan letters adorned the wall face.

"You must remember your training, slave," Tural said. "They will not be forgiving here."

"Yes, Mistress."

Several women approached the jurina and they had a brief, pleasant conversation. They all appeared to know each other.

Tural unlocked my wrist chains. "Off. You will walk now."

I dismounted. Tural leaned down and locked a long horse lead onto my collar, and then she led my leash behind her and to her right. She nodded to the jurina.

The gate guards seemed satisfied and waved us through.

They were heavily armed with swords, bows, and pikes. Reinforcements stood guard inside.

I jogged, barefoot, on the stone path. Several times I had to jump over small piles of manure.

Inside the wall, there were hundreds of one-story and two-story structures surrounding the castle. Several wells, made of metal components, were pumping something out of the earth. Six slaves were pulling a rather big wooden cart next to one of these pumps. I could not decipher what they were doing beyond that.

The actual base of the castle was still five-hundred yards away.

On the right was a large open parade ground area occupied by several rows of warriors on horses, all listening to orders. I counted the rows and made an estimate based on their nine-woman formation that there were three-hundred warriors present.

The pace of our column had slowed considerably, but it was still having me trot along at about the same speed as an eight-minute mile, while barefoot, on stone. Calluses had long ago formed on the soles of my feet, but they were not ready for this.

I heard what sounded like a battle cry. Warriors broke rank and rode out in an orderly manner through the main gate.

Several male slaves awaited our arrival at one of the buildings next to steps leading to a courtyard and, beyond, gigantic, metal-plated wooden doors.

The jurina gave an order, and we stopped.

Most of the warriors dismounted and left their horses with the slaves. Then they split up, heading in a variety of directions.

Other people passed by us; all of the women were dressed in military uniforms, either brown short leather skirts or brown leather pants. The slaves were wearing the solid color kimonos or, sometimes, long belted leather skirts without shirts.

"Tural, you will come also to see the Torino," the jurina said as she approached.

Tural secured my wrists behind my back and locked them into place.

One of the castle guards accompanied us as we went through the partially-opened door. She was wearing the military skirt, but all of the colors were of black leather and silver rank emblems.

The inside was spacious... palatial. Light beamed in from skylights and windows. Artfully crafted glass scattered colorful patterns of light on the stone floors. Candles were interspersed among the sparse furnishings, lighting the darker areas that the sunlight could not illuminate.

Vivid tapestries hung on the stone walls. There were thick, luxurious rugs under my feet. My toes curled into the nap as we stepped into the entry hall.

There were a couple of slaves cleaning statues and dusting art, all of it of females in valiant, defiant poses, usually holding weapons. The men turned and looked surprised to see me. Or us... maybe our entourage was unusual.

We entered another large room that had comfortable-looking furniture and many paintings on the stone walls. It was as I would imagine a sixteenth-century castle on Earth – except that it was colorful and bright. There was nothing foreboding about this place. Tapestries were made of brilliant colors; art was lively and energetic. It was "Japanese restaurant meets Disney meets King Arthur."

Tural led me to a side room where she handed my leash to a palace guard. "Go with her, slave."

I swallowed my fear. She had left me with strangers.

The palace guard led me to a stone room where she secured my collar to the floor with a chain and unlocked my wrists.

I recognized this design as she handed a bar of soap to me.

First, I used the chamber pot to urinate and then let her shoot me with the room-temperature water.

After a few minutes, I was clean and dry. The soap was softly perfumed. The towel I was given was plush and comfortable. Even the tooth cleaning goo was flavored with something, though I couldn't associate the taste with anything I had tasted before.

 The palace guard did not speak, whether by choice or orders, I did not know. I was given different clothes to wear. She'd handed me a skirt, a long, ankle-length, thin light gray leather skirt, slit widely open on both sides, held up with a leather belt. It was comfortable, airy, and I felt foolish wearing it.

My wrists were locked behind me again, and she led me back to Tural.

The jurina and Tural were wearing fresh uniforms, replacing the pants with black short leather skirts and dark gray sleeveless leather vests. It appeared that field uniforms were brown; the palace and castle uniform scheme was black and silver.

Tural had nice legs that were very attractive. I enjoyed the view, right until the second they caught me staring. Immediately, I studied the rug at my feet.

Tural took my leash and whispered, "The Torino would give you ten lashes for looking at a warrior as you did."

"Yes, Mistress."

We went down another hall and headed toward a closed wood door.

It opened and four warriors came our way.

"Jurina Erika," one of the women said, clasping shoulders with the jurina.

"Jurina Tharka," the jurina said. "It is great pleasure to see you. Are you well?"

Tharka? *Tharka?* I recognized her from somewhere.

"I am well. Have you heard about Renest? Have you heard about the attack?"

Jurina Erika stepped back, "Yes. I was informed when we entered the city."

"There were no survivors... three-hundred dead."

"When did this happen?"

"Five days ago. We met with the Torino this morning after we returned." Jurina Tharka looked at me with hard eyes. "The Torino must not be kept waiting."

"We will meet tonight?" Erika asked.

"I ride to Renest in an hour," Tharka said, walking past us.

"Who attacked Renest?" Erika asked.

Tharka turned on her heels. Then she said, "The Torino is waiting for you."

The Jurina Erika looked at Tural with a concerned expression. Then we knocked.

Two black leather-clad guards opened the door from the inside.

We entered a room that housed several large tables adorned with cloth maps. Maps hung on the stone walls. Several warriors moved about, carrying rolled-up maps, others painting on maps on the tables.

Lamps hung from the ceiling beams, illuminating every table.

One warrior stood with her back to me, talking about a setting a defensive line. A half-dozen other officers were circled around her, listening. She was moving small figurines of warriors along the map.

Two slaves knelt nearby, holding trays of drinks. One looked at me, his mouth agape.

The warrior ahead stopped talking and whirled around to face me, her short skirt swishing in the air.

She covered the ten foot distance in a half-second and delivered a powerful slap to my head. With my wrists locked behind me, I could not protect myself.

I was knocked down, sprawling on the rug-covered stone floor. My collar choked me until, I guess, Tural let it go. I landed on my side and elbows and tasted my own blood.

I needed help and looked at Tural, but her confusion was obvious. "Sklera Kretahla, I apologize for this slave."

The Torino stood over me, hands on her hips, glaring down.

It took a moment before recognition hit. The woman at KoVer. When I had been captured. Sklera. Queen of the Erskans. And, she was furious.

"Where are the rest of the raaa sticks?" Torino Sklera Kretahla demanded.

She opened her hand and let down a rain of empty bullet casings, several bloodied.

They fell to the carpet, making clinking sounds as some of them hit the others.

I watched a couple of them roll a few feet away. One spent shell brushed the booted foot of a warrior. She hesitated moving, and then uncomfortably lifted her foot and stepped a few inches to the side.

There was dead silence in the room.

"Where did you find these, Mistress... Torino?" I asked, blood running from my lip to my chin.

"Renest," she growled.

Chapter Eight
A True Erskan Slave

Using my shoulder, I wiped the blood from my mouth, careful not to get any of it on the rug. I was in enough trouble, and I didn't think Tural could do much to help me.

Torino Sklera clenched her teeth. She had a look I've seen many times before – nearly uncontrollable rage.

It was time to slow down the action a bit... ease the pace.

Lying on my side, I rolled over a and put my nose next to one of the spent casings, eyeing it for clues. "This is not one of mine."

"These are from Renest," Torino Sklera told me.

"This is not from my gun... not from my raaa stick."

"You are lying," she said, leaning over me.

"I know the penalty for lying," I replied.

There was a pause.

Jurina Erika broke the silence, "Slave, can you prove this?"

Torino Sklera snapped her head in the direction of the jurina.

"Torino," the jurina explained, "the slave has saved the life of one of my warriors. We could allow him the time to prove his innocence."

Torino Sklera looked back down at me. "How?"

"Please bring the gun that you have taken from me, and you can see."

Her face softened almost a fraction. She let out a long breath before turning to one of the officers and pointed to a door.

The officer disappeared into the next room and returned with a metal box that she placed on the map table. Torino Sklera produced a key and unlocked the box. Her breath was noticeably more regulated than it had been moments ago.

She pointed my StacGun to the ceiling.

"Drop the... clip," I said. "Uh... point the gun down to the floor... and press that blue circle. Use your left hand to catch a metal box will come out."

The ammo clip fell into her hand.

"Put the metal box onto the table. Then pull the top half of the gun back toward you. It will stay open."

Awkwardly, she pulled the slide back and exposed the chamber.

"Take the metal box on the table, and you will see the cartridges," I said, using English. "The metal cylinders. Pull one of them until it comes out into your hand."

Torino Sklera held a single round in her hand.

"Take it and drop it in the hole."

She put the cartridge directly into the chamber and it fit into the breech.

"It fits, yes?"

"Yes."

"Those are mine. Now, point the gun up and the round will fall out. Put it on the table."

I kicked an empty cartridge to her. "Try this one."

She lifted the cartridge and attempted to push it into the barrel. It was two calibers too large.

"My gun uses a nine millimeter cartridge. Those," I nodded my head toward the cartridges on the floor, "are from something different."

"How did they come to be here?" she asked, dropping the empty cartridge to the floor.

"Torino Sklera, I would be happy to tell you what I believe. We both want the head of the same male."

"Who is he?" she asked.

"Louis Corrigan."

"He is from Earth?"

I nodded. "Torino Sklera, are there Erskans that break your laws?"

"It happens," she said. "They are *trenama*."

"Corrigan is a trenama. He is my trenama, from Earth. It is my caste to find and take trenama to be punished."

It was a risk, but I was going to take it: I slowly got to my feet. I looked at Torino Sklera and wiped the blood off my chin with my right shoulder. "If Corrigan is alive, we need to find him. And kill him. Corrigan will want to rule your world."

Torino Sklera returned the StacGun to the box before facing me. "I will kill him."

"That will be fine. The Erskans are in great danger," I said, panning the room of warriors. "Corrigan is a trenama because he has been selling raaa sticks to someone. I did not know who his buyer had been. Until now."

"Treaslok." Sklera nodded. She cocked her head and asked the question I knew would be next. "How many weapons does Corrigan sell to the Treaslok?"

"It could be a hundred. I was chasing Corrigan in the space wagons when we both crashed down onto Aervanta. It is amazing that he lived."

"You are alive," Sklera pointed out.

"Yes. Corrigan's wagon was on fire before he crashed. He may have all of the guns, or only some. What would he do if the Treaslok found him? Do the Treaslok have the same life as you do?"

Sklera had a questioning look on her face.

"Male slaves," explained Tural.

"Yes, we believe so." Torino Sklera added, "We have battled the Treaslok for centuries."

"Then Corrigan may be using force to take control of the Treasloks," I said.

Sklera walked over to the large map table. She looked at the Jurina Erika, who nudged me toward the table to stand at Sklera's left side.

The map was similar to the one that Hula had shown me. But this included the continental outline of the eastern continent. There were only three towns or cities noted inside.

"The Treaslok know how to cross the water. We can not. Years ago, the Treaslok come to our land and attack our people. We have always sent them back to the water."

Sklera put her finger on the map of an eastern village identified as Renest. "Tell me about Corrigan."

112

"Corrigan is an evil, ruthless person. He will kill anyone and everyone that is in his way. The attack on Renest was a test. He wanted to test your warriors and your ability to fight. Were there any Treaslok bodies of the Treaslok at Renest?"

Another officer shook her head.

"After Corrigan and the Treaslok won the village, they took their own dead with them," I said. "Corrigan thinks that I am dead. He saw my space wagon explode – but I was in another smaller space wagon that he could not see."

Sklera stabbed at Renest with her finger.

"Jurinas, we must consider what the slave has said." She looked at Tural. "Take the slave to my chambers and wait for me. He is your charge."

I bowed my head, looking down at the floor.

"Slave," she said.

I met her gaze.

"I was in haste."

I knew that was the closest she would get to making an apology. It was time to be gracious and bank my chips for later.

"It must hurt the Torino greatly to suffer the loss of Renest. Her people would be glad of the Torino's passion to find the killers."

Torino Sklera chuckled.

Tural saluted her leader and then took my leash. As we went out the doors, we heard a swell of conversation among the warriors.

"Follow me," Tural said.

The chambers were within a few hundred feet, and we were led into a spacious room.

Tural let go of my leash. She unlocked my wrist cuffs and then pointed to a sink. There was a spigot and a valve there. I turned the valve and watched as warm water flowed.

There was a basket of scented soap. I picked a bar and washed away the blood. I dried my face with a towel and then turned back to see Tural.

She was sitting in one of several ornate chairs, legs stretched out in front of her.

"Slave, here," she said.

I walked over to her and knelt at her feet, my knees resting on the plush rugs.

"Slave, sit if you wish."

"Thank you, Mistress." I got off my knees and sat cross-legged.

Tural chuckled. "Slave, you were polite to the Torino."

"How?" I asked, seeking the confirmation.

She pointed her finger at me. "You know, slave. You could have made words to insult the Torino."

I smiled. "Yes."

"You are... " she said, then stopped.

"Yes, Mistress?"

"I am not permitted to tell you," she shook her head. "You must be unsure about my people... Erskans."

"Yes, Mistress. I have many questions."

"Do you want to go home to your Earth?"

"Yes, Mistress."

"Did you have many mistresses on Earth?"

"None."

The door opened and a palace guard entered.

I got to my knees and looked down as the guard approached Tural. "The Torino will not be returning for a time. She has issued an order."

"Yes?" Tural asked.

"The Torino says that the Netratoh will talk freely to the slave."

It was about time. Apparently, nothing will stir someone to generosity like the threat of an invasion.

"Please inform the Torino that the slave is thankful for her generosity," Tural said.

"Yes, Netratoh," said the guard, before leaving.

"It has been hard to not talk to you." She shifted her feet, moving them in front of her. "I will talk; you will pleasure my feet."

"Yes, Mistress." I moved closer to her feet, unlaced her boots and massaged her left foot, softly caressing the inner sole of her foot. She closed her eyes for a moment, taking in one long breath. I was getting better at this.

"The Erskans have been here for many centuries. The Erskans were of a ancient city and many small villages, and were victorious in many wars two-thousand years ago. Antrana was created almost one-thousand, five-hundred years ago. Between that time we had many great wars on the continent. Only recently have we moved forces southwest, to KoVer. It is our first growth in a hundred years and the first time we have reached across the baracha, where the yiminee live."

I nodded. So, the Erskans were an occupying force in KoVer.

"We say it is for the protection of KoVer, but that is not all true. There are no other villages hostile to KoVer."

"The Erskans?" I asked.

"Yes, the Erskans are hostile to KoVer." Tural pushed her other foot into my hands. "It will take us another fifty years until we have the KoVer people under our complete control. The distance and hardship to reach KoVer makes it difficult and slow."

"What is north of the Antrana?" I asked.

"There are other villages. We have peace with most of them. They are not under the control of the Torino, but we trade with them."

"Please tell me about the women and men of your world," I asked.

"Before our writings, there were equal women and men. No one knows what happened. Sometime, one-thousand years ago, the men became ill. Most died. The remaining men were not as strong. For the last five-hundred years, there are thirty women for every man."

Tural closed her eyes as I continued to rub her foot.

"As there were fewer men, women became more powerful in the affairs of the land. Women dominated every aspect of life. Men were wanted for their reproduction purposes and personal pleasure and, for a time, their strength to do heavy work. Then women fought over men and took men and kept them. Soon, men were denied rights and all were made slaves. The most powerful women could buy the best slaves. Fewer men in the world make the men who are left very important. But only as property, to be bought, sold, and used as the owner, the woman, wants."

"The wars," I said. "Those were about slaves, yes?"

"Yes. A city without slaves... frey... is a city that will die."

A genetic catastrophe created a situation that could be boiled down to a supply and demand problem. Keep the dwindling resource under tight control. If you want your family line to go on, you must have a male. Or, you need access and the financial means to rent one.

Tural dismissed my smile. "The men are the weaker sex. Slave Alexi is what we believe our men to be like two-thousand years ago."

"The women fight wars over men, and then enslave the men," I said. "Interesting."

"What does this word 'interesting' mean?" Tural asked.

"To look and wonder, Mistress," I replied.

The doors snapped open and the Torino walked in, flanked by a palace guard.

"You have been talking?"

"Yes, Torino," Tural said.

I stopped rubbing her feet and rose to my knees.

"No, slave, keep servicing her."

As I massaged Tural's feet, the Torino explained. "Netratoh Tural has given you the story of our people. My mother was Torino before me, and her mother before her. The House Kretahla has fought many wars. Far by our land, people have come to be in the Erskan way. Some by choice. Some by not choice.

"My armies fight small battles in the north." The Torino put her hands on her hips and drilled me with her eyes. "What I tell you is not to be told to anyone, under penalty of your death."

"Yes, Torino," I nodded.

"The House Kretahla has had the ways to crush our north enemies for many years. We keep the battles so that our armies may remain strong and may have skill for fighting. The Erskan warriors are strong. The Erskan leaders are great."

I nodded, not sure what was coming next.

"We are..." she grasped for more simple words for me. "We know good that Erskan armies will lose fight with Corrigan and the Treaslok. We want you to help us."

"What do you bargain me to give you for your help?"

"I want time to try to get home to Earth," I said, having practiced this speech a thousand times since the crash. "Torino, I believe that my people will search for me. But they are looking in the wrong place. It could be many years until they find me, a hundred. It could be a thousand years. I may never be found by my people. My space wagon will not fly."

She paused to digest what I'd asked.

I shook my head. "Then, Torino, my desire to go home may not happen. I see that the House Kretahla and the Erskans are great and have much of the land. The way of your world is that men are frey. I do not know what I want. Aervanta may be the only home I have for long time."

"We will help you if your Earth people come for you. You do know, slave, that you will not be allowed to be free in our culture?"

"Yes," I said. "I ask that if my people find me, I will be allowed to go to my home."

"Yes," she nodded. "If your people come for you, you will be allowed to go with them. Know this, that you are not free until I have Corrigan's head on a stake. Until that moment, you are frey."

"Yes, Torino, I understand."

Sklera turned to leave. "Netratoh Tural, I have heard reports from Jurina Erika. You have done well. All of the Erskan warriors will be preparing for war tomorrow and for many days. Use the slave for your pleasure."

"Torino?" Tural half-asked.

"Use the slave for any pleasure you desire."

"Thank you, Torino," Tural said, a gigantic smile flashing across her face.

"My chambers are yours until the morning. Bring the slave to the war council at eight." Sklera turned to me and said, "Corrigan's head – on a stake."

I looked at the two-legged piranha wishing the Torino had not left me behind.

"My pleasure."

I heard the Erskan growl I was coming to know all too well. A slight twinge of concern... no, *fear*, crept up my spine. Tural had just been given authorization do to pretty much whatever she wanted with me... to me.

An involuntary shiver ran through me. *Fear.*

Or was it?

Anticipation? Exhilaration?

Tural sat in the chair, her long lean legs reaching down to me. Her feet were so soft. She was very attractive, which made the sexual charge in the air even more potent.

"Lick my feet, slave," she ordered, tapping her hip.

I hesitated.

"Lick," she told me again. "I do not enjoy repeating orders."

"Mistress, I... I have not done this."

Tural glared at me.

"Yes, Mistress." Trying hard to mask my unfamiliarity, I took her right foot and licked her big toe.

"First, kiss, slave," she said. "I will teach you how to please me."

I kissed her big toe. Then again. Three times. She moved her foot slightly and brought her second toe to my lips. I kissed it thrice.

Tural shifted her weight in her chair.

I licked my lips and then kissed her middle toe, making two long, wet kisses. On the third kiss, I gently sucked her toe before separating my lips from her.

"Mmmmm," she moaned.

She was quiet as I kissed her fourth and fifth toes. She moved her left foot to my mouth.

"Slave," she said.

"Yes, Mistress?" I paused before kissing her big toe.

"You want to please me, yes?"

"Yes, Mistress."

"It pleases me to see you suffer," she whispered.

I did not reply, instead moving to suck her second toe. I did not know how to answer that question.

"You will suffer for my pleasure, yes?"

"Yes, Mistress."

"When I am pleased, and you have suffered, then, only then, will you be allowed to have your pleasure. You understand our culture, yes?"

"Yes, Mistress."

"What will you do to please your Mistress?" she asked.

"I will suffer for her," I said.

"For now, slave, you will pleasure my feet."

After a few minutes, she shifted, offering her other foot to me, "Long, wet licks on the bottom of my foot."

116

I kissed her heel and moved my tongue along her foot, ending between her toes, and then taking her toes and gently sucking the full length of them. It was a natural rhythm I fell into, drawing one toe into my mouth, then another, then another. Tural growled; I think I was getting the hang of it.

"Good, slave," she said, her voice nearly purring.

I was suddenly aware that my breathing was a little faster. My pulse was quicker.

Tural spread her legs slightly, again shifting her weight somewhat in the chair. She took her right hand and reached under her black leather skirt. She gyrated slightly and then walked her right hand down her thigh and to her knee, teasing me. "Here, slave."

I kissed her left big toe and got to my knees and leaned closer to her hand.

"Open," Tural told me.

I opened my mouth and she slowly put two of her wet fingers into my mouth.

"Suck, slave," she said, but I was already closing my lips on her fingers, gently sucking and pulling, subtly, until my lips shrouded the tips of her fingers when, I pushed forward again and enveloped her fingers.

"Good, slave."

My simple leather skirt had a noticeable bulge in the front. My body was responding to her commands... her instructions... her dominance.

"My pleasure," she growled, her voice pure seduction. Her left hand held my hair, and she firmly drew my head toward her knees.

My hands straddled her thighs as she guided my head to her skirt. Her right hand lifted the leather and revealed her glistening beauty. Quickly, with her left hand in my hair, Tural drew my lips to her.

"Now, slave," she breathed, "you know how to lick, and you know how to suck. Do not stop until I tell you to stop."

She was intoxicating – I had nothing on my mind but to please her. Gently at first, my tongue darted against her. And then, pressing firmly, our wet bodies meeting.

Her breath was becoming noticeable. Her ribs were rising – and her hips were thrusting into my mouth, pressing into my tongue until I felt it was right for me to penetrate. With a probing, hot and wet tongue, I pushed into her.

The Erskan growl erupted as I fully entered her with my tongue.

She moaned. "Good, slave."

She was in ecstasy – and I wanted to do more for her, to please her. To... care for her.

I made short thrusts into her, slowly at first. Then a little faster.

Tural's hips rocked with my thrusts. She continued to rhythmically pull my head.

My tongue thrust and thrust and thrust.

Tural panted, the waves of pleasure washing over her.

I realized that I had been thrusting my hips involuntarily into the air as I leaned over her, orally servicing.

My tongue was getting sore, but still, I licked. I blew soft puffs of air. I thrust deeply with my tongue.

Our play turned painful. But still, I wanted to please her... to please Tural... this beautiful, powerful woman.

She grabbed tightly onto my hair, writhing. Tural shuddered, her entire form shaking. Then a low-pitched growl came from her and she rose partially out of the chair. Promptly, Tural let go of my head and grabbed onto my collar with both hands,

"Stop, slave!"

"Mistress?" I asked, concerned. "Did I displease you?"

"I ask the questions." She slowly stood up, holding me to my kneeling position. "Crawl."

I crawled.

Tural led me to the next room.

It was a bedroom. An enormous bed was on the far side of the room. There was a metal cage near one wall. Metal chains and manacles hung from the ceiling in a couple of places.

"Stand," Tural ordered.

In a few quick seconds, Tural had both of my wrist cuffs locked above me, taut against the ceiling chains.

She pressed her body against mine.

I looked into her eyes.

What was she thinking? Did she see me as anything other than a piece of... meat? What was she going to do? I found myself both wondering if she cared about me and whether should I care if she did nor not.

Tural flashed her teeth at me and angled her head slightly, "Are you afraid, slave?"

"Yes, Mistress."

She put her hands around my hips and pushed her hips against mine for a moment. "Good."

Was she meaning "good" that I was afraid? Or that she liked pressing into me?

She reached around and expertly dropped the belt around my waist; the skirt fell to the floor and she nudged it away with her foot.

"Yes, slave. My pleasure." She put her left hand on my fully erect penis and held on for a moment. My eyes melted when she looked into mine.

She squeezed, then let go and walked around in a circle once, then twice, dragging her left hand around my waist. Deliberately, she stopped.

I moaned. It was involuntary.

"The slave wants me to touch?"

"Yes, Mistress, please."

Tural stopped in front of me. She pressed against my body, her thighs straddling my erection, pushing it into her leather skirt. I then pressed my hips into her... once.

"The slave does not... relax," she said.

"I am... I do not know what to feel, Mistress."

Tural made a point of looking to her left, then to her right. "Slave, you must accept your life here. You are frey. You are for my pleasure. You will suffer for my pleasure."

"Yes, Mistress." I nodded.

Tural went behind me. I sensed her breathing getting rapid again.

Then she dragged her fingernails into my shoulder blades and scraped downward.

I screamed. Every time she raked my back, I screamed. She tore down to my buttocks, ten deep scratches. It was searing. She lifted again and quickly dragged downward.

"You will suffer for my pleasure, slave."

"Yes, Mistress." I understood, but that didn't make it any easier.

Tural reached on either side of my shoulders and dug her nails into my biceps, dragging until reaching my forearms. Struggles were useless.

Then she came to my front. She growled as she plunged her fingernails into my pectorals and dug them into my skin, pulling down to my stomach.

I cried. I begged.

She smiled. "Good, slave."

She rubbed her right hand index finger on her skirt, and then reached under her leather and quickly thrust her wet finger into my mouth.

Like a crazed animal, I found myself sucking and licking her finger; trying to drink in her essence.

She pulled her finger out and then dove at my chest with her claws.

I saw long, angry red gouges down my chest.

Tural moved behind me. I tensed up, but she did nothing. Then she clawed into my back, criss-crossing and changing direction, slashing at me.

"Please, Mistress!" I begged, trying to pull away. The chains held fast.

"Slave, you want me to stop?" She slashed at my chest again with one hand. With her other hand, she held my chin and forced me to look at her. "You said you would suffer for my pleasure. Did you lie?"

"No. I mean, no, Mistress, I did not lie."

"What did you mean to tell me, slave?"

She held my chin firmly while her other hand went into her skirt again. No... instead she loosened her skirt, which fell to the floor.

Her hips invited me. Though it was a large room, I saw nothing else in the room but Tural. There was nothing else anywhere. My past... my name... none of it mattered. She was intoxicating. She was beautiful.

"Please, Mistress, I will suffer for you," I whispered.

"Yes, you will!" she said, raining her claws on my chest.

She struck at me again and again. I lost count of her scratches and my screams.

Then she stopped, a tremendous smile on her face.

"Good, slave."

I hung there, my arms fully outstretched, my legs bent. I was panting. So was she.

Tears ran down my cheeks as blood ran the length of my body.

Tural appeared with a cloth. She wiped my body and then brought another cloth to dry my skin.

"I am pleased, slave," she said, smiling. "You should be happy to see me pleased."

"Yes, Mistress, I am happy to see you pleased."

"You do not show that you are happy." She tossed the cloth onto the ground and grabbed my limp cock with both of her hands. She ground her naked hips against me.

In a matter of seconds, I was fully aroused again. I was standing on my feet again, pulling at the chains from above.

She turned around and pushed her buttocks against me, guiding my erection between her cheeks.

I thrust once but she stepped away, as I tried to thrust again against her. I begged.

"Poor slave." She came around behind me and let my right wrist down and locked it to my collar. Then she pulled my left wrist down and did the same.

Tural pulled me by the front collar ring to the bed and pushed me down onto my back. I sank down into the mattress.

It was the first real bed I had seen here.

Tural pulled me to the middle of the bed and then she appeared with chains that locked and spread my ankles.

She then unlocked my wrists, one-at-a-time, and spread them apart, flat and overhead with chains.

Abruptly, Tural straddled my hips with hers, and she grabbed onto my erect cock.

I tried to thrust into her.

"No, slave," she scolded. "I control."

"Yes, Mistress."

But she braced my cock and then thrust herself down onto me, taking my cock deep inside her. She was hot. Wet. I arched my back, wanting more. She put her weight down again onto me and lifted up, pulling me almost out of her.

Tural fucked me.

I tried to time it, but she took control of all the rhythms. I followed her lead. She hammered onto me, her hips gyrating. She would take all of my cock, and then nearly pull away the full length.

She was hot inside. I could feel her wetness dripping around my balls and inner thighs. Her hands grasped my upper arms, pinning me to the bed. A deep, long growl escaped her lips. Her leather-wrapped ponytail hung off her shoulder and brushed my heaving chest.

Tural's eyes were wild. They were radiant fires exploding one after another. She ravaged me.

I saw her build to orgasm. Her face was flush; sweat ran down her neck to her leather. She was beautiful in her agony.

The shudder was my undoing. I whimpered. I was coming.

"Yes, slave, you may." She increased her thrusting; her body rode mine. A second orgasm enveloped her body.

"Mistress! Thank you, Mistress," I shouted.

The orgasm hit.

I bucked hard, as I came.

Tural hammered me.

The chains strained as I pulled.

We gasped for air. Animals, that was all we were.

I came again, clawing the air, demanding all that she had.

Tural hammered her body into me again, her hips squeezing mine.

She fell down onto my body, slamming me roughly... wrapping her arms around my back.

We collapsed into a sated, panting heap. I kissed her neck and tasted tears, either hers or mine, I would never be sure.

She moaned, pushed my head to the side and she licked my lips once.

Our mouths melted into each other. I probed her mouth, her tongue. She bit my lip gently and then probed my mouth.

Why did I kiss her?

"You are my slave, yes?" Tural asked, gasping for breath as she broke the kiss.

Why did I kiss her? She was raping me. She was treating me like I was worthless. I was being abused. My body had been scratched and torn. She had used me.

She rocked her hips slightly and my half-erect cock moved inside her again.

Tural's body shuddered. Her thighs grabbed onto mine as she pressed our bodies together again.

I was still aroused.

I pulled on my wrist chains.

But... it was not just physical.

I looked into her eyes.

They were possessive. Eyes of an predator.

What had compelled me to kiss her?

Her eyes looked into my soul.

And I could not hide.

Tural knew.

Why did I kiss her?

"Yes, Mistress... I am your slave," I admitted, my voice a whisper. And I knew what it meant to be conquered.

Chapter Nine
In Defense of Home

"Did the Treaslok attack Renest for any reason?" I asked the assembled staff of twenty-two warriors. "Is there a beach that allows them to bring their boats to the shore?"

"The village can not see the shore because a line of hills," another captain said, taking her own chalk and drawing circles on my improvised map.

"There are seven other villages on the coast," I said, tapping my chalk on a couple of them. "Why Renest?"

"You do not know why Corrigan would kill my people there?" The Torino sat in a chair, leaning forward, eyeing my drawing.

"I am not a military person, Torino," I admitted. "The experience of your warriors is needed if we are to defeat the Treaslok."

"Brenada and Cirtolna are near the coast, but they are inland several miles," the first captain explained. "The Treaslok could be seen. These four villages are large in population. Constona and Renest have small populations."

"How many people live in Constona?" I asked of the group.

"Over two thousand," a captain replied. "We have a harfala based there for protection."

"Constona would be a good next target," Torino commented.

"Yes, but when?" I asked, leaning on the chalkboard. "When I was crashing onto Aervanta, I saw that the land of the Treaslok had a middle line of mountains that ran east-west. They must live in either the north or south. Since Renest and Constona are on the southern Erskan coasts, it seems a good chance that they will also attack Constona next.

Several in the room nodded. They had already seen the obvious.

"Now," I tapped the two cities on the map. "These are fifty miles apart. The question is, how long would it take a boat to get from Renest, back to Treaslok, attend meetings and reload supplies, and then go back to Constona with more soldiers? Do the Treaslok have sails?"

No one answered.

"Do the Treaslok boats have large clothes in the air?"

"Netratoh Tural?" a colonel asked.

Tural had been staying mostly over by one of the tables, looking at a map. "Yes, they have sails."

I looked at her and frowned.

"The Netratoh saw a Treaslok boat five years ago," the Torino said, walking slowly over to me. She stopped within an inch of touching me. "Do you know, slave, what 'netratoh' is in the Erskan word?"

"Torino, I believe it to be a military rank."

"It is a position, not a rank. 'Netratoh' is the warrior that learns... finds information."

"Intelligence officer," I said, using Erskan words.

The Torino nodded, smiling. "Yes."

Tural was smarter than she had been letting on. I thought she was merely a soldier. Of course, had I thought that Sklera was just a native Amazon warrior, too. She ended up being the leader of the whole damn continent.

"The Treaslok boat that I saw could carry twenty warriors." Tural lifted a cloth scroll from the table and tossed it at me. "These are drawings of it that I have made."

I caught it and unrolled the scroll onto the closest table. The Treaslok boat was actually a decent-sized ship. It had two square sails, plus a jib sail. It had a single-hull, wood-covered body with maybe two or three decks. It was a good drawing. All the more impressive considering that it had been done on cloth with ink brushes.

I studied her picture. How many knots could a boat like that make with a good wind?

"Ten days to make the trip, five days each way. Then a couple of days to prepare for a larger force," I said, closing the scroll and looking back at the map. "That is if the Treaslok have already put their warriors on their coast. And, if they are ready to attack."

Jurina Iona scrutinized the map. I recognized her as one who spoke frequently. She seemed intelligent. "Slave Alexi, you said yesterday that you believed Corrigan and the Treaslok were testing our forces at Renest. I am concerned that we face an attack with many Treaslok and guns. We must be ready at Constona. Now."

I frowned and paced. She had a point.

"How many of those do you require?" Torino Sklera asked.

"What, Torino?" I asked.

"The chalk sticks... how many of the chalk sticks do you require?"

I was holding six pieces of chalk. I set most of them down, laughing. "We are in a tough *strategic*... hard, situation. Corrigan and the Treaslok may have better weapons, but we can rely on better communication here. It gives us a slight advantage. Do you send messages only by horse rider?"

Torino Sklera nodded to Tural.

"We have a way – not many people know." She pulled a small glass mirror from her pouch and handed it to me.

"Uh, huh." I handed it back. "How many warriors will it take to relay messages from Constona to here at Antrana?"

"Twenty-five women. But they are not warriors. They are not fighters."

"How many days ride from Antrana to Constona?"

Jurina Iona answered, "Two full days at fast speed."

"How many days from KoVer to Constona?"

Iona replied, "Three days at fast speed."

"One day from here to KoVer," I faced the Torino. "Your weapons are useless against Corrigan. Now, he may have only a few guns, or he may have a hundred guns. But sometime, someday, he will run out of ammunition... bullets... those metal things that fly in the air."

"We do not want to run out of Erskans first," Iona said.

"True," I said.

"We have three of your guns," the Torino pointed out.

"Yes." I looked in her eyes. Was there a hint of fear in her expression? It was understandable.

I tried to put myself in their place: what if, one day, I was home on Earth when an invader took over a continent with extremely superior technology? And what if I had been the leader of a historically invincible society? It had happened before. I tried to recall history... did any of the defenders survive such an invasion? If so, what did they do? There was that one situation, way back in my mind, in Vietnam, where the defenders defeated the old United States. Of course, it fell with North Korea on the United State's second go-round... and it was a combination of strategy and superior technology.

I was not a military history aficionado. Equally, Corrigan was not experienced in the military. And, likely, he did not care much for old Earth history anyhow. He was relying on his brutality and overwhelming weapons technology to control the Treaslok.

Assuming it was Corrigan. I did not know that for a fact.

"Torino." I knew I needed to make a stand. "I need to get to my space wagon. There are ten guns there, five of which are more powerful than what Corrigan used at Renest. There are also special tools to communicate at a long distance. These special tools will allow a warrior to talk to another warrior."

There was obvious skepticism. I would deal with that later.

"What is your plan?" Jurina Iona asked.

"We might not have time, but I see no other option other than to try," I told the warriors. "One, we arms ourselves with my guns. Two, we put warriors with my special talking tools in Constona, Renest, and Antrana, to alert us about an attack. Three, we wait in a location between Renest and Constona for the alert. Four, we ride to the battle. Five, during this, a team will take more special tools from my space wagon to Antrana. These will be useful to us later. No matter what happens with the next Treaslok attack, we will need the other special tools."

There was silence while the Torino contemplated the plan. Finally, she nodded. "I agree. Iona, ready your harfala to proceed to KoVer and then to the waiting point between Renest and Constona. You will need wagons for ---?"

"About as many as you see in this room," I estimated, sweeping the room with my hands.

"Iona, then two wagons. Load them and return to the palace".

"Kreka, two harfala to Constona and hold position five miles outside. Divide your forces into six units and encircle Constona from the high ground."

"Juroh, ready two harfala for a defense position around Antrana in case this does not work, or if they are not fast enough."

"Istana, I want to see a report on Antrana defenses in an hour."

"You have your orders," the Torino told them.

The jurinas, the generals, dispersed and left the room.

A few remained, including Jurina Iona. She looked at Tural, "When will you and slave Alexi be ready?"

"Twenty minutes," Tural answered for us. "We will be dressing for the yiminee, yes?"

"Yes. My warriors will be ready also. Palace Stables Yanntro, be quick." Iona left the room.

Torino Sklera looked at Tural, "I will meet you at the Stables with the guns. Go

125

now."

I bowed to the Torino and then followed Tural. Once the doors closed behind us, she quickened her pace, her long hair swishing in its single, leather-wrapped pony tail. "Hurry."

In remarkably fast time, we dressed in leather pants and were mounting our leather-armored horses in the stables.

Eighty-one women were on horseback, with another nine riderless horses. Three heavy-looking wood enclosed wagons with six metal-rimmed wheels, were also brought up, lead by a team of six horses each.

"This is a harfala?" I asked.

"Yes," Tural nodded. "Nine units of nine. The wagons do not count as part of the harfala."

The Torino walked toward us, flanked by several high-ranking warriors.

To the right of our area, at another stable, I could see more harfala getting into formation.

There were over four-hundred heavily armed female warriors mounted on fierce horses within a few hundred yards of my sight. The morning sun shone on dozens of swords and other weapons.

"How do I know you will not use your guns against us?" the Torino asked, walking to me.

I bowed to her from my position on the horse. "Torino, I believe that if you did not know the answer to that question by now, you would not have allowed me to mount this horse without chains."

She smiled and put her right hand on the hilt of her sword, belted to her waist in a non-traditional manner.

"True." She tossed a leather saddle bag over the back of my horse and then secured it with leather straps and buckles. Then the aide did the same with Tural's horse.

"Shia-talso," the Torino said.

"Torino?"

"Good fortune," Tural explained.

The Torino nodded to a jurina, who then pointed to Jurina Iona. Iona waved her hand and our harfala continued its fast-paced ride to the way station at the edge of the bug field.

We stopped at the way station and took a break from the hot sun. This time there were several warriors on duty. The Erskans were definitely in a war status.

I was not shackled, but was led by leash to the barracks by one of the station's warriors. Once there, I was put inside a cage.

Everyone was obviously tired from the break-neck pace we had made from the palace.

Some of the first unit of nine warriors had appeared, marking out their bunks. Then the rest of the hundred-plus harfala cavalry unit arrived. Tural came over, without much of a word, removed me from the cage, and then locked my chain to the slave ring at the base of her bunk bed.

Then everyone took a nap.

It was amusing and confusing at the same time. There were over a hundred warriors in battle dress, completely crashed in the barracks. Too, there was quite a bit of snoring. It was definitely snoring, but not a familiar sound to me. There must

126

be something in the native vocal cords that was more animalistic. When awake and aroused, the Erskans growled. When asleep they... purred?

I tried not to think too much about it. If they were sleeping, then it was probably a good idea for me to try to do the same.

Later, Tural pulled on my collar to wake me up.

"Yes, Mistress?"

"We ride," she said.

"Why do we wait?" I asked.

Tural lifted her scabbard and sword diagonally behind her back and then buckled it in front of her breasts. She unlocked my chain and grabbed onto the leash.

"There are many yiminee in the middle heat of the day. Not safe to travel."

We mounted our horses and maneuvered a careful descent to the yiminee plain. I glanced over my shoulder several times, keeping watch on the wagons.

In a matter of minutes, we were flying across the mud-caked surface. Even though I had lived through it before – twice, of sorts – it still gave me the creeps when the dark swarm rose from the ground.

It crashed into us. We rode through. Thankfully, we passed without incident. I reminded myself that we would be going through here once more on the return trip.

On the other side, we did not slow, and continued in the fifty miles per hour range to KoVer. The harfala was strung out over a couple hundred yards, only two abreast on the narrower roads. There were few villagers outside. Even with our rumbling column kicking up dust as we went through town, they remained inside. I saw archers posted on the rooftops of several civilian buildings. The fort was surrounded by a dozen warriors stationed at tactical locations. It was the first time I had seen the gate actually closed.

Jurina Iona slowed the column and talked briefly with the gate guards. Then we moved inside.

I had only been gone four days. But it felt somewhat reassuring to see the fort at KoVer. It had been my home for almost three months.

We approached the stables and dismounted. Several slaves took the horses inside to care for them. I saw the leather armor being removed and packed onto the saddles.

Tural took my leather pack from my horse before a slave lead the horse away.

"We will be here for thirty minutes while the slaves water our horses and we change," she said. "I will hold your guns."

"Yes, Mistress." I started to walk toward the prison.

"Slave?" she asked, a bit curtly.

"Yes, Mistress?"

"You will come with me."

I cocked my head, frowning.

"No," Tural's face lit into a smile. "You are not to return to the prison. You are Erskan now, yes?"

"In a way, Mistress," I said.

"In the most important way," she told me, walking closely and wrapping her left index finger into my collar. "Yes?"

We locked eyes and – I melted into them. "Yes, Mistress."

In the crowd of a hundred women and horses and slaves, I did not notice someone approach.

"Has the slave been using his verbs properly?"

I turned to see Hula standing beside me.

"Mistress Hula!" I said, it almost coming out as an unabashed greeting. I knelt and kissed her right ankle boot.

"Yes. He has learned quickly."

"I believe that is because he speaks many languages," Hula said.

I got to my feet.

"No chains?" Hula remarked.

It was good to see her again.

Tural looked at me, imploringly.

"I am an Erskan slave," I said, my eyes slightly dipping downward.

"You say that as though it is something to be ashamed," Hula noted.

"I am not ashamed."

"Then look at me when you say that."

I looked at Hula and said, "I am an Erskan slave."

"Yes," she nodded. "You are." Then she smiled and clasped arms with Tural. "When will the great Torino allow me to return home?"

"You are riding with us to Constona. From there, to Aervanta."

Relief swept over her face. "Netra! Finally, home."

"'Netra?'" I asked.

Hula grinned. "We have not learned all of the more useful words."

Oh. Slang and profanity were language skills I'd have to grasp soon.

"We received the orders from the Torino early this morning." Hula turned, and I followed them as they talked. "You are going to his space wagon today, yes?"

"We are watering the horses and changing – " she looked back at me. "Then we ride."

A group of nine warriors jogged past us, going ahead on the path. Their swords and equipment jingled the metal touching. Attractive, all of them. I was looking at the tight leather pants that enveloped their toned legs and buttocks.

"Excuse me, please," I said after I shook the vision of the warriors from my head. "This may be not be a good time to say this, but I did not tell anyone about where my space wagon is located."

They stopped walking and faced me.

"It is on sand. How are the wagons going to roll in the sand?"

Tural laughed and walked to one of several buildings I had never entered.

Hula looked over her shoulder and explained, "We know where it is. We have been trying to get inside of your space wagon for seven weeks."

I silently followed them up the steps and into the building. It was a galley, with dozens of tables, in bench-style, forming long lines. A couple of groups of nine warriors were sitting down as slaves rushed to bring them food and drink. I recognized slave Mak as one of the men serving. He saw me and made a slight nod with his chin while he poured drinks for a table of warriors.

I smiled back.

"Slave," Hula said, "sit here."

We stopped at a bench table. I sat cross legged on the stone floor between Tural and Hula.

Hula's leather skirt draped over her bench and brushed my ankle. I almost moved my foot away, but decided to keep it there... feeling its touch was nice.

A different slave brought over three sandwiches and three tankards. Tural and Hula had only waited about twenty seconds, but were getting visibly impatient.

After each had taken their first bite of food, Hula picked up the third sandwich and asked, "May I?"

"Yes, of course. He is not my property," Tural answered, casually.

Hula twisted half-around and held out the sandwich. It did not have a "here, take it" feel. So, I leaned slightly forward and took a bite.

It was a meat and vegetable sandwich made of their cattle known as a "braesk".

She put the rest of the sandwich on her plate and then took a drink. After another minute, almost as an afterthought, Tural stopped eating and handed the tankard of water to me. I took it in my hands, swallowed a large drink, and then returned it to her.

"How is our Torino?" Hula asked, between bites.

Tural shook her head, "She is grieved by the loss of Renest. Yes, slave? Is that how you would describe the Torino's feelings now?"

"You took the words out of my mouth," I replied.

Hula handed the sandwich to me again... this time allowing me to take three bites.

Tural laughed.

"Yes? What is funny?" Hula asked.

"The Torino was at her old ways again," Tural smiled.

"Come close." Hula held onto my chin. "Not at all of her old ways. There is no scar."

Tural laughed again. "After the Torino was – passionate – the slave was generous in his words."

I grinned, as well.

Hula offered me the last bite of the sandwich. Tural gave me the last of the water.

"Ten years ago," Hula said, "the Torino would have tortured you until you were a bloody slave."

"And later she would ask for your help," Tural ended. They both laughed. There was a background story I was missing.

A group of nine warriors arose from the table and headed toward the door.

"We must go," Tural said, standing. "Do you want to ride to the space wagon?"

Hula stood. "Yes. My horse is ready. I will be there in five minutes."

They gave each other a quick peck on the lips.

I looked up from the floor, blinking.

"Come, slave," Tural said, walking to one door, while Hula headed to a different door on the other side of the galley.

I scrambled to keep up.

"When you walk with a woman," Tural said, "you will be on her left side, two or three paces behind. She will need her sword arm free."

"Yes, Mistress," I said, switching my position from her right side to her left side.

"You know the Erskan word 'civilian'?"

"Yes, Mistress."

"There are different rules for Torino's army when meeting a civilian. There are several castes in our culture, but only for the civilians. You know the military ranks?"

"I have been taught about some of the ranks, Mistress."

I followed Tural to one of the large barracks. Several groups of warriors moved in and out, those exiting having already changed into the field uniform of short tan skirt and tan sleeveless vest.

We went into the lobby, which had two doors. Tural walked to a cut-out in the wall where a slave stood.

"Yes, Mistress?" He glanced at me for a moment and handed a folded cloak and garments through the window to Tural.

Tural handed the garments to me and pointed to a door on the right.

I went inside and saw that there were ten males in the room, all dressed in tan leather ankle-length skirts, with slits on the outer legs. Most held a cloak of slightly varying shades of tan or white. They had been standing, talking to each other when I came in. They stopped and turned to face me.

There was an uneasy moment when no one said anything.

"Hello," I said, in the Erskan greeting.

"You are Alexi, the frey from off Aervanta?"

I wasn't sure what to expect. Did the men here shake hands? Did we hug?

"Yes." It was a small room with no chairs and windows. My reply echoed off the stone walls.

"I am Metrok," the closest man said, walking to me. He crossed his hands, at belt-level, and tipped his head slightly. He turned and swept the room with his right hand, "We are from the Torino's stable. We are here to help you."

I made a half-way successful attempt to duplicate the hand greeting.

"You should get dressed, Alexi," Metrok said.

I unabashedly removed my leather pants and then pulled on the skirt, wrapping the leather belt around my waist. I draped the cloak over my left arm.

Tural appeared near the door, having changed into her field uniform of short skirt, high boots, and tan vest. "Hurry."

Metrok and the other nine men passed by, going ahead of Tural, and out to the door at a brisk pace. She walked after them, and I followed to her left side, as instructed.

Now, nearly two-hundred and twenty horses were set up in the large grassy area, most organized in the Erskan nine-unit pattern. The wagons were being drawn from a side road. Warriors, attended by slaves, were mounting their horses.

I mounted my horse, which had been moved to the left center row of the nine-unit formation. Tural was on my right, in the center.

Hula rode up, positioning herself to the right of Tural, completing our formation.

I had never seen Hula in uniform. She had the equivalent rank of captain displayed on the bands around her bicep.

Metrok and his team were evenly loaded into two of the wagons. As they entered, I saw that they dropped three wood shades on each side, opening the wagon to a breeze.

Jurina Iona raised her hand and led the harfala out of the fort and toward the desert.

*****

Once we reached the sand, Iona stopped the ride. She rode past Tural and I, toward the back of the column.

I turned my horse slightly to see what was going on.

The wagons had also stopped. Metrok's team scattered and worked on the wagons. They removed equipment which they placed under the body of each wagon. After a couple of minutes, the six wheels were off the ground.

"Wow," I said.

"What is that word, 'wow'?" Tural asked.

"Mistress, it means... surprise. Fascinating."

Metrok and two slaves removed the wagon wheels and stored them inside the wagon.

Three slaves set down a long metal runner, which was bracketed to the axles. After another few minutes, the other runner was down. One slave made adjustments to the tackle on the horse team while the other nine men went to the next wagon and prepared the conversion.

"Wow?" Tural grinned, her smile flashing from under her hood.

"Yes, Mistress."

She moved her horse close to me and reached out to my collar and pulled me slightly off-balance, toward her. "Does Tural 'wow' the slave, Alexi?"

I moved my feet in the stirrups to steady my horse.

"Yes, Mistress, she does."

Tural let go.

A couple of warriors behind us chuckled.

Hula and Tural exchanged glances.

Jurina Iona rode back to the front and the column moved again.

Soon we were moving along the river. We came to a location where someone had sunk two four-inch wide wooden posts into the sand about twenty feet from the river, probably as a marker.

We moved at a surprisingly fast pace. The horses were well adapted to the sand dunes. In a matter of about fifteen minutes I saw the passenger side of the cracked clearsteel angled up into the blue sky.

There were several tents in the area pitched into the sand. Five warriors and a slave were there, shading themselves from the intense sunlight. They stood to attention, drawing weapons, and then relaxed when they saw us approach.

I could not hear what the jurina said, but the tone did not seem complimentary.

The harfala spread out around the Tamagra, taking a half-dozen positions around the sand dunes. Most dismounted – several rode over beyond the hills to scout.

I waited for Tural to dismount before I did so.

The first wagon came over the sand, gracefully sliding behind the team of horses.

We walked to the straight shadow cast upon the sand.

It was beautiful... even battered as it was. I rubbed my hand on the side of the craft. I couldn't help but sigh.

Jurina Iona walked up behind Tural and me.

There were dozens of new, light colored scratches around the door frame.

"It will not open," Iona said.

"This space wagon is called a Tamagra," I informed them.

They seemed to like the name.

Several curious officers joined our group.

"I do not believe our *engineers...* our people who make such things, thought of the Erskan language with so many words ending in the 'ah' sound," I explained. But it was one hell of a coincidence.

"Can you open the Tamagra?" Iona asked.

I moved my hand near the door. The white frictionless door panel slid to the right.

Everyone flinched, but only a little. They looked at one another as a wave of cool air gushed out of the Tamagra and rustled everyone's hair.

"Who is first?" I asked.

"Netratoh Tural is first," Jurina Iona said.

Tural tightened her lips.

"She is the intelligence officer," Iona explained.

Hula gave Tural a gentle nudge on her leather-covered ass.

I wiped sweat from my brow. "Mistress, be careful on the right side. There is broken *plastic*... uh, broken glass in a pile."

Suddenly, I remembered Roberts and turned to see the buried edge of the craft.

"We have moved the body to KoVer," Iona said. "You may perform your *entrata* for him later."

"Thank you."

Tural reached up to the floor and pulled herself into the darkness.

I had to admire her bravery. She was about to step into a completely unknown world of strange technology.

And, I had to admire the view.

Unfortunately, the field uniforms had a full leather bottom as part of the skirt. It wouldn't work well riding horses wearing a thong. However, I was thinking that were I anywhere other than on this planet, I might have to give a confidence-building boost with my hand.

Jurina Iona made the decision for all of us. She reached up and pushed her right hand up under Tural's skirt.

"Alexi!" Tural shouted from the inside.

I retreated.

Iona let go.

"Ten lashes!" Tural shouted back at me.

"You are next," Iona said to me, flashing that devilish Erskan smile.

I was dead.

Tural's boots disappeared, and then she turned around, her head looking down at us. Or, more specifically, she was looking directly at me.

I started to look over at Iona, and then thought that, perhaps, that was not the best course of action.

Hula nudged my ass.

I tossed my arms over the floor ledge and pulled myself up. I knew it was coming – someone put her hand hard into my ass and pushed.

Tural locked her left hand into my hair and helped me get to my feet.

I began to explain, when, suddenly, she planted a wet kiss on my lips. She turned, steadying herself by holding onto the narrow column that served as a delineator between the entry way and the bedroom.

I reached over to a wall panel and pressed the lighting control.

About half of the usual lights came on.

Iona and Hula crawled inside and stood.

They surveyed the inside of the craft.

"Netra," Hula uttered.

132

"Soh-da Netra," Tural added.

Mental note: ask Hula to teach me Erskan profanity.

"I am sorry, Mistresses, that the inside is so dirty. It is usually clean and everything is put into a certain place." I stepped past Tural and leaned to the right, trying to keep my balance. "It is also easier to walk when it is not pushed over to a twenty degree angle. Over there to the left is the *engine* room. That is what makes – or did make – the Tamagra go in space. To the right is the bedroom. Beyond that is the *cockpit*, or place where one sits and controls the Tamagra. In front of us is the kitchen and galley."

"Slave, where does the blood come from?" Iona asked.

"My face," I said. "In the crash."

Tural reached to the ceiling and barely touched her hands on the plastic panel light. "It is not hot."

Iona and Hula reached up and did the same. Tural pressed the palm of her hand against the light.

"It is not hot in the Tamagra," Iona noted.

"The Tamagra makes a false winter," I told them.

"You said there is a kitchen?" Tural asked. "Where is the food?"

"The Erskans dry their food to keep it safe," I said, moving my way over to the kitchen. I opened the bottom refrigerator door.

Two more ranking Erskans came in, wide-eyed.

I removed a container of orange juice. Then I grabbed five drinking glasses and poured the orange juice. "This is from Earth. A tree grows there that is like the Erskan yaban plant."

I gave everyone a glass.

Iona eyed me suspiciously.

I poured myself a few teaspoons of orange juice to take a sip. I wanted to show that I was not poisoning anyone.

Tural pushed my hand down and took a drink of the juice.

"Good," she said, licking her lips. "It is cold."

The others took initial sips before consuming the juice.

"What do we need to take?" Tural asked.

"Where are the guns?" Iona asked.

It was easy to tell which one was the field warrior.

I led the jurina over to a weapons rack. I waved my hand over the sensor and the door opened.

The other two officers approached behind me.

"None of these have bullets in them. They will not harm anyone. You should take good care of them, and wrap them in blankets." I took out nine of the ten guns and handed them to the officers.

"Are you not taking this gun?" Iona asked.

"It only works underwater," I said.

"The Treaslok boats..." Tural pointed out.

It was a reasonable suggestion.

I grabbed the MU-28 and handed to an officer.

"Ammunition... bullets," I said. I opened another case and exposed several dozen cases of ammunition. "We'll take all of them. There should be almost five thousand bullets there."

The officers shuttled items to the doorway and to other waiting arms on the sand.

Tural poured herself the last of the orange juice. Hula stood beside Iona and me, as we moved the last case of ammunition out of the craft.

"I have never been in a room where there were no slave rings," Tural said.

"I thought this Tamagra was not comfortable," Hula agreed.

These women were in a sixty-two billion dollar ultra-modern space craft from another planet, and they thought it was strange, because there are no metal rings mounted in the walls to chain the men. I laughed.

"We can also take the ammunition from the guns on the outside of the Tamagra," I explained, extracting the metal pins to drop the strips of bullets to the floor. "Jurina, this reminds me of something we could talk about. Do you have wagons made to go into battle?"

"They carry supplies," she said.

"This Tamagra is also a war wagon. There are guns on the outside that will send bullets to an enemy. Is there a way that we could put guns on top or inside of a Erskan wagon?"

She seemed intrigued. "It may be good to try."

I turned the hand crank, and the hundred-round strips extracted onto the floor where they were collected by officers.

"Other side," I said.

Jurina Iona followed me to the left side of the craft. After a few minutes, another cache of ammunition was being transferred to the outside.

I went over to the desk and communications systems that stored ten hand-held radios. I extracted nine of them and handed them to a new officer that had come inside to help. "Mistress, please keep these available, so we may use them in a few minutes."

Hula approached. "Why is the cockpit closed?"

"It was broken in the crash. Use the hand crank on the floor, there, to open the door and look inside."

Tural spun the crank.

They peered inside.

"It is hard to understand how the slave could live in this crash from the sky," Hula noted.

"My friend did not."

"What else has Corrigan done to make him a trenama?" Tural asked.

"Corrigan has killed. He has stolen. He has hurt. And now, he has done great harm to your world."

Iona walked up behind me, taking a peek inside the cockpit.

A strand of liquid electricity glowed from the fracture in the clearsteel windshield.

"It is called *liquid electricity*," I explained. "It is a light that will glow for seventy Erskan years."

"Can we move the Tamagra to the palace?" Iona asked.

I shook my head. "No. I do not see any way that you could move the Tamagra. It is forty-six thousand *brekas* in weight."

Iona frowned. "But it must be light to go into the sky."

"Allow me to show you something." I opened a desk drawer and pulled out two pieces of paper. I took one and crumpled it into a ball, and then handed it to the jurina.

She felt it with both hands, rolling it over.

"That is paper. Earth people use it to write. Erskans write with brushes on cloth. Earth people use pens." I took a red pen from the desk and, on the other piece of paper, I wrote *Jurina Iona* in large letters, using the Erskan language.

All of the women watched in silence.

"While it is light weight," I said, "the paper in your hand does have weight, yes?"

"Yes, slave," Iona replied.

I folded my piece of paper neatly down the middle. Then I bent the creases and lifted the paper into my hands. "Even though this has weight... it will fly."

With a little push, the paper airplane sailed across the room, traveling about ten feet before diving into the sink.

"That is a Tamagra paper?" Tural asked.

"Maybe, the last part." I smiled. "It went down and stopped flying, only because there was nothing pushing after I let go. The same thing happened on the Tamagra. Corrigan's friends fired their guns at the back of my Tamagra, and they broke the engine. The engine stopped pushing the Tamagra."

"And the Tamagra crashed," Iona finished.

I grabbed a stack of paper and a handful of pens. "Mistress Hula, this would be a good gift to the Torino. Later, I will help you make paper."

"Is there anything else that we need?" Jurina Iona asked.

"We can take these boxes," I said, pointing out the surveillance equipment.

"Do we need the food?" Hula asked.

Someone was a bit attracted to the Earth food, it seemed.

"No, sorry, Mistress. All of this food will go bad if it is not in the *winter* box. But, we can take these, also." I pointed to three leather cases, then to the ceiling. "Those are lights, like these. Another gift for the Torino."

I noticed that Tural was looking in the wardrobe closet. She ran her fingers over my uniforms and growled.

"One time ago, I did not have a Tamagra. I was on a *motorcycle* – like a horse wagon – and that was my uniform."

She held the black leather police shirt. Yellow and gold Earth Alliance patches adorned the shoulders. My rank "RANGER" was on the collar tips.

Tural fumbled with the hanger for a moment until she got the leather shirt off of it.

Maybe I had a sad look on my face, because Tural tucked the shirt under her arm and tapped my lips with her finger. "We will take this. A gift *from* the Torino."

"We must depart," Jurina Iona said, walking to the door.

I helped the two warriors, then Iona, and then Hula down to the sand. Then I turned to survey the half-emptied craft.

Tural was intelligent. I was sure of it. She reached over to the wall panel and pressed the same switch that cut out the lights. "Perhaps, slave," she moved close to me, "we will return to build a slave ring on that floor."

"Thank you," I said. I appreciated her sensitivity to my situation.

Grasping the different emotions of the Erskans was not easy. They could be brutal, tough, and uncaring in one moment, yet compassionate and sympathetic in the next.

"Now, out!" she ordered, half-pushing me off the ledge.

I jumped down to the sand and turned to help Tural land softly. With a wave of my hand, I shut the door on the Tamagra. It felt that I had closed a door on my past.

"What do the Earth people say to each other when one of them is thinking of the past and not of the future?" Tural asked me.

"They say 'snap out of it.'" I replied.

"Snap?" Tural grabbed onto my collar and pulled me close to her face. She drilled me with her eyes, "Snap out of it, slave, or I will come to believe that you deserve ten lashes for touching my rear."

I grinned. "Yes, Mistress."

She jerked on my collar once for good measure.

"Constona is waiting for us," Jurina Iona said, walking to her horse.

The slaves finished loading the last of the boxes of ammunition and supplies into the wagons.

I knew that being too somber could get me killed.

I helped Tural mount her horse. Then I assisted Hula.

Finally, with a slight burst of optimism, I side-mounted my horse, pulling myself with one hand.

"Snap?" Tural asked.

"Snap." I laughed.

The soldiers that had been left guarding the Tamagra had broken their camp and also joined the harfala.

The column fell back into formation as the jurina led us away from my craft. The wagons were slower to move, at first, but then were keeping with our brisk pace.

Later I watched in wonder as the slaves efficiently switched the sled runners back to wheels on the wagons.

We were stopped, awaiting the mounting of the last set of wheels.

"Where did the black *radio* boxes go?" I asked Tural. "There were nine of them."

"Maranna!" Tural shouted to a warrior in the nine-woman formation ahead of us.

Maranna broke her unit and rode back to my left side.

"We need two of those," I said.

"I need two of the black boxes," Tural said.

Maranna fished out two radios and handed them to me. I gave one to Tural.

"What do these do?" Hula asked.

"We can talk to each other from long distances," I said. "Here. See this? It is called a knob. You turn it. This is *on* so it will work. This is *off* so it will not work. I will turn both of these to *on*."

I looked around. "What warrior will be taking one of these to the Torino?"

"I will," Maranna said.

"Good." I handed a radio to Tural. "Mistress, ride over there about fifty yards. Then stop and hold the radio in front of your face, like this. And just talk to it."

Maranna frowned.

Tural smiled and backed her horse a few feet. Then she rode off and stopped. We saw her turn her horse to face us.

We looked at the radio. There was no sound.

I looked at the indicator panel – it seemed to be working.

"Hello?" came Tural's voice, in the Erskan greeting.

It was perfectly clear.

Hula's face broke into a great smile.

I handed the radio to her. "Hello, Tural."

"It is true!" Tural replied.

"How far can we use this radio?" Hula asked.

"It uses multi-modal reflective sorting and transference of stratospheric ozone to "

136

– I realized I had slipped into English. "Five-thousand miles."

"Tural, turn your back to us and talk," Hula said.

They wanted to see if it worked when you were not facing each other!

"Can you hear me talking now?" Tural asked.

"Yes!" Hula said.

I reached over and put my hand on the face of the radio, covering the microphone. "Mistress, ask Tural to close her eyes and then see if we can hear her talking."

"Tural," Hula said. "Close your eyes. I want to know if we can hear you."

"My eyes are closed. Can you hear me now?" Tural asked.

"Yes!" Hula replied.

I covered the microphone again. "Ask her to put her left hand on her head."

Delighted, Hula spoke into the radio. "Will it work if you put your hand on your head?"

We saw Tural start to lift her arm up. Then she stopped and whipped her horse around to face us.

"Can slave Alexi hear me whipping his ass?" Tural said through the radio.

All of us laughed heartily.

Tural rode to us. She pushed the radio into her pouch. "For your insolence, I will keep this radio."

"Yes, Mistress," I said.

"Maranna," Tural said, "take one radio to Jurina Iona and show her how to make it work. Then take a radio to Otra at KoVer. Take two radios to the Torino and another to Juroh. One radio here to the slave. I will deliver one to Kreka at Constona, and I will keep one extra."

Maranna handed over the radios. I clipped one to my belt. Tural saw that, and slowly removed her from inside her belt and repositioned it, clipping the metal pins to her belt.

"Ride fast," Tural said.

Maranna made the Erskan salute and then rode up the column to Jurina Iona.

The slaves were converting the last wagon.

"Netratoh Tural?" we heard Iona's voice on Tural's radio.

Tural removed her radio and spoke, "Yes, Jurina."

"Can you hear me talking?" Iona asked.

"Yes, Jurina."

There was a pause. Tural was about to put the radio back onto her belt, when the jurina spoke again. "I believe the radio works well without one having to put a hand on the head."

Tural snapped her head around to me.

I owed Maranna for that one.

"Beh-teska Maranna!" Tural said.

"Mistress," I said softly, "you need to put your hand over that part if you do not want anyone to hear you... or press on that part with your thumb."

"We can hear you talking," Jurina Iona's voice came over, laughing. "Beh-teska?" "These may not be a good idea," Tural said, pressing over the mute button. She put the radio back onto her belt.

Maranna broke away from the column and rode ahead.

The slaves loaded the sleds into the wagons.

With weapons, ammunition, and supplies, and communications equipment, we headed to KoVer at a faster pace.

We had only gone about two miles when we heard Maranna's voice over the radio. "Treaslok!"

Chapter Ten
The Interrogation

There was a pause. I guess that for a moment, I was expecting Jurina Iona to respond. It was not a lack of confidence on her part but, more likely, unfamiliarity with the radio.

The sound of five gunshots came from the north.

I snapped my radio and spoke, "Mistress Maranna, are you where you can watch without being seen?"

Tural pointed ahead. The formation of the front of the column was just starting to lurch forward. Iona had used a hand-signal.

I looked at Tural, "We can not go to KoVer yet! We have to find out which ones have guns."

Hula nodded in agreement.

Rapidly, several options flashed through my mind. Would I have to ride up to the jurina and block her? Would she strike me down without a thought? Would I need to resort to using my weapons against her?

If the harfala attacked, blindly riding into KoVer, they would be cut down.

"Yes. I am on a hill. They can not see me... or hear me talk. I can see them. There are forty warriors on foot; there are twenty warriors on horse. They are on the east and northeast of KoVer."

Iona brought her horse to a halt. It was so sudden that one of her senior officers ran into the back of her horse.

"There are two Treaslok who have guns. They have killed two archers," Maranna related. "We have killed four Treaslok, but they are moving through the village now."

We heard a dozen or more gunshots.

Slowly, the column moved again.

"What happened?" Iona asked, her voice tense on the radio.

"Fighting on the streets," Maranna said.

"Tural, Alexi, come forward!" Iona ordered.

We rode to the front of the column.

There were more gunshots.

"Our sisters need our help!" called Maranna, her voice desperate.

"Do not change your position," ordered the jurina , her command solid and direct. She looked at me, "I understand the good use of the radio. If we can move you to the rear of the Treaslok with the guns, can you kill them?"

"There is a Treaslok patrol coming toward me," Maranna said. I heard the sound of her sword being drawn across her back.

"Our force will approach from the south where Maranna is," Iona said, waving and charging forward on her horse. "Tural, take Alexi to the southeast!"

The column of warriors stormed past us, heading over to the first small hill. Two warriors remained behind with the wagons and slaves.

"This way!" Tural said before turning her horse away.

The sound of more gunshots echoed from ahead.

Hula rode on with Iona. I looked concerned as she went past.

We turned slightly to the right. I followed Tural as she guided her horse through the brush on trails I did not know existed.

We turned and popped up on a rise.

To the left, several hundred yards away, I could see Maranna on the ground, sword in hand, fighting with two other women dressed in black pants and black bra-type tops. One had a beige cloak still wrapped around her waist.

Maranna was being pushed back, the three swords glinting in the sunlight.

Then the hill was overflowing with Erskan warriors. They crashed down onto the two Treaslok women. One of the Erskans routed an adversary with a sword blow to her shoulder. Blood and skin showered up into the light as she went down.

I lost sight of the other Treaslok as the Erskans surrounded her.

Tural had curved and we headed down onto the level of KoVer.

Iona was a tactician, no doubt. Their attack to defend Maranna had attracted the attention of all of the Treaslok.

"Jurina," I said into the radio, "I suggest fewer of your warriors fall back; the rest should dismount and lay to the ground."

Tural rode to a KoVerian house, dismounting quickly. She tossed a leather bag to me.

I dismounted as I caught the bag.

We pressed ourselves against the side of the house.

Tural's sword sang as she withdrew it. She looked around the corner of the house to our right.

I checked the magazine of the StacGun. It was full. I removed my gun belt from the bag and wrapped it around my waist. Then I checked the four backup magazines.

"Ready," I said.

We moved to the left of the house and saw that Iona's forces had followed my suggestion. Their archers had come up and were firing arrows down on the Treaslok.

The Treaslok had stopped their advance to the fort and they were now dealing with archers shooting deadly arrows from the west and south. Treaslok warriors took positions behind other homes and shops. They were not firing arrows back, however.

"The Treaslok do not have bows?" I asked.

"They do," Tural said.

I pointed to a shop that had two young Erskan girls crouching by wood barrels outside. "They are in the middle of this."

Tural looked at them. "They know to stay still."

Several of the Treaslok appeared with bows and fired a volley up to the hill.

I watched the arrows arc over the houses and land onto Iona's forces.

Several women shouted cries of pain as the arrows landed on the defenseless Erskans.

One of the Treaslok moved forward, toward Iona's forces. She was flanked by two swordswomen and an archer. I saw her steady the MTL-38 on the shoulder of a swordswoman.

She was about forty yards away.

There was no wind.

It would be a pretty easy shot.

I fired.

The Treaslok fell over, half her skull blown away.

The crouching swordswoman had only a moment to look at her fallen comrade before I took her down with a single shot to the chest.

The other two looked over at me, and then they darted out of sight.

One reached for the rifle as it lay on the dirt.

I missed with the first shot. The second shot blew away her hand.

"The other one will come now," Tural said. "We must change our position."

"Tural," Iona's voice came over the radio. "Other Treaslok are going to you. *Shetah*!"

A volley of arrows left Iona's archers and flew down to Treaslok positions among the houses. Several screams pierced the air.

"Follow me!" Tural said. I turned to follow her around the right corner of the house.

The flash of metal stunned me.

Tural had run into a Treaslok warrior.

Both drew their swords, the metal colliding in a spark and a clash.

Tural screamed a charge as she rained her sword down on the woman.

The Treaslok back peddled, her sword taking defensive blow after defensive blow.

Tural's back was to me, blocking my shot. I leveled the sights on the two, waiting for my moment.

Tural gasped and stepped back, slow to get her sword up.

I fired, hitting the Treaslok in the chest, dead center. Her body reeled back before falling to the ground, blood spurting from the chest cavity.

Tural stumbled back into my arms. I caught her and pulled her back toward the building.

She had a small amount of blood on her lower abdomen. I was terrified for a moment.

"It is not bad," she said. Part of her skirt had been cut through. She poked at herself with both hands. "Not bad," she said again. "Hurts."

She saw my expression.

"It is not bad," she said again. It seemed she was trying to reassure herself.

A bullet ricocheted off the side of the building.

I jerked Tural back, literally lifting her from the ground and tossing her behind me. She rolled into the dirt, cursing.

The Treaslok was two buildings away, positioned on the front doorstep of a home.

I pulled back and peeked around the corner of the building.

She fired again at me.

Arrows flew around, most bouncing off the stone walls.

A quick-peek around the corner; I saw her begin to move again to my right, trying to out-flank us.

"I don't think so," I said in English.

My shot exploded in her stomach. She fell down onto her own intestines.

Another Treaslok ran from the side of the same building. I let her get within a foot of the gun before I cut her down with a shot to the chest.

The battle had concentrated on the three closest blocks of KoVer. I saw that most of the Treaslok had moved into positions across the street.

One of the Treaslok stepped out onto the road. I managed only to get her in the shoulder.

Tural came behind me.

"There is one," she said, pointing further down the street.

"That's pretty far," I explained. I fired twice, missing with both shots.

We heard a tremendous shout from our left.

Iona and her warriors were moving forward, coming down to the street, mounted again on their horses.

The bulk of the Treaslok forces appeared about ten structures away. The cavalry was twenty-some strong; the infantry was about thirty in number.

A single Treaslok across the street fired an arrow at me. I ducked back and returned six shots in her direction.

She fired another arrow.

Then another bounced at my feet.

I could hear the shouts from the Treaslok cavalry.

Another arrow was shot.

I fired five more rounds at the edge of the building.

The Treaslok drew back an arrow.

My shot hit her left hand, shattering bone and skin.

I looked down the street.

Tural came around my right side, looking as well.

The two forces collided nearly in the middle of the road, with warriors engaging between houses and shops.

Iona's forces had overrun the Treaslok, blending in that it was impossible for me to fire.

Tural ran to the street, toward the fighting.

I ejected the magazine and snapped another one into my gun. Then I chased after her.

Horses screamed.

Women screamed in pain and in anger.

Swords clashed.

Blood flowed.

Then I was close enough to pick targets.

I crouched onto the road and fired at any Treaslok I could find that was not engaged in combat.

It was over in thirty seconds.

I had killed ten women. Fifteen in all today.

The Erskans had killed or captured the others.

Two Erskan warriors lay dead.

Injured Treaslok horses were screaming horribly.

One of Iona's warriors began the grisly task of killing them.

I stood in the street, gun hanging down at my side.

Tural walked back to me, blood splattered all over her vest.

"Are you well, slave?" she asked. Her breath was labored. Sweat and blood was on her forehead.

"How much of that blood is yours?" I asked.

"Just down there," she pointed to her skirt.

I watched two of Iona's warriors go to a wounded Treaslok. She had been gashed on the side of her head, blood spilling from the wound. It was a mortal wound.

She did not seem to know that, however. She crawled on the ground, her fingers digging into the dirt and gravel road, trying to get away.

One of the Erskans stepped on her ankle, while the other, her teeth clenched, plunged her sword into her spine.

I heard the bones breaking as the blade crushed them. Her final scream shook me for a moment.

"Are you well, slave?" Tural asked again.

The Erskan had to put her foot on the lower back of the corpse to leverage herself before she could extract the blade.

"Better than some, Mistress," I said.

One of the bloodied Erskan junior officers approached, "Netratoh Tural. We have two prisoners."

Tural held my gun hand while she guided the StacGun back into my holster. "Now, slave, it is my time to work."

I followed her as we skirted the edge of the street, somewhat around the carnage.

It was... a catastrophe. Bodies – half of bodies – littered the road. I nearly lost my footing on the slippery blood that soaked the dirt and gravel.

Eight horses lay dead, caught in the sword fighting. One Erskan horse was among the fatal casualties.

People were starting to appear on the streets, hesitant at first. Several were looking at me.

"You look ill," Tural said to me, looking over her shoulder.

We walked past the scene and headed up the road to the fort.

Other warriors rode past us, from the direction of the fort, heading toward the battle scene.

"I have never seen anything like this," I explained.

"If it was not for your gun, I would be one of the dead on the road," she told me.

That much was true.

Jurina Iona rode up, leading a horse. Behind her was Hula, leading my horse.

"Maranna was injured, but she has already left to deliver the radios to the Torino," Iona said, stopping. She handed the reins to Tural's horse. "How are your injuries?"

"They are not bad injuries," Tural said as she mounted her horse.

"Someone almost caught us," I said. "Tural was very brave."

"I had a good teacher," Tural explained. She touched her stomach with her free hand, "I will need bandages soon."

"I will take care of you, Mistress," I told her. There was a little bit of pride in my voice.

"Has Renya told you about the two prisoners?" Hula asked. "They are in the prison."

"Yes," Tural answered.

"Jurina Iona," I said.

She turned to face me.

"Our view of the Treaslok is not good," I explained.

"Yes, they did not move as we had planned," she agreed, grimacing.

"There could be a large Treaslok force already on your continent," I warned. "KoVer and Renest are south of the yiminee plains. KoVer on the west, Renest on the eastern coast. Constona is north of the yiminee. It is the next logical target. They would have to take and secure Constona before moving onto the capital."

"Constona may have already fallen," Iona said.

Hula noted the sky, "It will be dark in one hour."

In the rush of events, the time had completely slipped my mind. We had spent the entire afternoon moving from one event to another.

"There are a few things," I said. "First, is that the Treaslok had two guns, called *rifles*, here. If they had many rifles, say, one-hundred, then why not arm this force with more than two rifles? Are they holding back, saving many rifles for use on the larger Erskan cities? Or do they have a shortage of bullets? Or do they need more rifles on the Treaslok continent?

"Two, how did all the Treaslok get here? Are these Erskan horses from Renest or are they different? How many boats do the Treaslok have? Where are they? Is there a chance we can cut them off from their boats? There must be dozens of boats someplace.

"And if so, the supply routes for the Treaslok are getting very long.

"Finally, why are they coming here?"

Iona wiped blood from the right side of her leather skirt. She rubbed it between her fingers for a moment before answering. "We do not know about the guns. We have found two wagons from Renest that were used to deliver the foot warriors here. The boats are not known to us."

Tural gave a questioning look to Iona. Iona nodded.

"The three-hundred dead at Renest," Tural told me.

"Yes?" I asked.

"They were all women."

"How many men were killed?" I asked.

No one answered for a full five seconds. I guess I was not figuring out the meaning.

"They were all captured," Hula told me, moving her hands in front of her in an Erskan gesture for *"Can't you understand?"*

"The Treaslok are here to take slaves?" I asked, my eyes widening.

"Why else would they attack?" Iona said, more of a statement than a question.

"Corrigan might have something to do with that," I suggested.

"We need answers," Iona told Tural.

"Yes, Jurina, you will have answers," she said. "Alexi, come."

Iona and Hula rode down the street while I followed Tural to the fort.

We made a quick stop at the infirmary. There were eight Erskan warriors being treated. One was serious and was not expected to survive. Tural was going to leave the infirmary, feeling her injury was not serious enough to warrant waiting. I had to gently insist that the Torino would be unhappy, if Tural had died without completing her mission.

I stood in the doorway, watching two Erskan women medics perform nineteenth century Earth medicine.

Tural sat on a chair, holding her abdomen, speaking with another wounded warrior.

"Mistress," I approached. "Veronda is dying."

"Yes," Tural frowned. "She is bleeding to death."

"In one of the cases on a wagon is my medicine. It will cure her... today."

"Go. Get it," Tural ordered.

I started to walk out of the infirmary.

"You will not be hindered. Just remember to mind protocol," Tural said. "I am hurting too much to escort you. The wagons are by the third building on the right after you turn."

"Yes, Mistress. Thank you."

I stepped out onto the porch.

It was dark. Torches lit the area, flames flickering on all of the roads. The front of the buildings glowed with porch lights. Small groups of warriors moved about on the roads. Every now and then, a slave or two would go by, carrying something.

Stars had come out. They were brilliant.

One of those was mine, my home.

Since being captured, it was the first time I had been alone... the first time I was outside at night.

I was so lost that I could not even figure out where my home star was. Even the location of Celion was a total unknown.

I walked into the road and headed for the wagons. Twice, when warriors came toward me, I stopped off the road and looked down to the ground until they had passed.

Two warriors were standing guard by the wagons.

"Mistress," I said, "I have been sent by Netratoh Tural to get a box of medicine."

I recognized one of them from earlier in the day. She waved with her hand to pass by.

As I moved past, she pinched my right buttock.

I stopped, surprised.

"Yes, Mistress?"

"No, slave. The answer is 'Thank you, Mistress.'"

"Thank you, Mistress," I said.

Her eyes dissected me, moving from my neck down to my groin.

"When this war Is over..." she said.

It was time to move. I stepped slightly away from her and then proceeded on to the second wagon.

I fumbled around in the dark until I grabbed the case with the lighting. I took out an electronic torch and then grabbed one of the three medical kits.

"Thank you, Mistress," I said, walking past them.

Both laughed, as I headed back to the infirmary.

One of the medics met me inside. She wore a blood-splattered cloth apron that covered a field uniform. "What do you have for Veronda?"

"Mistress, this will tell me what is the matter," I explained, holding the case in the air.

The other medic beckoned us.

Several warriors, including Tural, appeared behind us to watch.

Veronda lay on a cot. She had a gash wound from a sword on her left bicep. The cut was deep, maybe two inches. It had cut into her bone. Blood soaked bandages encircled her bicep. She rolled her head over at me, her eyes unseeing.

"We can see what is the matter," the first medic said.

"If you are going to do something, do it fast," Tural told me.

I sat the medical kit on a table, and I unsnapped the seal.

"Okay. I do not want to frighten anyone," I said. "But we need more light in here. These torches are not good enough." I sat the electronic torch on the table. It was a typical model: one inch diameter, four inches high, tapered from the base to the top, like a small cone. On the top was the liquid electricity light.

I pressed the button on the base.

The entire room lit up.

Several of the warriors actually gasped.

And, frankly, it was pretty cool to show off.

"It is not even hot," Tural said. She reached past my elbow and touched the light with her hand. "See?"

I lifted a sensor out of the box and moved it near Veronda's arm, scanning from her shoulder to her elbow. Then I presented the handheld device to the medic.

It quickly scanned her body. It noted peculiarities about chemical makeup, but otherwise, it detected her as mostly-human.

"That is a *picture*... a drawing... of what her arm looks like. You can see where the sword broke into the marrow... the soft part of the bone inside. Even if we stop the bleeding on the outside of her skin, she will bleed inside."

"What can you do?" another warrior asked.

"We have to do three things. First, we must heal the bone." I took out a syringe from the kit. It had mixed the correct chemicals and dosages automatically. "Pull off all the bandages. She will begin to bleed a great deal, but we will stop the bleeding in a moment."

The medics removed the soaked bandages. Blood spurted out of her jagged wound.

I gritted my teeth, and then I plunged the needle directly into the wound, pushing down until the needle hit bone.

Even in shock, Veronda stiffened her arm.

I pressed the plunger. Then I pulled the syringe out. My hand was covered in blood.

"Now, we stop the outside bleeding."

I took out a small bottle of coagulant. I poured a capful of it onto her wound.

"Those are clean bandages," I pointed to a roll. "Can you open it and pull out three of them?"

The medic lifted the package.

"Just take the corner and pull on it... there," I instructed.

She opened the sterile package.

"Put them here," I said, pointing out the wound.

The bandages were applied to the wound, which had already stopped bleeding.

"Now, something to keep her from getting ill." I gave her an injection of an antibiotic.

"This will work on an Erskan?" Tural asked me.

"Yes. It works with all kinds of Earth people and the animals of Earth people. It will make the medicine as needed."

"Now," I said, putting the syringe back. I listened to the kit clean the syringe and prepare it for another solution. "The spare blood is back in my space wagon... and I do not believe we are the same blood type. Erskan blood is different. Not much, but slightly different. This will make a medicine that will help her body to make more blood faster."

The medical kit flashed a "finish" light. I took out the syringe and put an injection in her left hip.

"Now what?" the medic asked.

"We wait." I put the scanner back into the kit.

"How long do we wait?" the medic asked.

"She will be better soon."

Without warning, Veronda screamed. Her eyes blinked, and she looked at me. Then a burst of Erskan words, which I assumed were expletives, were aimed at me.

The medic chuckled. She put her hands on Veronda's chest. "She sounds like Veronda now."

"What has he done to me?" Veronda demanded. She reached over with her right hand to feel her left bicep.

There was blood all over her body and on the cot.

It did look like a failed medical operation. If I woke to see that, I'd be unhappy as well.

"He has saved your life," Tural said.

"A frey saved me life?" Veronda said. "Someone, please kill me."

"Help the others," Tural said. "I must go to the prison."

"Mistress?" I said, puzzled.

"Do not look at me with that face," Tural said.

"Just one minute of your time, please," I said.

The medic nodded.

I sprayed medicine on Tural's abdomen.

She stood there, hands on her hips.

"That should stop the pain," I said, packing up.

"The pain is gone," she cocked her head.

"It should be completely healed in 16 hours," I explained.

Tural walked to the door, but turned to face me and jerked her head. "Coming, slave?"

"Yes, Mistress."

There were a half-dozen Erskan warriors in the prison. There were also two that I had recognized before from my recreational stay at KoVer.

I had to check my guns and equipment in the intake area. But so did everyone else. I followed Tural through the familiar hall. My feet almost skipped a beat when I approached my old cell.

The group of warriors stopped at the last cell door. One warrior on the inside unlocked and opened the door for us.

"Are you prepared?" Tural asked the warrior.

"Yes, Netratoh. All is prepared."

"Good," Tural nodded.

I was behind her, but I felt her piranha teeth flash.

Inside was a sight that resembled nothing less than an old twenty-first century horror vid. There were two Treaslok women in heavy chains, ankles and wrists, each bound to a ceiling spreader bar and floor-hook chains. They were at opposite ends of the room, about fifty feet apart, facing one another.

They had been stripped of all clothing.

The Treaslok were not too different than the Erskans. Treaslok women were a little bit paler in complexion. They both had brown hair, instead of the Erskan black, and it was cropped short; whereas the Erksans usually wore their hair tied up in various manners, but was generally shoulder-length.

Tural looked at me, "This must be done for now."

"Yes, Mistress?"

Two of the Erskan women firmly grabbed onto my arms and, not roughly, steadily pulled me back to the stone wall. They each locked one of my wrists to a ceiling manacle. Then one of the warriors went over to a table and removed a gag.

"Open," she said.

I opened my mouth.

She pushed a leather-coated ball into my mouth, pulling the straps around to the back of my head and securing it with a roller-buckle.

"Yes?" the warrior asked me.

I suppose she was wondering if I could do that and not choke. Or, did she want me to test my speaking?

"Mumff," I nodded.

"Frey, if you begin to fill with your mouth juices, swallow them."

I nodded.

This was not very comfortable.

"Ureketa!" one of the Treaslok women shouted at Tural. It was the Treaslok that was closest to the door.

Tural strode to her and delivered a stunningly quick fist to the woman's mid-section.

She made a muffled noise as the air ran out of her.

Tural walked up to her and put both of her hands around the prisoner's neck, squeezing. "Treaslok, you will not speak until I ask a question. Do you understand?"

The prisoner tried to shake away.

Tural delivered a right-handed blow to the woman's left side, at the ribs.

"Do you understand?" Tural asked again.

"I will... not talk to a ureketa huraj," the woman huffed. It was in a heavy accent. I almost did not understand it at first.

A *huraj* is an animal similar to an Earth dog. I did not know the word *urekta*.

Tural delivered three rapid-fire punches to the woman's left ribs again.

The prisoner shouted, her sound of pain echoing off the walls of the dungeon.

I found that I was clenching my fists, trying to lean forward. What was I doing? Was I trying to stop Tural from doing this? I tried to ease myself back to the wall until my shoulders touched the stone again.

One of the Erskans looked at me and then crossed her arms in front of her, returning her attention to the interrogation.

Tural turned from her and walked to the second prisoner. She looked younger. She had a wild eye expression. She was barely covering her fear. Her right shoulder had a large bruise, probably from the battle.

"Wenata," the first prisoner said, "do not speak!"

Tural turned to one of the Erskans and made an expression of putting an index finger into her mouth, and then turned back to the second prisoner.

The second prisoner actually shivered for a moment, her chains clinking.

148

Two Erskans produced a gag. It was much different than the one I had in my mouth. This thing had a large protrusion, on the mouth-side that was about two inches in diameter and maybe four inches or so long.

The first prisoner tried to shake her head away, but one Erskan held her still while the other took the gag and held it below her own head. Then she spit on it, and pushed the thing into the prisoner's mouth.

The second Erskan pulled the straps tight as the gag reflex on the prisoner kicked in.

I squinted my eyes as she made horrible choking sounds. Tears streamed down her face.

The Erskan finished locking the gag on to her head and stepped back.

The prisoner continued to make choking sounds. Saliva spewed from the corners of her mouth.

"Quiet," the first Erskan said, elbowing the woman in the solar plexus, having the desired effect. It seemed to calm her down for a moment.

She whimpered, as the saliva continued to run from her mouth. I could hear her trying to breathe, to control it, to relax her throat and try not to choke.

"You," Tural said, walking to the second woman, "are going to be more reasonable, yes?"

The prisoner shook her head.

Tural produced a large knife with a four-inch blade.

"A 'Weneta' is what?" Tural demanded. Tural put the blade of her knife against the tip of the prisoner's left nipple.

The prisoner did not talk.

Tural slowly dug the tip of the blade into the woman's areola.

She screamed.

"That is not deep," Tural said, pulling the blade out. "I just barely cut you."

True. It was not very easy to see from my distance, but it did appear that a fine trickle of blood was all that was there.

"If you do not tell me what a Weneta is, I will cut this off." Tural grasped the woman's breast.

The woman did not speak. She closed her eyes, shivering.

Tural turned to face the first prisoner. Head bowed, tears on her face, saliva on her breasts, the first prisoner looked at Tural with absolute hatred. "If this one is a weneta, then you must be at least a rejella, yes?"

Both prisoners blinked.

Tural had known the answers all the time.

I had not seen Hula walk in. She was standing a few feet to my right.

"This one is a new warrior," Tural pointed to the second prisoner. "And this is their Jurina."

"The Rejella will not talk," Hula said, stepping forward.

"We should give her one more opportunity," Tural said, walking back to the first prisoner. "Here is what I will know: how many of you are attacking my land? How long have you been here? Where are your forces? How many guns do you have? Where is the frey that has given you the guns? Will you tell this to me now?"

The first prisoner shook her head.

"If you will not talk, then I have no use for you." Tural grabbed onto the woman's left ear. "If you do talk, I will release you, after we have sent the Treaslok back in flames."

The first prisoner shook her head again.

"Here?" Hula asked, approaching.

"No. I do not appreciate blood on the stones," Tural said.

Four of the Erskans approached to release the ankle chains of the prisoner. They chained her legs together, tightly. Then they lowered her wrists. They unhooked her from the spreader bar and chained her wrists tightly together. When she tried to swing out, Tural delivered a knee kick to the woman's middle again. She collapsed into the arms of the Erskans.

Hula walked back toward me, standing slightly in front. She looked over at me. "Are you well, slave?"

I nodded. Drool rolled out of my mouth and left a long drip on my chin before breaking and landing on my chest. Hula scrunched her lips for a moment before looking forward again.

They took the first prisoner, the rejella, and pushed her face-down on one of the nearby torture tables. They unlocked and pulled her legs and arms out, spread-eagled, and then shackled them to the heavy wood spars. Hula was partially blocking my view. And two of the Erskan warriors were also on this-side of the table. I could see glimpses of what was happening.

"Turn her around," Tural said to one of the Erskans near me.

She left my side and went over to the warrior. She reached up and rotated the woman one-hundred and eighty degrees... and then lashed a chain from the overhead spreader bar to a wall. The prisoner would not be able to see behind her.

I looked back over at Tural.

The rejella made frantic sounds.

"No. You have had your opportunity to talk to me," Tural said.

I could not see what was going on.

Then I saw a sword blade flash in the air for a moment.

A solid sound of it hitting wood filled the dungeon.

Then a high pitched scream from the first prisoner, that lasted almost twenty seconds.

She was sobbing through the gag. Screaming.

Tural walked away from the table, over to the second prisoner. She went to the woman's right side and opened her hands.

"Right hand," Tural said. She dropped four fingers and a thumb onto the stone floor. Blood filled Tural's hand, which she wiped on the prisoner's right breast.

Tural walked back over to the small crowd of Erskans.

The rejella protested through her gag.

I saw Tural pulling on the sword. Then it made a *clang* and went into the air before descending.

The prisoner howled again.

I felt Hula's left hand on my chest.

I looked at her. She seemed calm. Her lips were drawn into a fine line. She patted my chest four times. How could I have loved these savages?

This was unconscionable.

Blood soaked Tural's uniform. She walked over to the prisoner and tossed five more digits onto the stone at the woman's feet. "Left hand."

I could hear the second prisoner choking back tears. Her shoulders shook.

150

Tural walked back to the first prisoner who was making incomprehensible noises.

My bowels had turned to water. I could not breathe. I strained to look, although I knew they would not let me see.

The blade was extracted from the wood frame, and again it flashed in the air, before diving down out of my sight.

One more high-pitched scream, and the prisoner was silent.

Had Tural stopped the vicious mutilation? Was she done butchering the prisoner? I was repulsed. Why had I promised to help these people?

"No, let it bleed out," Tural said. Then she walked over to the first prisoner.

She carried a blood-covered arm with her, severed from the bicep.

I choked for a moment in my gag, saliva spurting on both sides of the leather.

"Back," Hula said, resting her hand on my chest again, gently pushing me.

I remained taut against the chains.

"Back," Hula ordered, pushing on my chest firmly.

I relented and moved back again.

"Stay," Hula said icily, with a definitively aggressive expression.

Tural tossed the arm down onto the floor, on top of the fingers. "Right arm."

"Please!" the second prisoner begged. "Please, stop. I will tell you if you will tend to her now."

Tural walked to the woman's side and wiped her bloody hands onto the woman's breasts.

"Kimera, tie off her hands and the arm... for now."

"Yes, Netratoh," an Erskan said.

At least the horror was over.

I felt dirty, soiled. I had had intercourse with Tural. Tural... she was... brutal. I was almost incapacitated by the repulsion that washed over me.

I also felt a measure of fear. Tural could have slit my throat at any time, and few would seem to care.

"How many of you are attacking my land?"

"There are twenty-thousand warriors here in Ureketa."

All of the Erskans in the room looked at each other.

"How long have you been in my land?"

The woman sobbed. "We arrived four days ago."

Tural looked pleased. She looked at the woman, grabbing her throat. "You will be kept as our prisoner until we have sent you back to your land. If anything you are telling me is a lie, you will be cut into pieces. Small ones. Do you understand?"

"Yes. If you will tend to my rejella, I will tell you all the truth."

"I am bound by honor," Tural replied.

I could hear the first prisoner trying to say something.

"Where are your forces? What is the strength of each?"

"I do not know all of this," the prisoner said. "We have one large force, and three smaller forces."

"How many guns do you have?"

The woman did not answer.

Tural specified, "The weapons that *raa*,"

"I do not know. I have seen two with my eyes. There are stories that we have twenty of the *itarankas*."

"Where is the frey who has given you the guns?"

"Frey? There is no frey."

"When and where will you attack?"

"I do not know."

Jurina Iona was let into the dungeon, followed by two of her lieutenants. She waved a finger to Tural.

"Do not go anywhere," Tural said to the prisoner.

Tural walked over to the jurina. The four of them went into the corridor.

This was a dangerous place. Several escape plans rushed through my head.

Hula looked at me, and our eyes locked.

"Do not be afraid, Alexi," she said.

My eyes widened, and I nodded my head toward the butchered prisoner. Her groans were pitiful.

Tural entered the dungeon. "Put them into separate cells, at opposite ends. Assign the prison guards to watch them. And assemble immediately." Tural pointed to a warrior and then at me.

"I will take him," Hula said, reaching behind my head. "Do not talk until we are outside. Do you understand?"

I nodded.

Hula pointed to a cloth that was beside one of the warriors. She tossed it over.

"Spit into this," Hula said, taking the gag out.

It seemed like a pint of saliva oozed out of my mouth. I spit it into the rag, which Hula then wiped on my mouth.

"Do not talk," she said again.

I nodded.

Hula unlocked my left wrist.

Tural and five warriors headed for the cell door.

"This one, Netratoh?" one of the remaining four warriors asked.

"Dump it into the fire. Be quick!" Tural said. She and her small group headed for the door as Hula released my other wrist.

The Treaslok general was lifted to a seated position on the wooden table. She had all of her fingers and body parts intact. The Erskans chained her wrists behind her back.

Then they shoved her down to the ground and chained her wrists to a floor ring. Gag still in her mouth, she looked furious.

I did not know whether to be furious or relieved. I felt a bit of both.

One Erskan pulled a body from the floor toward the cell door. It was missing a right arm, hands, and had a skull carved from a sword blow.

The tattered remains of a Treaslok warrior's uniform identified the corpse as an enemy.

The Erskans turned the second prisoner around as they let her down. She saw her floor-chained leader.

The Erskan warriors laughed and jeered as the foolish enemy gasped and tried to make sense of the cruel joke.

"Hula?" Tural said.

"Go," Hula said, pointing to the cell door.

I rushed after Tural and the other warriors.

We went down the hall and into the intake room.

"Maranna has reached Antrana," Tural said, snatching her weapons and equipment from the racks on the wall. "The enemy is one hundred miles southeast of the city. We believe their strength to be fifteen thousand or more."

"A morning attack?" Hula asked, as she handed my StacGun to me.

I holstered the weapon in a natural motion.

"No. They could not move that fast tonight."

"Respectfully, Mistress, I believe they are moving quite fast," I said.

"Yes. We have... what is the word you would understand? We have under planned what the Treaslok are doing."

"Antrana is alerted?" Hula asked.

One of the jurina's lieutenants nodded. "Yes. The city is preparing for a siege. Jurina Juroh has moved the citizens into the protection of the palace. Jurina Istana has summoned all of the forces that are available."

"You do not approve of the interrogation?" Tural suddenly inquired of me.

The room, full of a dozen warriors and myself, fell quiet.

"I believed you were cutting their jurina into pieces, Mistress."

Tural walked over to me. She was a half-inch from my face, looking into my eyes. "And, if I had been cutting that Treaslok dog into pieces?"

"I would be surprised," I told her. "I thought the Erskan warriors to be fighters of great honor."

"I will do everything to protect my people and my Torino," Tural said. "Everything."

"Yes, Mistress. I understand."

"The other Treaslok had died in battle. Rinita felled that dog," Tural explained. "Tell me, as you have chased the law breakers of your Earth. Have you not used threat of death or injury against them so that they may be encouraged to talk to you?"

I thought of my experience on Taleon with the two smugglers.

"Um, well, I, maybe."

All eyes were on me.

"Yes, Mistress."

"You will pay for your disrespect to me later." Tural reached a finger into the ring on my collar and pulled me down an inch before turning to the dozen warriors. "When we have killed all the Treaslok that have touched Aervanta, each of you will come to a celebration where," she jerked on my collar once, "slave Alexi will be the entertainment."

There was a fairly hearty round of applause and approval.

"Assemble outside!" Tural said. "Jurina Iona is ready to ride."

All of the women went outside, securing their swords behind their backs.

Hula stood behind Tural, who continued to grasp the ring on my collar.

"I apologize, Mistress."

Tural laughed and placed a small kiss on m left cheek. "I am not displeased. I knew that you would be angered."

"That is why you were chained, yes?" Hula explained.

I nodded. "Well done, Mistress."

"Jurina Kreka to Torino Sklera," we heard coming from both Tural and my radios.

"Speak," Sklera replied.

"I have lost a harfala to the enemy. They have four or five guns. One thousand warriors attacked us from the north. We are retreating to the southwest."

"Jurina Iona," Sklera asked, "Where are the guns?"

We heard the jurina's voice reply, "They will be on the Brenta road by this time."

"Jurina Istana," Sklera called, "Send fifty warriors to meet them."

There was about a ten second delay before the reply was returned, "Yes, Torino."

I followed Tural and Hula outside.

Night had fully taken over. Stars sparkled high ahead. It had been a long day.

Our military unit had grown. There were now three hundred warriors assembled on horseback.

We mounted our horses and moved into the formation on the parade grounds.

"How will we cross the yiminee plain?" I asked.

"We have found the lights you have," Hula explained. "They have been given to many riders."

"We are not wearing any armor," I noted.

"The yiminee do not fly at night," Tural told me.

"Maybe they are attracted to light."

Two flashlights, near the front of the column, were activated. They were extremely powerful. One was aimed down the road. It lit the entire block. A handful of residents came out of their doors to see what was happening.

Tural frowned.

"This could be suicide," I warned.

"Netra!" Tural exclaimed. She pounded her right fist into her left palm. Then she grudgingly pulled her radio to her face. "Netratoh Tural to Jurina Iona."

"Speak."

"Jurina, please hold. I have information."

There was a pause.

"Be quick."

Tural broke and rode toward the gate.

"We could send one or two riders to see what happens," I suggested.

Hula nodded.

After a minute Tural's voice spoke on the radio. "Slave Alexi, give the radio to Hula."

I handed over the radio.

"Yes, Tural?"

"Send my unit here. And bring the slave with you."

Hula handed the radio back to me.

I followed her. The other six women of the unit followed us to Tural.

Iona did not look amused.

"We will ride ahead and send Frenda's unit into the field with the lights," Tural explained.

A group of nine warriors had placed their horses slightly out of the larger formation. I recognized the leader of the unit, Frenda, from our ride to KoVer. She held one of the two flashlights that still illuminated the street. She turned it off.

Iona handed one of my flashlights to Tural. "This makes the sun. This makes the night."

Tural took the light and pressed the *on* switch. She practically blinded everyone on the front row, until she pointed it toward the street.

"Ride," Iona told us.

We gathered into our two nine-person units and headed for the way station.

"How do you want to do this?" Frenda asked.

Tural and Frenda were on their horses. We had just approached the ridge and were shining two flashlights down onto the dried mud.

We were illuminating about a three-hundred yard square area.

"One of us will have to ride out there with these day sticks," Tural said.

Hula looked at me. "What are these called?"

"*Flashlights.*"

"Flashlights?"

"Your English is very good, Mistress," I said.

"When we take control of Earth and have all men as frey, we will abolish English," Tural said.

I looked at her face. It was illuminated by the backflash of the light. She was grinning.

"How many is your forces?" Tural asked me.

I calculated the Erskan language equivalent for a few seconds. "There are twenty-eight million in our military."

All of them looked at me as if I were lying.

"There are not twenty-eight million Erskans," Hula said. "How many Earth people?"

"Oh, Mistress, I do not know the name for that number in Erskan. What are the next four places? Eighty-six of those."

"Eighty-six billion?" Hula stated.

"Yes, Mistress," I said. "We are on two hundred worlds now."

They were silent.

Maybe I should not have been telling them this. I probably made everyone feel very insignificant.

Tural broke the reflective moment. "With twenty-eight million warriors, we could capture all of the Treaslok men by tomorrow morning."

Everyone laughed.

"Penises for all Erskan warriors and citizens!" Hula said, pointing her fist into the sky.

"Penises for all!" Frenda laughed.

Damn. Sometimes, these blood-thirsty Amazons were funny!

"No ride tonight," Tural said. Her grim delivery of the statement caused all of us to break the mood and look ahead.

We could hear a massive amount of buzzing. Then the edges of our lighting became instantly blacked by an opaque wall of the yiminee. They flew toward the light. In five seconds, there was an ocean of vicious little monsters forty feet below us.

"I have never seen this many before," Frenda said, her voice wavering.

The yiminee were so thick they were making their own wave-like patterns. Light was reflected off an uncountable number of flying wings.

"Mistress, if I may?" I took Tural's flashlight and directed the beam to the right, along the bottom of the ridge.

The entire field of view of the light was blacked out by the bugs.

Frenda moved her flashlight to the left and saw the same thing.

Then I moved my light outward.

Even five-hundred yards away, the bugs packed the plains.

The rest of the warriors rode up behind us and stopped.

"What is the noise?" Lentara asked, raising her voice to overcome the buzzing of the insects.

Frenda lifted her head at Tural. "You will go first, yes?"

"Netra!" Tural exclaimed. She pulled her radio from her belt.

"Netratoh Tural to Jurina Iona."

"What is your report?"

"We are headed back to KoVer."

"Jurina Iona to Jurina Istana."

"Noween Tika to Iona. I speak for Istana at the moment."

"Relay to the Torino," Iona said. I could sense her disappointment in her voice. "Yiminee not passable tonight. We will arrive in Antrana at ten in the morning."

There was about a thirty second delay.

"We will have little time to learn how to use the guns," came the Torino's voice. "I believe the Treaslok could attack Antrana tomorrow at any time."

"When we return to KoVer," Tural looked at me, "can you use the radio to teach our people in Antrana how to use the guns?"

"We can try. But I am afraid they would get hurt. It is not only about having the guns, but it is about where to place the guns. And it is also about when to fire the guns. This must be learned, as by your sword fighting, by using the gun."

"We shall await your arrival," Torino Sklera said. Her voice sounded heavy.

"What do we say when we are done talking?" Tural looked at me.

"You say 'over.'"

"Over," Tural said into the radio.

"I heard you, Netratoh," Torino Sklera said.

Tural put the radio back into her belt. I watched her push the mute button on.

We turned about and joined the two units, riding back.

"If this was not so depressing," Tural said to me, "I'd take you tonight."

I grabbed a little tighter to the reins. I wasn't sure how to take that. As a compliment?

"Tonight we should rest," Hula said. "Tomorrow, we ride early. And then we fight."

Despite the late evening heat, a chill ran down my spine.

156

Chapter Eleven
On the Eve of Battle

How often does someone witness forty-thousand women warriors fight to the death?
It was a question I never dreamed considering. I was curled-up on four blankets that padded the cold stone floor. My collar was chained to the post of Tural's bunk bed.

The barracks at KoVer were jam-packed with troops. Small lamps flickered in the room, their wicks low, casting dozens of small flashes of light about the stone walls. Several Erskan women snored, in the native manner, but most were dead-silent.

Tural's hand reached over the side of her bed, fingers waving in the air, one at a time, until they found my head. She placed her fingertips on my forehead and slowly stroked my hair.

I did not even think about standing or coming over to her. If she wanted me, she would indicate her desires.

So I remained laying still while she petted me.

How often does someone witness forty-thousand women warriors fight to the death?

*****

The morning update from the Torino was not all bad news. Several small towns had fallen to the Treaslok; there were no civilians or military units coming back from the southeast. Presumably they had been killed or captured.

However, we had two scouts providing detailed troop surveillance. I was concerned that if one of our radios had been compromised, we would be equally broadcasting our own activities. Tural established an imaginative challenge-answer system. And I advised them how to switch frequencies, which we decided to do every two hours.

The wagons with the guns and supplies were in the palace walls.

We ate a quick meal in the morning darkness.

Armored in light leather, our three-hundred-twenty-four person unit was at the ridge of the yiminee plains just as the sun broke the horizon. After a break-neck pace, we reached the other side in time to receive the first radio reports that the Treaslok had moved into the city of KarTona.

There had apparently been a significant argument about what strategy to employ for KarTona. We knew it would be attacked today by far superior numbers and firepower. However, if the Erskans evacuated the city, the Treaslok would suspect that their efforts to keep their advance on the capital and palace had been detected... and might then charge on-ward.

A counter argument was that trying to conceal twenty-thousand troops and support staff was no longer a concern because the Treaslok would have an overwhelming technological advantage in firepower. Too, the distance between KarTona was just long enough that the Treaslok would have to ride a significant distance and then fight. Better to make a short jump when engaging an enemy already entrenched.

In the end, it appeared that the Torino was not going to accept civilian losses, nor that of her valuable warriors. She evacuated the entire city and pulled most of the units back to the palace. A few units were sent to the flanks of the Treaslok, though we did not have enough radios to communicate with them.

Our ride through Antrana was, again, at a dangerously-fast pace. Several times I felt my horse's pads slip.

Instead of the bustling, festive atmosphere I had seen just a few days ago, the city was boarded with makeshift sheets of wood. Street-side shops were covered with sheets. We passed several different columns of women citizens in loose formations.

"What are they doing?" I shouted to Tural.

"They are the *ten-tatay*... the home guard. We will arm them with weapons. If we should fail in battle the will fight!"

"They would not surrender?"

Tural glared.

I guess not.

Twice, on our ride to the palace, units rode opposing us, whisking by. I shuddered at the thought of these two columns making a mistake and crashing into each other at fifty miles per hour each.

There were only a few archers at the top of the palace walls. Security was heightened, however, at the gate. Our unit slowed down to a walking pace and then came to a stop while Jurina Iona spoke with one of the Torino's general staff. I looked ahead, about fifty horsewomen in front, trying to see whom Iona was speaking with.

Then the column moved again, at a brisk pace.

One of the gate staff passed orders onto each of the three harfala's leaders. Our unit, attached to the Iona, continued forward to the actual palace; the other two units broke off and headed to one of several of the stable buildings.

Hula explained, "They will change into field uniforms and take supplies on their trip to the battle lines."

We rode to the palace entrance and dismounted. Many of the warriors discarded their leather armor there, on the parade field. A dozen slaves appeared from the slave quarters carrying small packs and bags. One slave took my horse from me; he looked surprised that I had the illusion of freedom.

"I do not like the effect you might have on our frey," Tural said, as I followed her and Hula inside the palace.

"There will be few to see him now," Hula said.

"Why is that, Mistress?"

"They are in the palace to keep them safe," Hula told me.

"All of the Erskan males are here?" I asked.

"Inside the walls of the palace, yes," Hula said, impatiently.

"We have an old Earth saying. 'Do not keep all of your eggs in one basket.'"

Tural came to an abrupt stop and turned on her heel. "What do you – " and she cut herself off as quickly as she had started to speak.

Hula drew her lips into a thin line. And then she nodded.

"What is wrong?" Jurina Istana demanded, approaching us from the outside. "The

Torino is waiting for you."

Tural saluted. "Jurina Istana, we were discussing the wisdom of keeping all of the frey in the palace."

"The safety of Antrana is my concern."

"Yes, Jurina," Tural acknowledged.

"Making the slave teach us to use the guns without *nirodo* is your concern."

"Yes, Jurina. Slave, follow me now."

Hula hung back for a moment, blocking my ability to follow Tural.

We were approaching the last hallway that led to the war room.

"Why did you not press your view?" Hula whispered.

"Alexi, do you know the word *nirodo*?" Tural asked me.

"No, Mistress."

"To make stuck," Hula said.

"Jam?" I asked aloud, in English.

"Do your guns jam? They may have been using them this morning." Tural asked.

"If they are not cared for properly – if they get dirty they, can jam." I had to stop my conversation as we entered the war room.

The Torino Sklera Kretahla stood at the large map table, flanked by several aids. She had on the Erskan brown field uniform, adorned with several small symbols of honor. Her right hand brushed small figurines a few inches to the right. "Move this harfala. I want the lines for the archers to be solid. If we have to retreat to here or here, their sight-lines will be good."

The Torino turned toward us.

"The radios are giving my warriors an advantage." She seemed to force a half-smile. "Thank you, slave."

"It is in service to the Torino," I replied, bowing my head slightly.

"What do you think?" she asked, stepping back from the map.

I instinctively looked at Tural for permission. She rolled her eyes to the map.

There were figurines in several groups southeast of the capital. They appeared to be hastily-painted and poorly crafted. They probably had not needed this many representations of massive enemy formations before.

There was a slightly smaller number of figurines represented the Erskans.

The Treaslok were spread out on only a narrow face. The terrain between KarTona favored their advance as it was flat, slightly hilly, and provided no choke points for an ambush by the Erskans.

But there was a point where the terrain elevated slightly on the approach to Antrana; it was that location that the Erskans would draw their defense, taking a slight advantage of height. The two Erskan scouting units were on the flanks of the approaching Treaslok, monitoring any flanking actions they may take.

"I believe the Treaslok will hold at KarTona and then advance to this point between two o'clock and four o'clock." The Torino put her index finger on the line painted on the fabric. "Here."

"It will be hot for a battle," I commented.

"That is why I believe the Treaslok will attack. They know that we are inactive during the heat hours," one of the jurinas explained.

"With this, how do you see the best way to use the guns?" the Torino asked.

"Two of the guns would need to be mounted to wagons. They are much too heavy for any warriors to carry. The other ones – " I pointed to the map. " – would work best if we put two here. They can cover a line of fire across this area. Two guns here, which would give them cover from archery. If we could get a good gun shooter to be in this place, she could fire down. My concern, though, is the guns. Where are the Treaslok going to put their guns?"

"How many of our warriors can they kill with their guns?" Jurina Istana asked aloud.

"Jurina, they could kill three or four hundred warriors with each gun."

"If they have as many guns as we do," the Torino said, "I could lose one-quarter of my warriors."

The psychological aspect was chilling.

"We have thirteen guns and the two large guns for the wagon," Tural noted, wading back into the small group of officers.

"We have no training," I said. "Torino, we should begin training now."

She looked at me. "What do you favor that the guns will make a difference in the battle?"

"I can not give you an answer, Torino, until I begin teaching."

I caught Hula's eye for just a moment. She tipped her head and then walked out.

"Report to me in an hour," Torino Sklera said. "Netratoh."

Tural saluted and exited. I followed her outside and back to the parade grounds.

"I will have food brought to us," she said, as she caught a palace slave and instructed him to bring lunch. "Do you need to use the toilet?"

"Please, Mistress."

I stepped into a side room and took care of business. I went to the wash basin and rinsed my face with water. And I looked at myself in the ornate, gold-trimmed mirror.

My hair was long.

There still was no need to shave yet.

"Does the fate of these people rely on what I can do in the next four hours?" I asked aloud.

I stared into my own eyes, looking for answers.

There was more than self-preservation at stake here. Corrigan had been negatively influencing the Treaslok. I did now know how long he had been coming here. Perhaps once before. Maybe twice. Was he on the other side of the planet? There were no frey in charge of their operations, according to our young prisoner. Maybe Corrigan was keeping a low profile.

But why were the Treaslok attacking? If Corrigan was, in fact, running a dictatorship, why would he care about attacking the Erskans? What did the Treaslok have that would be bartered for guns and ammunition?

What about the upcoming battle? If we should win, what would happen to me? And most importantly, *why did I consider myself a slave to the Erskan women*?

It was not merely a feeling of accepting my fate, being unable to escape the planet and return home. It was like the irresistible attraction of a moth to a bright flame. These powerful, sensuous, and intoxicating women drew me into their inescapable aura of influence. I had always felt a measure of respect for powerful, confident people, male and female. Here, the powerful were the women, and they used their positions to influence, control, and dominate the men.

The disproportionate sexual demographics also created something that surprised me. My initial theory had been that the Erskan women treated the males with disdain and as lowly creatures; but the opposite was true. Due to the scarcity of the males, the women protected and fought over the males.

But where did that leave me? I was not only a foreigner to these people, but an alien. They automatically trained me and controlled my socialization into their culture.

I was dodging the question of why I considered myself a slave. I had an intellect and knowledge centuries ahead of the women here, yet I was willing to accept a subservient position.

"Slave?" Tural had approached from behind, putting her hands on my hips and pulling close.

"Yes, Mistress. I was thinking."

"About what have you been thinking?"

"Three thoughts, Mistress. One, my feelings that I am your slave. Two, to ask why are the Treaslok attacking. And three, why is Corrigan, the trenama, involved?"

"The Treaslok want our men,"

"Yes, Mistress. That is what everyone has told me."

I watched the reflection of her face, over my shoulder, in the mirror. She looked into my eyes, "What do you believe?"

"That is what your people have believed for centuries. But this time, there is something different. There is a trenama from another world here. Corrigan would only do what is good for Corrigan."

"If Corrigan is alive," Tural noted as she ran her fingers through my hair. "Why do you feel you are a slave?"

"Mistress, I do not know the answer. I was a strong man in my world."

"And do you believe you are weak now?"

"I think it could be viewed as being weak now."

"If you were a weak male, you would not be our slave... a slave of the warrior caste. We do not have frey that are without value. True, our frey are of less physical strength than Alexi, but they are males who have the inside heart of power. You are a prize catch, Alexi. No warrior believes you to be weak."

"Thank you, Mistress," I said, genuinely pleased.

"Do you remember how you met the Erskan people?" she asked.

"A boy found me."

"That was one of my stable frey. He had requested to go on a hunt. The Torino had been on a tour of KoVer. I offered her to go on a hunt for *inatooh*. We were returning from the hunt with two kills when you were found. It was a most fortunate meeting. One could have imagined what may have happened if someone with less forethought than the leader of our people had met you. The Torino is a woman of great thought. Once she recognized your intelligence, she ordered that you be trained as quickly as possible. That is why she assigned Hula to teach you our language."

I nodded. The sequence made perfect sense to me now.

"Do you miss your old life on Earth?" she asked.

"Yes. I miss some of it. I had a good life. My work helped people."

"Did you have a Mistress or – woman in your life on Earth?"

"No."

"Did this make you happy?"

"At times, no, I was not happy. My work was by myself."

"If you could go home to Earth today, would you go?"

"I promised my help to the Torino to protect your people from Corrigan and the

Treaslok," I replied. But I knew that was not the answer Tural wanted.

In the mirror I saw her cock her head slightly... waiting for the truth.

"I do not know, Mistress."

"That is an answer that I can respect, slave." She put her arms around me and held on for a few seconds, a bit possessively, but a hug nonetheless.

Our reflection in the mirror was one of warmth and intimacy.

Then I reached my left hand out to the mirror and pressed my pointer finger against the glass. "I have seen these mirrors before. One was in the infirmary at KoVer. I saw one in the Torino's bed chambers. Now,... this one. I know the Erkans can make glass. But... what is on the other side of the glass that makes us see each other?"

"*Det*," she said. "We can make glass, but to make glass this flat and perfect costs many *Querla*."

"What is *det*?"

"The frey dig it out of the ground," Tural said.

From the time I was a baby, I have been looking at mirrors. The scarcity of them here had not really jolted my observations until now. "Mistress, may I use your knife?"

Tural drew her four-inch double-edged dagger as easily as she batted her eyelids. She handed it to me.

"Cover your eyes," I said.

Before Tural could protest, I plunged the hilt of the knife into the mirror.

"Slave!" she huffed.

Broken pieces of glass fell to the counter, several shards splashing into the bowls of soapy water and rinse water.

I took a piece of the mirror and flipped it over. I dug into it with the knife.

"How much of this det is dug out of the ground?"

"It is not good for weapons. Sometimes, the poor will melt it and make trinkets. The det is on one side of the coal mine and it gets in the way of digging for coal."

I scraped pieces of it from the glass and let it rise on the blade.

"Damn," I said under my breath. "Your people dig up the det and then heat it and pound it into flat plates. Then you put a layer of glass over the top. Very smart."

"Slave?" she asked.

"I might be wrong. *Metallurgy* was a small study of mine once. My people call this *platinum*." I handed her knife back. "How much of this det is pulled out of the ground?"

"Every week, we have wagons of it that we dump back into the ground."

I ran my hands through my hair and breathed a sigh.

"Gun training," Tural said reminded me.

I followed Tural out into the late morning sunlight. Thousands of Erskan women were in various stages of grouping into formation. The formerly-well trimmed grass area was now a pock-marked dirt field.

"Platinum, is it good for the Earth people?" she asked.

"Yes," I said. "It is very good. We use it to make our space wagons fly."

Platinum was a critical ingredient of corona oil due to its outstanding catalytic properties and excellent high temperature characteristics. It was now very scarce. I had not seen a piece of platinum jewelry in twenty years. A simple earring was worth tens of thousands of dollars.

I followed Tural to an area set up by the palace walls. Twenty warriors, all with bows slung over their shoulders, stood in a loose formation. A senior officer spoke with

162

them as we approached.

Two young men were resting on their knees, flanking the group. They wore the simple cloth belt and loin cloth. Both had a small arrow-type pendant locked onto their collars.

"Netratoh Tural," the officer said, saluting. "Hemtre Virona."

The archers came to attention.

Tural returned the salute. "Virona, this frey is Alexi. The Torino has granted him a temporary position to teach the great archers of Aervanta in the use of guns."

"Yes, Netratoh."

"Mistress." I nodded to the officer.

"Frey," she said, then turned to Tural. "These are among the best of my archers."

Tural made one reviewing pass of the archers and told them to relax.

"You know why we are here," Tural told them. "This is a great responsibility. Do not let your emotions about having a slave teach get in our way of destroying the Treaslok. They are our enemy. Alexi is my slave, and he is devoted to helping his owners defend Aervanta and the Torino."

I looked at the wood crates to the right of us. The lids had been removed and the firearms were resting on simple wood tables. Ammunition was piled in small stacks on the tables.

"May I, please?" I asked Virona. After she nodded, I picked up a Crest-Leeland full-automatic machine gun.

I surveyed the other ten guns on the table. None of the safety switches were in the "on" position. None of the magazines were loaded.

I pulled a magazine from a crate and, after being sure it was charged, snapped the magazine into the handgrip of the Crest-Leeland.

"We need something to shoot at," I said to Tural. Virona looked at one of the slaves; he leapt to his feet and ran about twenty yards to a building.

"There are different kinds of guns," I said, pulling my StacGun from my right holster. "This is a small gun that only has twenty bullets in it. This one in my left hand is an *automatic* gun. *Automatic*."

Several of the archers voiced the word.

The slave returned, dragging a cart with two mannequin-like burlap shapes, both stuck on a pole secured to the cart.

"Good, take it over there," I said.

He pulled the cart to the wall and then returned to his place on the ground.

"There is much difference between these two guns. This automatic has one-hundred bullets. The StacGun has twenty bullets. A bullet is like an arrow tip. It will fly out of the gun so fast that you can not see it. The StacGun only shoots one bullet every time I squeeze this here, which is called the *trigger*. Trigger. But the automatic will shoot many bullets every time you squeeze the trigger."

I looked at Virona, "Mistress, how many of these bags on carts do you have?"

"We have twenty carts, frey."

"We need all of them. Also, please make sure there is no one on the other side of the wall."

Virona pointed to both slaves who immediately headed in two different directions.

"Mistress, how many arrows can your fastest archer shoot per second?"

"Two per second."

"With the small StacGun, I can shoot four bullets per second," I told the warriors.

"With this one, I can shoot twenty per second."

There was shuffling of feet.

I walked to the right of the warriors and put the strap of the Crest-Leeland over my shoulder.

Tural walked up beside me.

"Mistress," I said, looking at the two targets, drawing a line on them with the StacGun.

"Yes, slave?"

"You said that I am your slave."

"The Torino asked me if I wanted to keep you when the war is over."

"I am honored, Mistress."

"We will have a collaring ceremony soon."

"Thank you, Mistress." I flipped the safety on the StacGun. "Mistress?"

Both slaves returned, one helping the other wheel a tethered set of five carts out to the crates.

"Yes, slave?"

"None of these guns have been fired yet."

I looked away from the target and over my left shoulder at her.

Tural bit her lip and then tapped her right hip for a few seconds.

"Ready?" I asked.

"I have seen this before," she said, taking a few steps away.

The gun lurched three times in my hands. Pieces of straw blew out of the back of one of the target dummies. The second shot had ripped big holes in the shape. But the straw, packed as it was, made good repetitive-use target practice. At least for this gun, the straw remained intact.

All of the warriors stood wide-eyed.

"The automatic uses a special bullet," I explained, flipping the large weapon over my arm and then laying my cheek along the sight. I drew in on the second target.

The staccato from the gun shattered the peace of the courtyard.

I destroyed the second target dummy.

Pieces of stone exploded from the wall, fifty feet away, showering the dirt below with white-hot rock.

"We will learn how to use the small gun first," I said, putting the Crest-Leeland back onto the table. "The best shooters will get to use these two automatics."

My goal had been to exercise patience in teaching the use of the weapons and to try to ignore what was happening outside the city.

That was becoming more difficult to do. Tural wore her radio, as she floated in an out of the lessons, but I had kept my radio on a table. It was distant enough that I could not detect the words being said. However, the tone of the voices made me realize that things were gradually coming to a head.

I had just watched Merina punch a near-perfect quarter-inch group of three shots into a cloth strip when Tural walked over to the table and turned off my radio. She knew it was a distraction, but she knew I did not want to leave the situation either.

"Mistress Merina, let us see how you do with this one." I hefted the big gun into my arms and walked over to her. "This is where the 'safety' is on this weapon. You can move it to make it shoot one bullet, like the hand gun, three bullets, or all of the bullets. First, you will shoot one at a time, to get familiar with the weapon. And then three bullets. And then we will have you empty the whole magazine."

Merina was positively ecstatic. It was easy to tell that she was a natural armory expert. In a matter of minutes she was unloading the entire clip, with absolute precise accuracy, into the dummy.

I addressed the entire group. "Mistress Merina is one of the best shooters I have ever seen. In two hours she learned what takes most Earth people weeks to master. With your permission, Mistress, Merina, I would request that you help Milaya and Nitrayva with bettering their shooting."

Now I had a teaching colleague, and that could possibly double our teaching effectiveness.

After awhile, one of the frey brought drinks and food to all of us. Tural had rejoined us and walked over to me, holding my drink and food until the warriors had all begun their meals.

"Alexi, let us walk," she said, as I finished my food. "Warriors, have a twenty minute time."

We walked toward the palace.

"You have been teaching for three hours without a rest," she said.

"Most of the warriors are good, Mistress Tural, but others need more time." I surveyed the grounds and estimated approximately a thousand warriors making final riding preparations for battle. "What is happening?

"It appears that the Treaslok will be moving from KarTona shortly. Their forces have mounted, and they have sent several scouts ahead. We have used the radios to avoid them. If it were not for your radios, Alexi, we would lose the war. Thank you."

"You are welcome, Mistress. Where is Mistress Hula?" I inquired as we walked back to the makeshift firing range.

"Hula has been busy. She is concerned with the well-being of the freys."

"I was worried about that. The way that Jurina –"

Tural cut me off: "— it could be dangerous for a frey to voice suspicions."

"Yes, Mistress."

"Hula has been busy," Tural repeated.

Both of our radios interrupted with an urgent transmission. "The Treaslok are beginning to ride."

"Torino to Tural," we heard Sklera's voice.

"Yes, Torino," Tural replied, speaking into her radio.

"Dispatch all of the trained warriors whom you believe can help."

Tural looked at me.

"We can dispatch all of the warriors."

"Torino to Alexi."

I took Tural's proffered radio. "Yes, Torino?"

"How are my warriors?" she asked.

"Torino, there are warriors who are better than others. But all of the warriors are good enough that I would go into battle with them."

Sklera gave the orders to Tural. "Dispatch all of them to their positions."

"Yes, Torino."

"I will see you both at the front lines," Sklera said.

I walked to Merina and handed the Crest-Leeland to her. "You will need a frey to carry those boxes of ammunition with you."

She nodded.

I lifted carried the other big gun to Nitrayva. "Mistress, you have learned much in the last hour. Merina is a good teacher."

I passed out the other guns to the warriors. "If anyone has a problem, send a runner to a radio warrior. My people of Earth have a name for warriors who ride horses and carry guns. We call them the *cavalry*. The cavalry on Earth has a history of hundreds of years of riding into battle and saving the day. You are the first Erskan cavalry unit."

Tural addressed the women. "This is a great honor. You know the future of our people rests with you. You are dismissed."

I expected all of the warriors to shoulder their weapons and walk to their tethered horses. Instead, Merina walked over to me. "Alexi, do not speak of this."

I was about to ask for a clarification; however, she quickly gave me an Erskan military salute.

The other warriors nodded in agreement; then they broke as a unit and walked to their horses.

"Merina lost her sister at KoVer," Tural told me. "She will do everything she can to defeat the Treaslok."

Tural then dispatched orders to the dozen military frey there. She also assigned four warriors to protect the precious ammunition of the frey. Within a minute, ammunition was crated and loaded onto horses to attend to each of the respective cavalrywoman.

"Now?" I checked my holster for the StacGun. Then I slung my sniper rifle over my shoulder.

Radio traffic was nearly non-stop as the Erskans coordinated their positions based on the advance of the Treaslok and the arrival of the armed cavalrywomen.

"We ride to the front line," Tural said.

The last of the Erskan mounted warriors and support teams rode out of the palace walls. Small units remained, preparing for riding to the front line, but the majority of the fighting force was already there or riding to meet the onslaught of the forty-thousand Treaslok invaders. I saw a couple of light mounted warriors ride by; they were carrying long brass-like instruments that looked similar to a bugle.

"We have changed our way to allow for the use of the radios," Tural explained, observing my interest. "A junior warrior will be near each radio to pass commands to the unit leaders."

Tural looked at me as other warriors headed over to us, all riding high in their saddles. "You do not know much about the Erskans. You have only seen the world of the military. You have not seen civilian life."

Tural and I mounted our horses. The rest of our group of eight other warriors formed our unit.

Tural adjusted the buckle on the straps across her breasts and pulled the scabbard lower on her back. She turned her horse to face the palace.

She looked at it for a long thirty seconds, engaged in private thought. Then she turned her horse and rode out.

We followed her break-neck gait through the deserted streets of Antrana.

Before we knew it, we would be engaged in battle.

Chapter Twelve
Concert of War

I followed Tural as we ran, half-crouched, up a slight rise in the terrain. We looked ahead. Our field of vision was clear for about a quarter mile. There was no movement ahead.

We continued running until we were down again.

Dozens of senior warriors were actively issuing orders around the roped-off area that served as Torino Sklera's field command post.

One of the palace guards let us by the opening in the ropes. We stood looking at large cloth maps.

"There are three Treaslok scouts approaching from this direction, directly ahead," the Torino said, pointing to a small figurine. "Most of their army is spread out behind them. They may suspect we are aware of them now."

"Why?" Tural asked.

"They are rotating a scout every five minutes. One rides from the front line to replace one of the scouts. They can then assume, if a rider does not return to them, that they have been attacked."

Smart.

"Torino," I asked, "are your forces fast enough that we can split as the scouts get here, and let them ride through us?"

"Yes. I have moved one third of my army to the west and one third to the east. There is a five-hundred yard distance between them. That is room for the scouts to ride through."

"The other third, Torino?"

"The remainder of the forces have moved one thousand yards behind us. The Treaslok should ride into a three-sided box. We will kill all three of the scouts, and then send one of them back, tied sitting up, to the horse. We shall have extra horses ready in case we must kill the Treaslok horse. This will give us more time for the Treaslok to move into our trap. Before the Treaslok show signs of concern, we will attack."

"This is a great plan," I said, nodding.

"The cavalry warriors are here, and here, and here. They will not shoot their guns into each other," Torino Sklera pointed to the lines of figurines.

It did look like a great plan.

"All warriors on the north front of the advance must cross that hill and lay in waiting for the scouts. We will move to the corner where our north and west flank meet now." The Torino lifted her radio. "Torino to Urala, are we safe to cross?"

"Urala to Torino. Yes. The three scouts should be fifteen minutes until reaching the north flank."

Torino Sklera nodded to one of the generals. That jurina walked up the hill behind us and waved, before turning and returning.

A wave of brown leather-clad warriors came over the low hill, toward us. They jogged by, going over the other low hill.

The warriors ran out onto the grass and dirt-covered plain, taking positions flat onto the ground. Unit leaders ran by, ensuring that all of the reflective swords and gear were covered by the warrior's body or that of a colleague.

The Torino moved to the right, and our group of a dozen officers shadowed her aside the top of the ridge.

My jaw was still half-dropped. There were about five-thousand warriors well-concealed on the ground. The entire movement and placement had taken fewer than two minutes. And it had been utterly silent.

I looked over my shoulder and saw three cloaked Erskan warriors riding horses come to a stop, on the other side of the low hill, in the valley, out of view of the advancing Treaslok. The three horses were each of a different color. Again, it was an example of Erskan military prowess.

We ran a couple of hundred yards along even ground until we reached a point where it sloped slightly downward. As I came over to the top of the ridge, I could see thousands of Erskan warriors lying down next to their horses that were also laying down.

The Torino and senior staff had assumed position along the ridge, peering over the edge.

We crouched down along the same ridge, on the end, with all of them out to my right.

"Four minutes," Urala said.

"Make all of your radios more soft," the Torino ordered.

I reached down and lowered the volume with my hand.

Tural had to roll onto her left side and pull her radio out, looking at the volume control before lowering it to about twenty-five percent.

"Three minutes," Urala advised.

About thirty yards to my right, along the ridge, was Merina, flanked by three frey. She had the Crest-Leeland sitting in front of her. The tri-pod was collapsed, ready to be hoisted the two foot distance to the top of the ridge so that the gun could rain fire down upon the Treaslok.

"Two minutes," Urala advised. "They will be able to see anyone that moves."

Several hundred yards to my right were three small figures, moving slowly through the scrub brush. Small waves of heat blurred their images for another minute until they moved close enough that we could see them as three distinct, cloaked riders, closely grouped.

One of them turned around to face the rear as a fourth rider approached. It was the cyclical replacement.

The four of them stopped.

My breath seemed loud. Tural fixated on the four Treaslok warriors, so I supposed that my breathing was not actually noticeable.

At least I could see what was happening. I looked down and saw that there were about eight-thousand Erskan warriors waiting to attack; they could not see what was going on.

The rider exchange was taking longer than I expected.

As I had seen before, Tural tapped her left index finger on her thumb. She also

168

thought this was taking too long.

Then the third rider broke from the group and rode south. The other three riders proceeded north.

I sighed.

Tural pointed to the southern rider. "Alexi, kill that rider, now!"

"What? –"

"Kill that rider!"

There was a ripple effect along the officer line as they heard Tural speak. Her voice had risen significantly. Perhaps loud enough that the three approaching scouts, still a hundred yards away, might pick up on her voice.

The Torino glared at us. One of the generals crawled in our direction.

I raised my sniper rifle and fixed the warrior in my sights as she rode away. It was nearly one-hundred and fifty yards.

"Now!" Tural shouted.

The three scouts would have heard her shout the command.

I fired.

The single shot echoed across the area.

I saw the head of my target explode. Her lifeless body fell forward off her horse.

"What are you doing?" screamed one of the jurinas. She half-crouched over me.

Tural pointed to the three scouts. Still closely grouped, they continued riding forward, maintaining speed.

Decoys. They were decoys.

"Tural to Urala," Tural said into her radio. "Tural to Urala!"

There was no reply.

The jurina crouched over me slowly stood to her feet, looking to her left.

A chill run down my back.

"Fuck!" I looked around.

The silence was shattered by automatic gunfire from a half-dozen locations around us.

Our flank was being ripped into pieces as bullets from below crisscrossed over the laying Erskans and their horses. Women and horses screamed as rows of blood and flesh skyrocketed upward.

I looked down and saw two women, lying beside trees, firing at us. Two white-hot muzzle flashes raked our warriors to pieces.

Women and horses were trying to stand up, only to be cut down.

I turned around and aimed at the closest Treaslok and put a bullet in her face.

Merina had gotten her bearings. She turned her heavy machine gun around and opened fire on the other Treaslok. The trees around the adversary blew apart as the chain gun exploded. Screams filled the air.

Everything was still for almost ten seconds.

Back home, before a thunderstorm, you can almost feel the pressure of the wave of cold air rushing across the surface toward you. Here, I could not see anything. But I could feel the pressure of another wave rushing toward us.

Battle cries filled the air. From below... no,... from behind us!

Then there were thousands of Treaslok warriors running up, swords drawn. The Erskan warriors were dazed. Those closest to the advancing line of the Treaslok hardly had an opportunity to draw their swords.

I could hear automatic machine gun fire from across the field over on the eastern flank. On our side, Merina was firing into the advancing Treaslok, cutting down scores of them.

Tural pointed to the Torino standing among her senior staff. Thousands of mounted Treaslok were coming into view. Treaslok in the front were firing light machine guns into our flanks.

"Down!" I waved both of my hands to the ground.

The Torino and the others hugged the ground.

Merina continued to fire.

The advancing center column of Treaslok targeted the closest line of the Erskans. Dirt ripped skyward and tracer fire arced down upon the crouching Erskans.

A line of machine gun fire danced near Merina. She and one of the frey dove to the ground.

I sighted in on one of the mounted Treaslok. She was looking back at me, squeezing the trigger of a Stemmons 6mm Rapido in my direction.

I snapped off two shots, blowing a cavity in her chest as she was swept from the horse.

The Treaslok below and to the right had taken an opportunity in the break from Merina's defensive fire to instead advance into the mayhem that was the Erskan warriors. The close quarters effectively prevented Merina from firing.

I watched her turn around and begin firing into the mounted Treaslok.

One of the jurinas near Torino Sklera shouted orders to a group of warriors to protect the back of Merina.

Barely heard over the sound of machine gun fire, clashing swords, and the screams and cries of thousands of women came the sound of a bugle.

A wave of the Erskan warriors from the north flank crested down the hill onto the flat field, charging toward the mounted Treaslok.

"Merina will not be able to fire!" Tural shouted.

"Not in a moment, that's right!"

Our west flank was involved in hand-to-hand sword fighting.

I picked out individual Treaslok and fired. Then I handed my StacGun to Tural. "Just aim into the crowd of Treaslok and squeeze the trigger!"

I fired twenty times, striking attacker after attacker.

Tural was firing, in a two-handed stance. Her shots were mostly wild, but they were higher than the heads of the Erskans, and I was certain she was hitting Treaslok.

Over my shoulder I saw the impending collision of the charging mounted Erskans and mounted Treaslok.

One Treaslok in the advancing line on the eastern side was firing a machine gun into the Erskan line. Dozens of Erskans were falling before her, creating a pile-up of bodies and horses.

I had no clear shot. There was going to be a massive collision of nearly ten-thousand warriors.

"Alexi!" Tural shouted.

The Treaslok had broken past part of the Erskan line nearest us. We had been the most severely harmed by the initial machine gun attack. It had been a terrible and destabilizing blow to the Erskans.

Carnage.

I turned to face Tural and saw that our position was in danger of being overrun. The two forces collided on the field in a thunderous noise that echoed across the sky.

170

The low rumble slowly increased – it was the sound of screams and cries of battle.

I saw hundreds and hundreds of warriors fighting. Many remained on horseback. Others had fallen to the ground and were slinging it out, metal blow by metal blow.

Blood and body parts littered the ground.

Horses screamed. Several were wandering, headless, their legs not aware that they were no longer attached to a head.

There was a non-stop clashing sound of metal as thousands of swords crashed. I shuddered.

Still more riders approached from both sides, pushing into the fray.

Heavy weapons fire had subsided. The close-quarters combat made machine gun fire useless.

Someone was shaking my shoulder.

I had been mesmerized by the calamity.

Tural pointed to my right.

More than thirty Treaslok were trying to approach us. Erskan, outnumbered two-to-one, were fighting with swords, knives, and fists.

It was too close for Tural to shoot.

I had to drop a clip and reload.

I sighted and fired and fired, again and again. My trigger finger ached.

One Treaslok prepared to deliver the killing strike to a wounded Erskan, but I put a shot through her throat that decapitated her.

Tural and I moved back a few feet as the line surged toward us.

They were attempting to take me out of the battle.

A Treaslok got within ten feet of me. I killed her as another two Treaslok took her place.

I killed another.

Then another.

I felt something being pushed into my leather pants... it was the StacGun. Then Tural pushed my barrel to the left, as she stepped in front, her sword drawn.

A sword blade flashed toward me. I gasped and retreated a foot.

Tural intercepted it with her own sword, sparks flying.

I let the rifle drop to my left hand, as I pulled out the StacGun.

Tural countered the sword strike and caught the Treaslok in the chest.

Blood spurted out, spraying Tural in her face. She backpedaled, wiping her face with her free arm.

A Treaslok fought past an Erskan to get to Tural, drawing back for a killing strike. Tural recovered and cut down the enemy. The Treaslok let out an ear-piercing scream as Tural hacked her body into three parts.

From our left additional Erskan warriors arrived, flooding the space between the Treaslok and our forces. They repeled them.

It gave me enough distance to begin firing again.

"I'm running out of bullets!" I shouted to Tural. I had killed at least two hundred Treaslok. My gun barrel was smoking. I dropped the fifteenth magazine to the ground and snapped number sixteen in.

Hair matted with blood, her face smeared, Tural nodded. She tried to get the attention of a frey who hugged the ground, terrified. Tural ran behind the line toward the ammo crates. The "line" was no longer an accurate description, though. The north flank had filled out and spread so much that it was now blending in with our west

171

flank.

I had not heard Merina's machine gun fire in quite a while. It was time to reclaim it and put it into action.

Because I think... we were losing.

I had no idea what was going on over at the eastern flank, but without someone of my skill there, I assumed the worst.

Tural was headed back carrying a handful of pre-loaded magazines to me.

"We need to find Merina!" I took the magazines and stuffed them into my pockets. "Follow me!"

We threaded through the small gap between the back of the west flank and the west side of the northern flank.

Combat of the northern flank was going better for the Erskans. They had not suffered the surprise attack and were gradually overpowering the Treaslok.

Tural pointed sixty feet away, where Merina was engaged in a sword fight. With the shifting of a dozen combatants, I instantly lost sight of her.

The Crest-Leeland was left on the ground, undamaged.

I slung a sack of ammunition drums to Tural. "Take these. Move me up to—"

I was knocked to the ground onto my face. Dirt filled my mouth, and all I saw was darkness. I put my hands out and tried to push up. My head was spinning. Someone pushed down on my back.

Then, without warning, it rolled off. The screams and clash of battle again filled my head. I had been knocked out for a moment. I think... I opened my eyes and tried to roll to my side.

An Erskan lay next to me. It was Jurina Kreka. Three arrows protruded from her back, one buried deep just to the right of her spine, near the shoulder blade. She was dead.

I sat up.

Several Erskans had taken a crouching position and were countering the volley of arrows with their own shots into the Treaslok archers.

Tural!

Sprawled on the ground a few feet away, she propped herself up with her left hand and looked at me, blinking. She shouted something and stood, half-limping on her right leg. An arrow left a gash in her leg.

I shook my head, trying to throw off the cobwebs. I got up and lifted the heavy machine gun. "Can you carry these?"

"Yes."

"We have to move down to the line!"

"Follow me." Limping, she pushed her way into the thinning line of Erskan fighters. Finally, about thirty-women deep, Tural was brandishing her sword again, cutting into the Treaslok warriors.

"Clear a path! Then get out of my way!" I shouted.

Tural sliced the arm off of an enemy and promptly retreated behind me. Blood splattered onto my chest as an enemy died at my feet.

I hefted the machine gun and let fly on the trigger. The gun whirred, the belt feeder spinning. Cartridges ejected into the air by the hundreds, streaming into a golden arc. I walked forward as I mowed down the advancing Treaslok.

"Come, get some!" I shouted in English.

I created a buffer area of dead bodies in front of me before sweeping the perimeter, expanding the fire zone. Erksans were aware of this and retreated from the periphery.

Then the gun let out a small burst of tracer rounds, signaling the end of the ammo drum. "Get ready for a reload!"

There was a click, and the gun stopped. I dropped the drum and grabbed a new one from Tural's outstretched hands.

Before the Treaslok could recover, I was shooting a cyclic rate of over one-thousand rounds per minute. It was a completely overwhelming tactical advantage. By the time I loaded the third drum, the western flank was ours.

Treaslok, hundreds of them severely wounded, threw down their swords and knelt in shame.

Erskan warriors moved in, separating their weapons and locking long loops of chain around the necks of the defeated enemy.

Tural pulled on my arm.

The northern flank was still in heavy combat. We climbed the slight ridge.

The front line had moved to our right by about fifty yards.

Freed from the battle on the west flank, hundreds of Erskan warriors streamed past us, helping their sisters.

One of the warriors stopped to look at Tural and inquire about her. Tural shrugged her off and waved for her to engage the battle. I tore a piece of leather from a fallen Erskan warrior and bent down to tightly wrap Tural's calf.

Tural nodded and then led me to the edges of the northern flank. Additional Erskans carved and sliced a path for me to get near the front lines.

Then I was able to open up on the enemy. I had fired over a thousand rounds when I felt the enemy change directions. The Treaslok were retreating.

Tural ordered, "Continue firing!"

The Treaslok were retreating, running away. I hesitated.

"Do not get in front of me!" Tural took the gun from me, leveled it and fired.

Dozens of retreating Treaslok were cut down by the explosive bullets.

The Erskans on the northern flank moved east, enjoining the battle there.

It was all over in another few minutes. Tural stopped firing and dropped the gun to the ground. She put a hand out to steady herself, and then sat down.

A haze of smoke enveloped us. The barrel of the gun smoked.

I was exhausted and, likewise, sat down next to her. Spent brass cartridges were strewn over the blood-soaked ground.

I looked at my shoulder and realized I had been cut. Not too deeply. I couldn't remember how it had happened. Or where. Or when. My clothes were blood-splattered. I gingerly brushed off blonde hair that was matted onto my left thigh.

Other Erskan warriors, on a kind of mental high, sang war songs. They were rounding up prisoners and chaining them together by their necks. Several moved through the jumble of limbs and torsos looking for seriously-wounded Treaslok. A metal-tipped pike was thrust into the chest of the dying.

I was almost unable to fathom the carnage. It was reprehensible. Bodies of women and horses were scattered everywhere.

My left forearm was cut. Or scratched. I wasn't sure. It was a cut. I squeezed it with my right hand fingers and watched a small amount of blood come to the surface. My leather skirt was half-torn away on the right, exposing from ankle to knee. My knee was scuffed and bleeding. I felt no pain.

I realized that I was sitting down on what remained of someone's left hand, severed at the wrist.

I brushed it away, pushing it next to a leg of a horse. A leg of a horse. The smell of blood filled the air. Other horrific odors I could not place. I had never realized that so much blood could actually have an odor.

There was a ringing in both of my ears. The sword fighting, screams. The high-pitched firing of thousands of rounds of gunfire.

Too close to me, two Erskans pierced the lungs of a dying Treaslok. Her death scream left me shaking.

Strong hands clasped my shoulders from behind. I looked up to see the Torino.

"You are trembling." She continued to squeeze me for another moment, in reassuring manner, possibly the closest an Erskan warrior could offer in place of a hug.

"Yes... I'm sorry. I've never seen anything like this..."

"Most of my warriors have never seen such a battle," she stated. "But they fought bravely. As did you."

Looking up, I noticed that her face had been cut. A gash ran from her left ear to her left chin. Actually... her left ear had been partially cut away. She had a bandage around her head; but it had so much blood and was so dirty that it wasn't initially distinguishable as a bandage.

"Istha," the Torino said, standing. "Collect the weapons. Take Netratoh Tural and Alexi to the palace immediately."

Istha, who was muscular for an Erskan, approached. She was covered in bloody, shredded uniform. Her face was puffy. When she grinned, I noticed that three of her teeth had been knocked out. "Yes, Torino!"

The sun was at its highest, most debilitating intensity now. The scope of the carnage was in-estimable for me at the time.

Erskan warriors sang their victory songs, tears flowing down their cheeks, while gathering the corpses of fallen comrades.

I turned my back on the sea of death and staggered down the hill to the wagon.

There was a steady stream of wagons carrying the injured back to the palace.

Our open-top wagon was in the line of dozens. We had gathered six wounded Erskans, each in a dire situation.

Tural and I did our best to administer aid; I introduced the concept of a tourniquet to Tural which was likely to save the lives of three of the wounded. I was fairly certain that one of the women would be dead before we reached the palace. One was sitting upright, her ankle crushed from a falling horse. The sixth had expired almost as soon as she was loaded.

"Could you try to hit more of the rocks in the path!" the warrior with the broken ankle shouted to the wagon driver. "You missed one back there!"

"How is your leg?" I asked Tural.

She was replacing the make-shift leather knot I made with a new strip of cloth she took from the Spartan medical kit in the wagon.

"It does not feel well," she admitted, displaying her leg. "The arrow cut the muscle."

We rode in silence for another moment.

"Did you see what Jurina Kreka did?" I asked.

174

"Yes. She saw the arrows headed for you and blocked your body with hers."

"I do not know how to thank her for the sacrifice," I admitted. "Nothing is – I do... I do not know what to say or do about that."

"You helped us win the war with the Treaslok," Tural told me. "That is what Kreka would have wanted." Tural closed her eyes for a moment. "We should have heard from Hula by this point in time."

A junior officer was headed toward the scene of the battle when Tural stopped the wagon. She flagged the junior officer and ordered her off the horse.

The junior officer dismounted.

"Take the next horse," Tural told the junior officer. "Ride to any officer and deliver this message: Netratoh Tural requests the Torino dispatch help to the palace for Hula. Understand?"

"Yes, Netratoh!"

Tural mounted, grimacing as her calf banged into the other side of the horse.

She reached her hand down to me. I put my foot in the stirrup and lifted myself behind her.

"Hold well!"

I held to her waist tightly as she turned the horse and galloped toward the palace.

"How did the Treaslok know our exact position?" Tural asked me.

"They rotated the last real warrior from their scouts at exactly the right time," I noted.

"Because they knew where we were. We did not set that position until forty minutes before the scouts arrived. And no one left formation to share the information."

"Did someone capture our radio warriors?" I asked.

"No."

"Then someone was listening to our radio transmissions and notified the Treaslok."

"If the Treaslok sent out a replacement every five minutes, they had to receive at least a thirty-five minute notice, yes?"

I nodded. "Yes."

We practically ran another wagon off the path as we continued toward Antrana.

"How long would it take a rider to get from Antrana to the Treaslok? If that rider had to avoid the Erskan lines and not draw attention to herself?"

"Thirty minutes," I replied.

"With five minutes of time to spare, yes?" Tural said.

"Where were all of the radios?"

We could see the first structures of the outskirts of Antrana.

"All of the radios were at the battlefield – except for one," Tural frowned. "We were suspicious of Jurina Istana. Hula stayed behind to watch her."

We rode hard for another five minutes, warriors and wagons scattering before us.

The closer we got to Antrana, the fewer wounded we came across. Finally, we approached the palace.

Tural dismissed the guards with a sweep of her hands. We rode past them and headed left, toward the main palace entryway.

Three warriors and two frey were walking toward the door when I brought the horse to a sliding stop.

"Frena, what is your name?" Tural asked the low-ranking officer.

"Frena Nashitah, Netratoh," she replied, turning around.

"We must find Otah Hula at once. Do you know where she is?"

"No. I have not seen her."

"Do you know where Jurina Istana is?" Tural asked.

One of the other warriors replied: "The jurina moved the frey to the lower chambers, in the *ritahn*."

"It is one of the safest places of the city because it is underground," Tural explained to me.

"What is a *ritahn*?" I asked.

"It is where we clean the water for the city," Nashitah replied.

"How many frey are there?" I asked, dread welling inside me.

"Almost all of the frey from Antrana."

"How many is that?" I pressed.

"Several thousand."

"Can the ritahn be flooded?" I asked.

The three warriors looked at each other for a moment. The one that had seen Istana spoke: "Yes. I have been there many times. There is a way to flood it."

"She is going to drown them," Tural said.

"Who is going to kill the frey?" Nashitah asked.

"Jurina Istana," Tural said flatly.

The three women and two men inhaled sharply.

Nashitah observed a palace guard walking by and called her.

"Kara! Find Jurina Istana and report back to me or the Netratoh. Tell no one what you are doing!"

The guard nodded and went back inside the palace door.

"I know the fastest way into the ritahn," the warrior told us.

Tural and I dismounted. We handed the reins of the horse to one of the frey and then we followed the three warriors inside.

*****

We ran into several halls, past the war room, and then headed toward the central corridors of the palace.

After about two minutes of solid running we descended a twenty-foot wide curving stone staircase. Tural made introductions as we continued heading downward.

"We are near," said Karhan, the junior warrior that knew the underground area.

As we finished the last turn in the staircase we were abruptly met by two fully-armed black leather-clad warriors securing a massive wooden door.

"Open the doors," Tural told them.

My finely-honed law enforcement instinct told me that we were going to encounter resistance.

"Netratoh, you have no rule here," one of them sniffed.

"We have a problem. Open the doors."

"I will not open the door."

"Who has given you the order to lock the door? These doors are always open," Karhan asked.

"Jurina Istana has ordered the ritahn to be locked to protect the frey."

"The battle is over. We have won," Tural said.

"Jurina Istana has ordered us to wait for her return. Now, go back to your horses and play in the dirt."

The last had a decidedly disrespectful tone.

"Where is the jurina?" Tural demanded.

"Jurina Istana left five minutes ago – the frey are safe."

"That is what I wanted to know." She stepped back and turned to walk away.

I looked at the other three warriors, who both had a confused look. We were anticipating the confrontation to escalate. Instead, Tural capitulated.

We retreated about ten feet before Tural whispered, "Give me your StacGun."

I obeyed. She rotated swiftly and drew down on the leader of the two guards, one of whom raised her sword.

"Drop your weapons or die!" Tural shouted.

Still armed, one guard ventured, "You do not know how to use the raa stick."

Tural fired.

The gun blew a four-inch section of the wood door, just missing the guard by a couple of inches.

"Drop your weapons!" Tural told them again, jabbing the gun once toward the leader.

Weapons clattered to the floor, and the guards were overpowered.

"It is locked," one of the warriors said, pulling on the door latches.

Tural handed my gun back to me. "Can you open the lock?"

"Yes. Step back." I put five bullets through the lock, shattering the metal pieces. The door swung open.

We pushed through. A dimly lit antechamber that ran another twenty feet. A second set of doors.

There was a constant low pounding coming from the other side.

We lifted the beam blocking escape to find a dozen panic-faced warriors on the other side.

"What is happening?" Tural asked the highest ranking one.

"Istana – she locked us inside and opened the gates. We have been flooding for the last few minutes!"

"Everyone out! This way!" shouted one of the warriors.

A steady stream of women, and then men, scrambled out. Several of the warriors took up positions along the hall.

"How can we stop the flood?" Nashitah asked the freed warriors.

A warrior returned, blood on her hands, and interrupted. "Istana's officers were on the other side,"

"Brecka and Yurin?"

The first warrior nodded. "I cut their throats."

"Good. Traitors to Erska." The warrior looked at us again. "I have sent someone to turn off the water on the outside."

"We are looking for Otah Hula." Tural asked, "Has anyone seen her?"

By now, well over two thousand people had gone by. I noticed that the feet of many were wet.

"I have not seen any Otahs here."

"We have to stop Istana from escape," Tural said.

Several warrior officers were now standing around us. One of them had a senior rank, but was still subordinate to Tural. "Mranda," she said, saluting Tural.

"Mranda, I remember working with you at Renest," Tural said.

"Yes. And now, we must kill the trenama Istana." Mranda pointed to the warriors nearby. "Marka, Yasta, Nashitah, Karhan, you will go with us. Brena, you are in charge of the evacuation."

The Erskan military efficiency had regained traction. Everyone nodded, and we followed Tural as she raced up the stairs.

We commandeered a half-dozen other warriors and dispatched runners to relay the news to gate guards. We wanted to contact the Torino, but knew our radio communications had been compromised by Istana.

We reached the surface, where we had several frey bring horses.

A rider approached. "The trenama Istana was seen riding to the east gate a few minutes ago!"

Ten frey, drawing two horses each, arrived. I saw that my horse had survived the battle. It rubbed its nose against my chest. It deserved a name.

"It nuzzles you? A frey?" a warrior asked as she mounted a horse. "Frey do not own horses."

"My horse, my slave," Tural said, swinging herself onto her horse. With a wave, she took off.

There were nearly twenty warriors riding east through the town, vengeance foremost in their mind.

*****

At about forty miles away from Antrana, Tural raised her hand and we came to a stop.

Mranda rode up beside Tural. "What is the matter?"

"I am uncomfortable," Tural said simply.

I could hear wind rustling through the grass. Our horses were silent, even their breathing minimal.

Then, east of us, I heard it.

"What is that?" Mranda asked.

Tural shook her head.

I cocked my head and strained to listen to the growing sound.

"Oh, hell!" I turned my horse calling to the warriors. "Ride, everyone turn back! Retreat!"

"What are you doing?" Tural demanded.

I slowed my horse to speak with her. "Look to the east. We can not escape that."

Several hundred feet away, skimming over the grass, was a Clayton CargoBoss 9300 dual-surface industrial cargo craft used for light-weight loads.

"Ride!" Tural told the other warriors.

The warriors headed west. Mranda stayed beside us.

"You do not want to fight?" Mranda asked.

The Clayton was moving about thirty miles per hour. It would be upon us in about five seconds.

Tural looked at me. "It would be suicide to fight that, yes?"

That thing could run us down and the driver wouldn't even feel it. "Suicide."

"Go," Tural ordered.

"I will not leave your side," Mranda shook her head.

178

The Clayton slowed, hovering to a stop about twenty feet before us. The grass was completely undisturbed by the craft – winds continued to ripple in waves under the wide-bodied craft. Our heavy caliber guns could take out the Clayton, but my StacGun was next to useless.

The distinctive whirring sound of the Clayton lessened in volume as it stopped. "Drop your weapons!" The female voice coming from the Clayton was female, and the language was Erskan.

"Istana!" Tural hissed under her breath. She removed her sword and, reaching close to the ground, let it drop into the grass.

Mranda, likewise, disarmed herself.

"Drop your knives."

Tural and Mranda each tossed two knives each into the grass.

"Throw down the StacGun," came the same voice, in English.

Tural looked at me.

"She speaks English." I rolled the gun-belt and then dropped it to the grass.

I heard the sound of metal... a door. Then a dozen Treaslok warriors and five Erskan palace guards approached from the rear of the Clayton, swords and bows drawn. Quickly, they confiscated our weapons.

"Down. On your knees!" ordered one of the palace guards.

I did not recognize her. But Mranda did.

"Iona," Mranda growled.

Encouraged by the drawn bows, we dismounted and got to our knees in the grass.

I saw Istana approaching, two palace guards flanking her. She marched to Tural and looked down at her.

Tural met her gaze with gnashed teeth.

Istana laughed. "In my hands, I have not only the Earth man frey. But another prize."

My wrists were bound behind me with leather cuffs. Then a leather thong was connected from the cuffs to my neck collar. It was pulled up uncomfortably high and tied. I remembered this feeling well.

Tural was cuffed and a chain wrapped around her neck to secure her.

Istana moved closer to Tural and put her hand under Tural's chin, lifting it even higher. "What will Torino Sklera Kretahla pay to have her young sister returned to her?"

I turned toward Tural in disbelief.

"The Torino has given the story to only her most trusted," Istana laughed, pointing to herself. "She wants her sister to become the next Torino by virtue of her own success. Your mistress is the second most-powerful woman in all of the Erskan lands. Or, she was."

Istana moved to Mranda. "Deliver the message to the Torino that I have her sister and her slave from Earth. The Earthfrey is not for sale. But I will sell her sister back to her for the last of the Erskan frey."

Mranda did not move.

Istana delivered a powerful backhand slap to Tural's left cheek. She went down.

Mranda jumped to her feet – a palace guard restrained her while another prepared to execute her.

Tural rose to her knees.

I realized that I had half-risen to my feet also. Two hands pushed my shoulders down.

"Do I have to kill her?" Istana asked Tural.

"Mranda, there is nothing good by your death. Go, ride to the Torino."

Released, Mranda got to her feet and accepted the cloth scroll. "Yes, Tural. I will do as you order." She had emphasized "you" while glaring at Istana, who chose to overlook the slight.

Mranda was offered her horse. She mounted, saluted Tural and rode west to where she knew reinforcements would be riding.

"How many of these do you have?" I asked.

Istana looked at me. She said something in Treaslok.

Two warriors held my head while a third pushed a large leather ball-gag into my mouth and secured it tightly around my head. The leather strap cut into my skin and edges of my mouth. I shook my head to try to toss it off, but it was much too tight. In only a few seconds it began to hurt.

Tural's eyes locked with mine.

We had achieved our goal of defeating the Treaslok; yet now we were doomed. Tural's face was, for a moment, an expression of defeat. But then she smiled. I raised my eyebrow at her and cocked my head slightly. I could see that she was not willing to accept failure. Therefore, neither was I.

"Where is Louis Corrigan?" Tural asked.

Istana waited a moment before turning to look down at Tural.

Tural pressed on. "Now that *my* people have defeated your new friends, we will be at the door of the Treaslok to take our revenge."

Istana laughed. "It is a three hundred mile voyage to the shore of the Treaslok lands. There is only one cart that can move any people across the ocean."

"It is no matter. We will destroy you."

Istana reached down to Tural with both hands and slowly choked her. Tural tried to roll back on her heels to get away, but Istana continued to squeeze.

I tried to move toward them, but two guards latched onto my collar and neck strap and pulled me down hard.

Helpless, I watched as Tural's eyes fluttered. Then, as suddenly as she had begun, Istana released her hold and shoved the gasping warrior to the ground.

I lunged and remember very little until someone's boot pressed on my neck.

It was Istana. "Tell me, human, why you care so about your mistress. This is not your land. Yet... I feel you would die to protect her." Istana put the sole of her boot on my head and applied pressure. "You have killed many Treaslok – your torture and execution will... "

Istana stopped talking, let her boot up, and walked over to several of the others to discuss something.

"On their knees," Istana said after a moment.

I was lifted to my knees.

Tural was on my right, also brought to her knees. She had a fresh bruise developing on her left cheek bone.

"Louis is not your concern, Tural. He has plans for the human. However," Istana grabbed onto the chain around Tural's neck. "I have plans for you."

"The Torino will not trade for my life," Tural said.

"She will try. But I will take the frey and you. You will be my torture pet."

180

Several guards held me still on my knees while Istana went behind me. She grabbed my left hand and singled out my index finger. I tried to pull away.

Slowly, almost gently, she applied pressure until I screamed into my gag. At the moment I gasped for air, I heard it crack. The bitch had broken my finger.

I wasn't going to die like this, one broken part at a time. Using strength I never knew I had, I got to my feet. I elbowed one of the guards, and then I swung around with my left foot and delivered a vicious kick to Istana's chest.

I head-butted another guard. Three women were down.

The next spinning kick caught another warrior in left side. Four warriors down.

Three more approached.

"Stop!" I heard the order from Tural.

I chose to obey.

A Treaslok warrior stood about ten feet away, an arrow cocked and aimed at my face.

Istana slowly stood to her feet. She looked at the armed warrior. Then she looked at me.

"Istana," Tural called.

Istana ignored her, looking back at the warrior.

The warrior's eyes were on a line straight into mine.

I held my breath.

Another second passed.

"Istana!" Tural called.

One more second. Like an invisible pressure wave, I knew the instant Istana made the decision to kill me.

"Fire," Istana ordered.

I saw the warrior's fingers twitch.

Caught in slow motion, I was not moving fast enough.

The warrior's fingers were beginning to release the arrow.

I heard Tural scream, "No!"

Something moved on my right.

It was an arrow.

Coming from above and right.

I was going left. The warrior moved left also, suddenly twisting at her waist.

She was falling as she let loose her arrow.

She was off-balance.

An arrow pierced the warrior's right wrist.

I had heard the warrior's arrow swish by my right ear.

My left shoulder crashed into the grass.

I heard a scream. Then a shout.

More shouting.

I rolled, practically choking myself with the neck-to-wrist strap, and came to a crouching position on my knees.

The Treaslok and Erskan guards crouched in the grass, looking around wildly. Istana turned away from me, searching to my right and her left. Before anyone had fully set their positions, an arrow shot up from the grass and hit Istana in the chest.

The impact knocked her from her feet.

In an instant, the trenama was dead.

Two Erskan palace guards approached her; one was cut down instantly with an arrow that shattered her skull. The other guard dove for the grass, but was hit in the neck.

Several Treaslok fired arrows at various distances to my right.

Tural rolled away from the hostile women, but I could not get to her.

Another sniper arrow took out a Treaslok warrior.

I lay flat on the grass and then inched toward the general area of our unseen ally, my face scraping along the ground.

"Slave, I teach you our language and then you have to get one of these stuck in your mouth so that you can not talk?"

I recognized that voice. Hula was covered with green face paint, and her hair had been marked with streaks of green. Waves of long grass blew around her.

Then Hula produced a knife as unconsciously as I would blink. She cut the leather strap from my gag. I spit it out.

"Thank you, Mistress." I couldn't enunciate, but she understood. *Oh, god, thank you.*

She cut the leather strap from my neck to my cuffs, and then cut the leather straps holding my cuffs.

I brought my hands in front of me and rubbed them together.

"That looks like it hurts," Hula said, looking at my finger. It was twisted backwards.

"Istana broke it."

"I saw. You were brave. Now, hold out your hand and bite this." Hula handed me a cut leather strap.

I put it into my mouth and shook my head. This was going to be terrible.

Then she grabbed my hand, extended my finger, and jerked on it.

The finger was wrenched back into place. It was as terrible as I had imagined.

"Do you want this?" Hula handed a StacGun to me.

I spit the leather strap out of my mouth. *Fuck, that hurt.* "The gun... it will not work against the Earth wagon."

"Follow me," she said, crouching and moving along in the deep grass.

We curved around until Hula held up her hand. I waited.

Then Tural rolled into our view. She grinned when she saw Hula.

"I knew you would be here," Tural whispered.

Hula cut the leather binds.

"The lock can not be broken," Hula said, pulling on the metal chain around Tural's neck.

"We will worry about that later."

Hula handed her sword to Tural.

"Where is Virona?" Tural asked.

"Here, Netratoh," I heard. It was Virona, the expert markswoman from the palace.

I heard the engine of the Clayton engage.

"This gun is useless," I told them again, using my left hand to pointing to the StacGun in my right.

"Quiet," Virona snapped.

The Clayton was headed our way. Several archers lay on the top of the unit, bows pointed downward, scanning for us.

Virona reached behind her in the grass, pulled out a metal tripod and fixed it on the ground. She pulled the Crest-Leeland out from its hiding place and sat it on the tripod.

"We needed more time to get this heavy gun here."

I watched as she expertly loaded the drum onto the side.

"Where is the best side to hit?" Hula asked.

"Anywhere but the smoke glass front," I said. The clearsteel screen would be nearly impervious to this.

"Fifty yards," Tural said, listening.

"Now," Hula told Virona.

Virona pressed the pneumatic switch and let the stalk of the tripod lift up. She rose with the Crest-Leeland machine gun and squeezed the trigger.

I lifted my head above the blades of grass and saw Virona rake the lower front and left side of the Clayton.

The rapid dual explosions of the firing rounds and the impact on-target was a near-steady staccato.

She targeted the archers and shredded their bodies into a dozen pieces.

Warriors tried to escape from the back, but Virona cut them down. She returned her fire to the side of the Clayton.

It exploded.

Pieces of metal flew overhead.

All of us crouched, looking at the fireball. A wave of heat washed over us for a moment.

Grass caught on fire around the burning machine.

Virona saw one woman trying to flee to the right.

"Kill," Tural pointed.

There was a quick burst of gunfire and a small explosion of bullets as they found their target.

Virona lifted the Crest-Leeland into her arms and walked toward the flaming wreckage. I held my StacGun and, flanked by Hula and her bow, and we moved in.

It was a bit of a flash-back – I remembered walking to the stolen craft, making an arrest... that was months ago. A different life.

"Slave," Tural asked. "Is there anything we can do with this?"

Everyone was dead.

The Clayton was a complete loss. We had to stand twenty feet away from it due to the intense heat. A piece of the engine unit was on fire, propelled thirty feet to our right.

"No, Mistress."

"Did you find your answers?" Hula asked Tural.

"No. Istana would not talk. We did learn that Corrigan is alive. I believe this to be the only wagon they have."

"We were captured... by plan?" I asked.

"Istana would only share information if she believed she was going to keep us as her prisoner," Tural explained.

From the direction of home. . . Antrana... dozens of riders approached

"You look unhappy," Hula observed, facing me.

"Yes," I holstered my weapon. I was about to complain about being captured, but decided it was a useless argument. I was a slave.

"You were easy to find," the Torino said to Tural as she waved away the billowing smoke. She dismounted and returned the salute.

I bowed my head.

"Not a word about what you know, slave," Tural said, looking at me.

"Yes, Mistress," I answered.

The Torino looked approvingly at me.

Mranda rode up beside us leading Tural's horse. She tossed flasks of water to each of us. The water was cold and wonderful tasting.

We were all silent for a very long time.

Finally, Tural mounted and held her hand out to me. I pulled up behind her and sat on the end of the saddle, my feet dangling without stirrups.

Virona had disappeared, but returned leading her horse, which was tethered to Hula's horse.

Tural rode over to the lifeless Istana. Her hands were wrapped around the shaft of the arrow protruding from her chest.

Tural spit onto the corpse.

"Mranda, bring the bodies back to the palace," the Torino said, riding to her sister's side. "Brenah, scout ahead. Report on the radio every half-hour. Do not attack. I want to know how many they are, and if they are leaving."

"Yes, Torino," Brenah led five warriors along the road, disappearing from view.

"Are you well?" the Torino asked Tural.

"Yes, Torino. We are all well."

"Ride with me and tell me what you learned from the trenama."

Despite the pain from my finger, I found myself holding Tural tightly on our ride back to the palace.

Chapter Thirteen
The Great Hall

The palace was a hornets' nest of activity when we arrived, even late at night. Search parties had found and captured additional Treaslok forces, which were being chained en masse to one another in groups of a hundred. There were nearly five-thousand prisoners, heavily guarded and shackled, lined outside the palace walls, all dimly lit by torches mounted on the palace walls.

Following the Torino and her entourage, we rode past several hundred prisoners before entering the palace. The women were chained about the neck with heavy pad locks. Additional metal shackles chained their ankles together on the right leg of each prisoner, with a chain connecting their right shackled wrist to their neck chain. Many were injured slightly. Those who were severely injured had been executed on the battlefield and burned.

"Mistress, what will become of the prisoners?" I asked.

Our group of sixty separated once we arrived at the inner palace doors. One of my lights was suspended from a twenty-foot pole in the center of the parade ground. It brilliantly illuminated the expansive area.

Tural brought her horse to a halt. A frey took the reins from her and held the horse still as I slid off. Tural came down into my outstretched arms.

"Hand over your gun," Tural said.

I removed my gun belt and handed her the weapon. I wouldn't be seeing that again soon.

"Slave, do you want the truth about the prisoners?" she asked.

"You are going to execute them," I said flatly.

"We shall interrogate each prisoner. Those with the most useful information will live the longest."

"My people have rules of war."

"Any invader will die," Tural explained. "Any traitor will die. Those are the Erskan rules of war."

Hula dismounted her horse, gave it over to a stable frey and wiped her left cheek with the back of her hand. She might have applied more grime than she removed. "A shower will be good."

I realized then how terribly filthy all of us were. My clothes were torn. I had a copious amount of dried blood on my leather. I guessed the time to be about two o'clock in the morning. My finger throbbed.

Several wagons with medical staff and injured passed by. While not much advanced, Erskan medicine was, at least, better than that of medieval Earth.

Tural looked at me. "Slave, tend to your finger with your medicine. Then, come to the third floor, room A-52."

185

Everyone looked exhausted.

"Yes, Mistress."

I bowed to Tural and Hula and then, with heavy shoulders, trudged toward one of the doors. It took about ten minutes to find a palace slave that knew where our packs and gear had been stored. A palace guard let me into a locked storeroom where I had to push boxes of ammunition aside to find the metal-cased medical kit.

After treating my finger and several minor cuts, I took an antibiotic to counteract potential infection from the open wounds and exposure to blood and metal cuts. I packaged a small quantity of topical medicine for Tural and Hula's wounds before leaving the room and thanking the guard.

I passed several dozen Erskan warriors on the second floor; most were officers of the medium ranks. For the most part, they were wearing the thin black leather skirt and sleeveless vest. Some were walking with wet hair tied into knots or wrapped with cloth towels. Many had been treated for minor wounds and had clean white bandages on their bodies. While their mood were that of relief or satisfaction of their victory, their faces betrayed imminent emotional and physical collapse

I found room A-52 and opened the door.

Inside was a nicely-apportioned room: stone walls, ceiling, and floor, with heavy rugs and colorful tapestries. A slave cage. The center of the room held a double-sized bed. The left side of the room had various bondage and torture items hanging on a wooden rail with pins; below it was a wooden dresser. Twenty candles flickered throughout.

"Slave, come here," Tural's voice ordered from the unseen room.

I obeyed.

Tural was standing with one foot upon a small stool. She had already stripped of her clothing and was wearing only a black soft leather sarong. She was using a sponge to wipe around the arrow wound on her calf.

In a hammered brass tub, amidst a mound of bubbles, sat a contented Hula. The Erskan palace was a marvel of architecture and engineering. Hula kept her eyes closed. Waves of steam wafted past me. I could feel the warmth and moisture of the hot bath.

"I have medicine for you, Mistress," I said.

"Do I use it now or after I am clean?"

"Earlier is better, Mistress."

She bared her calf for me.

I knelt beside her and rubbed the medicine onto her calf. There would be a scar, despite the effect of the medicine.

"How is your finger, slave?"

The flickering candlelight illuminated her beautiful body. I almost licked my lips.

"It is good. Thank you, Mistress." I finished attending to her. "Is this better?"

"Yes, it no longer hurts." She put her leg down onto the rug and then patted my head for a moment. I looked down.

"Are you going to be in there all night?" Tural asked Hula.

Hula's eyes popped open. She had fallen asleep.

"Towel," Hula said to me, pointing behind me.

I stood and took one of several towels from a row of pins. Hula stepped into it and wrapped herself. Then she walked into the bedroom.

Tural pointed to the bathtub.

I found the plug, and, after it drained, I filled the tub with hot water. Tural handed a flask of soap to me that I added to the water. The water pressure and volume were high and the tub was filled with bubbles in only a few minutes.

Tural removed her sarong and then eased herself into the tub, moaning softly.

I remained on my knees, awaiting her command.

"We will have a big meal tomorrow. For now, there are fruit and dried meats in that bowl. Eat – but remain where you are."

"Thank you, Mistress."

I ate while she soaked. She occasionally splashed water over her hair. I drank heavily from a large tankard of water. Then, I realized I had fallen asleep while on my knees. My arms jerked, and I reached for the floor with my palms.

"Slave? The towel," ordered Tural.

I was not sure if she had called my name once or several times. I stood and retrieved a towel for her. When she was dry, she wrapped herself in the cloth and walked to the bedroom.

"Clean yourself – and be quick."

I drained the water and filled the bath.

My leather skirt nearly fell apart when I removed the belt. My vest was torn in the back and the left front sleeve. I dropped the smelly clothes into the floor hole that was the trash chute. My right boot was trashed on the heel – there was a chunk of the hard leather missing. I tossed both pair into the trash.

I could smell smoke from extinguished candles wafting in from the other room.

The water was hot. My toes tingled when they touched it. I slowly immersed myself until I was completely submerged into the water, holding my breath for almost ten seconds.

I came up and held my head barely above water. The bar soap was soft and unscented. After a couple of minutes, I was scrubbed clean.

There was a soft conversation outside in the bedroom. I stood and was drying myself when the Torino walked in. She was clean and wore the black leather kimono-like outfit, embellished with a minimal amount of gold trim and jewelry.

"Torino," I acknowledged, bowing and looking to the floor.

"Follow me," she said, handing a simple black leather belted long skirt to me.

"Yes, Torino." I stepped into the skirt and fastened the belt around my waist.

She had already stepped out and was near the bedroom door.

I intercepted the door latch and opened the door for her. I glanced inside the room as I shut the door; Tural and Hula were apparently asleep, both covered under sheets. Most of the candles had been put out.

The Torino walked to one hallway and ascended a circular staircase. Finally we stopped climbing flights and went out to a balcony. The view was impressive, especially at night.

The Torino walked over to the half-height stone ledge and leaned onto the wood rail. I came up slightly behind her.

She looked over the city – I followed her gaze.

Antrana was spread out, seventy-five feet below us. Directly below was the main parade ground, where a brilliant white light was cast for five-hundred yards in every direction. Lining the high stone palace walls were small torches. Outside the palace grounds, the street intersections were illuminated by oil lamps that hung on rope lines stretched between wood poles.

Caravans of wagons and horses moved slowly through the streets. Many residences and businesses had oil lamps on their porches. I saw hundreds of windows dimly illuminated by candles. Above the city, the night stars twinkled over the city, brilliant and clear.

There were sounds in the city, even at this time of night. Somewhere, I could hear the sounds of sobbing and crying. Those sounds were carried away by the next breeze – and I could hear singing.

"What I see always changes," the Torino told me. She was silent for a moment and then finally added, "and what I hear always changes. But the smell and taste of my city – it is always the same."

I inhaled deeply.

The odor of grass... wet from the dew, was strong. As was the scent of wood fires and cooking.

The Torino turned to look at me. "I must honor our agreement."

"We did not capture or kill Corrigan," I noted.

"No." The Torino looked at the city while she spoke. "When we made our agreement, we did not know that the Treaslok would attack us with such numbers. It will be many years until the Treaslok can come to us."

"Corrigan does not like to lose," I said. "He will soon begin working on another way to transport the Treaslok here."

"I have already interrogated several prisoners," the Torino said, looking down to the city again. "Corrigan used his guns to make the Treaslok bend to him. The prisoners believe that the *yarino* – the leader – of the Treaslok will not receive their defeat well. They expect that Corrigan will be removed from power... at any cost."

I hoped she were right.

"There was only one Earth wagon that could cross the ocean – it is now destroyed. There are two Earth wagons that move on the ground." She looked at me again, "I will agree that, for now, you have come to meet your part of the agreement. Tell me, what do you want?"

My options seemed, still, to be quite limited. I could not go home. That meant staying here on the planet. And the best place to be was where I was already established and had some, if minor, credentials about me based on what I had done and, more importantly, about what I could do.

"Torino, I would like to stay here... with Tural."

She chuckled. "Is being my sister's slave important to you?"

"Yes, Torino."

"Why?"

"I feel... I am close to her. We have been through much together."

"I heard you have risked your life for her."

"Yes. She also put herself in harm's way for me."

"Tural knows the value of a frey." She smiled wryly. "Look at me. This is important. Tural just may take you as her slave – that is her right with her rank. It does not mean that you are a life-long slave. She could sell you the next day, if she chose. You must be pleasing to her and serve her. Soon, I will inform others of her lineage. There will be greater demands placed on her slaves."

I nodded.

"You know that being her slave does not mean that you are only for her use. There are no slaves in this land that are the use of only one woman. All owners offer their slaves to women for use in many ways. Being the slave of a powerful woman does grant you more responsibility in the slave caste – responsibilities you must earn and continue to demonstrate. Greater responsibilities lead to greater punishments, if you fail."

"The good about this," she explained, "is that you have a Mistress who knows how to treat her property correctly. She will use you – and protect you at all costs – even her life. That is the added responsibility that Tural will have for taking a slave that is not from this world. You are a difficult slave."

"You have more knowledge than we – and you can help us, if you choose. I have made a decree to my jurinas – and to the civil leaders – that they are not to force you into sharing information. It will be your choice."

"Thank you, Torino. I know that granting the right of a choice to a slave is rare. I can tell you now that I choose to help you."

The Torino nodded. Then she smiled at me for a moment before placing her hands on the rail. Looking over the city, she had a far away gaze. Then, she touched her cut ear and came back to reality. "I must rest. We have much to do. The injured must be healed. And we must prepare to take the battle to Treaslok before they attack my people again."

There remained one big problem ahead. Corrigan. We had won the three-day war in a decisive manner. But, there would be trouble in the future. There were many things I had planned for advancing the technology of my new home. Many things.

I looked again at the stars of Antrana.

"This is my home now, Torino," I said. "I am at your service."

"I believe Tural is waiting to be served. You are dismissed."

Both grateful and exhausted, I retired.

Despite my attempts to be quiet, both Tural and Hula awoke as I entered the room and closed the door.

Tural stretched on the bed, the sheets partially covering her lower body. Hula was beside her and looked over Tural's head for a moment before rolling away and burying her head in a pile of pillows.

Tural pointed to the floor beside the bed. The soft rug tickled my knees as I knelt beside my Mistress.

Tural pulled one of the several sheets from above and pushed it over the side of the bed to me.

Hula grumbled a bit as two of her pillows were fished out and dropped over the side to me.

It was hard to see in the dim, candle-lit room, but it appeared Tural winked at me before turning over to wrap her arms around Hula.

In a moment both women were making the typical, rhythmic Erskan snoring.

One part of my consciousness wanted to stay awake and think about the day's events. But my subconscious succumbed to physical exhaustion.

*****

After breakfast at Tural's feet in the Palace I asked Tural if we could visit the infirmary to assist with the wounded.

She stopped walking on the stone pathway. "Slave, do you have supplies to treat a thousand wounded Erskans?"

"No, Mistress. There is limited medicine." No other options came to mind.

"The entrata in two days will honor my lost sisters. Three-thousand warriors. We have two-thousand injured."

That meant the Erskans had five-thousand casualties out of twenty-five thousand warriors. One-in-five hurt or killed.

"Treaslok dead numbered at least eight-thousand. Four-thousand were captured. We estimated their force to be twenty-thousand."

Tural continued walking. We arrived at the armory where I spent an hour with the staff demonstrating cleaning and care of the firearms.

One of the Crest-Leeland heavy machine guns had been damaged by a sword's blade; the barrel was bent, and the muzzle was covered in dried blood.

"Where is Mistress Nitrayva?" I had asked the assembled group of twenty women and two men.

The Torino's Mistress of Arms pointed to the weapon. "Nitrayva used the open end to strike into the heart of a Treaslok. Nitrayva is not badly injured."

I looked inside the muzzle and saw that there was rotting human tissue inside. "Hmm. The bent barrel is a problem, but we should clean this as well." I unscrewed the cylinder and handed it to one of the men.

Later we field-stripped all of the weapons several times until all of the staff had accomplished it twice without guidance.

I followed Tural to the stables where she inquired on the status of her horse that had been loaned to a cavalry officer. Both had survived but had already moved onto Renest for a clean-up operation.

Outside, Tural began to walk in one direction, but then suddenly changed course. She headed behind the central castle structure to an enclosed courtyard.

Once there she sat on a bench and sighed.

I sat on the grass, near her left boot deciding to say nothing.

The grass was neat and perfectly trimmed at the stone edging. A dozen trees lined the squared-off area, with vines and other foliage covering the castle wall that was to our right.

Water from a line in the ground poured onto a black sculpture of a warrior, female of course, in a pose with a sword in her right hand, about to strike a blow from above.

It was so quiet in the area that the sound of the water trickling around the base of the sculpture could be heard.

Tural looked at the water and closed her eyes. She appeared to be relaxing.

An Erskan warrior walked by the entrance and stopped. Her slave almost ran into the back of her.

She was about the same height as the typical Erskan, but her biceps and legs were quite large. Her hair was a brownish-shade of black, which was pulled into a pony tail and wrapped in brown leather strips. Her face was fetching, but she had a severe expression.

She came into the courtyard, her brown sleeveless vest adorned with the rank of a jurina. I had seen her somewhere previously but did not know her name or position. She pointed at me and then moved her finger to my left. Her fingernails were painted in a dark gray.

I moved over and she sat down beside Tural.

Tural, startled, turned to the woman, "Jurina Cinzia."

"Tural," she replied.

190

"You have not returned to Constona?" Tural asked. She blinked and then finally seemed to regain her composure.

"My harfala will ride tomorrow at first light." Cinzia looked down at me.

I looked away from her face and fixated my eyes on her booted feet.

"Our history has no record of a frey fighting as a woman does," Cinzia noted. "This will make for interesting discussions among the civilian population." She laughed for a moment. Then she grabbed onto my collar with her left hand and pulled my neck slightly toward her.

Of course I did not resist. Instead, my eyes locked on her forearm. I could detect several small scars on her arms. Visible through the cleavage of her vest was a three-inch scar high on her right breast, near the sternum. By now it was obvious that I was inspecting her so there was no point trying to avoid looking at her right shoulder, which had a scar as well.

"Jurina Cinzia does not know how to avoid sharp blades," Tural snickered.

Cinzia took her right hand and, while holding my collar, pulled my hair slightly down until my nose was almost touching a scar on her lower left bicep. I was half-crouching now. "What do you see there, slave?"

"A scar, Jurina Cinzia," I replied.

"Are you curious about this scar?"

With my face pressed against her at that moment it would it would certainly appear so.

"Yes, Jurina."

"Cinzia, you were too slow," Tural snapped, flashing teeth.

Cinzia released her hold on me. "It was a gift from Tural."

Cinzia patted my head as I crossed my legs under me.

"Does he play *chase* like a huraj?" Cinzia asked, referring to me as an Erskan dog.

Tural leaned forward and looked at me. "Not as yet. But that is a good idea."

Cinzia looked at Tural. "You are troubled today. You are aware this is normal."

"Yes, I know, from prior battles and our schoolroom classes, that there is a pause time.

"But yes, it is something we must live by." Cinzia turned again on her hips and looked at me.

I resisted the urge to shuffle a bit under her gaze.

"It is calm and quiet today," she said to me. "Slave, how do your warriors recover from battle?"

I was not exactly sure. "Jurina, I do not know."

Cinzia rose to leave. Her slave got to his feet and stood ready to follow.

"Our people have a great celebration. We will drink to victory, sing songs to our sisters, drink again honor those that have died in the battle, and use the frey for our pleasure."

Like many things in Erskan culture, this could be good or bad. I tried to remain optimistic.

"In battles past," she continued, "we would have newly captured frey. Our regard for their suffering would be, perhaps less so than our own." She shrugged before leaning in to me, "Tonight? We do not know what will happen."

Tural saluted her.

"Get to your feet and your duties," Cinzia told her before walking out.

"Tonight?" I asked aloud.

Tural did something that I had not seen in several days; her piranha-grin flashed at me.

It was both comforting and disconcerting.

*****

It was time for me to be reminded of my place, of my stature in society. Surely that is why two palace guards appeared after I had dressed Tural for the celebration. With a nod from my Mistress, they bound my hands behind me and snapped a leash onto my collar.

We were met on our way through the castle by other palace guards that had over a dozen house slaves in tow. Before walking outside the guards paused. Two frey were put at the front of the line while the rest of us were chained, neck-to-neck, in single file fashion. As we stepped outside two guards removed clothing until we wore only collar and chains. It was easy to understand the reasoning for having males wear the belted, slit skirts; we could be bound hand and foot and yet be easily stripped for use or punishment.

It was late afternoon in the primary yard of the castle, which was almost deserted. There was little pedestrian movement save palace guards and several chain lines of naked frey. It was hard to resist asking the man behind me what was going to happen, but one guard was keeping her eye on the entire line.

We were marched to the Grand Hall, a building I had only seen from the outside. Walking in a line like this was not easy, especially when climbing steps. After a moment we were led inside beyond massive, tall metal-plated doors.

Rows of carved-stone columns flanked the sides of the long, rectangular room. The enormity of it caught me by surprise, and I caused a small ripple in my line.

My left outer thigh was struck from the rear by a leather strip. I made small protest and continued looking around.

Slave rings were mounted on the outer walls in frequent intervals. Candelabra were stationed between slave rings and at the ends of tables.

There was enough room here to accommodate over a thousand people. I estimated there to be two-hundred chained frey.

Hundreds of rows of benches and tables stretched end-to-end almost the entire length of the hall. Large colorful tapestries hung from the ceiling beams to the walls. Strips of red and blue cloth were tied around the base of each column, spiraling upward to the ceiling.

My gaze moved toward the farthest area of the Grand Hall. There was a raised dais, flanked with two large open-flame torches. Beyond that was... I blinked to be sure. Beyond that was a considerable collection of torture equipment.

Each frey was being removed from the chain line and secured to a slave ring. Metal manacles were locked onto my wrists, and they were closely chained to the slave ring that was about chest-high.

Then a black leather hood was pulled over my head. It had a hole for my mouth, but no visibility. It was tightened with laces.

After a few more minutes, probably after all the frey were secured, the noises in the room subsided.

The leather hood obstructed my hearing; I listened intently for any tell-tale sound.

There was a snap of a leather strap somewhere; likely a frey had said something without permission.

Then, came the sound of boots marching on the stone floor. The sound grew until the tapping of the boots, in unison, echoed from the stone floor and vibrated the chains to the manacles.

My bare feet tingled as the warrior's entrance shook the stone floor.

The army dispersed throughout the Grand Hall, with boots passing behind me.

Someone stopped behind me, perhaps three feet back, marching in place for another thirty seconds until, I presumed, there was an Erskan woman behind each frey.

There was a double-paced march of four beats and then everyone stopped, the echo reverberating for a moment.

I became aware of my breathing, which was unexplainably rapid. Energy. Apprehension. Excitement. I pulled against the chains for a moment just to reassure myself that I was connected to something besides air.

"Warriors of Antrana," boomed the voice of the Torino.

The response was deadening as each pair of boots made a one-two then three-four claps on the stone floor.

The Torino waited until the echo subsided. "This evening we celebrate a great victory."

The boots stomped twice.

"We celebrate the lives of our fallen sisters."

The boots stomped twice again.

"We celebrate the continued ownership and subjugation of our frey."

The flat part of a boot was suddenly pushed into the small of my back, slightly above my buttocks, until my body was pressed flat against the cool stone wall. The owner slightly twisted her boot, pressing deeply into my back.

The boot was removed, and I relaxed slightly.

"The citizens of Erska shall recognize your heroism and loyalty for many years to come. I shall honor you tonight." She paused and then shouted, "*Gat ta chim!*"

The Erskan word for "ride"? Perhaps, I misheard.

The warriors stomped their boots four more times, and then a hum of conversations buzzed around me.

Fingers latched into my collar from the back, pulling on the leather hood, and stretching my arms out against the chain to the slave ring.

"Slave," Tural said. "I have selected two of my sisters to partake in the ceremonial punishment. You will receive three strikes of the cane from each of us. This is a great honor. Do not disappoint me."

I half nodded.

The hum of the room died away.

I could tell it was coming.

The first one landed with expert precision across both sides of my ass. I yelped and involuntarily shuffled my feet about a half-inch before returning to my original position.

And caught another one in the same location!

Fire leapt up my back. I squeezed my eyes and let out a long breath to hide a groan.

But I held fast.

The third one landed in the same location again. This time I groaned and pushed my hands out against the wall to try to keep my feet from moving forward.

There was a pause. I heard shuffling around on both sides as, presumably, the canes were being handed off to another warrior. I expected the cane to land on my already welted ass.

Unexpectedly, my right outer thigh burned. My right foot came off the ground, and I practically screamed. It was still burning from the cane strike when it was hit again, seemingly in the same location. I put my foot down and felt a booted foot step onto my bare toes keeping me firmly in place. Then again!

My eyes watered, and I ground my teeth against one another. My hands rolled into the chains and clenched them tightly as the first strike hit my outer left thigh.

I resisted the urge to cry out loud.

The second strike seared into my bone.

I pressed my foot down hard to the floor, steadying for the final one.

Pain! It hurt so much that my left leg almost collapsed.

A teeth-clenching cry escaped from my lips as I pulled up to stand.

It was over.

Tural was at my side. "Good slave."

I started to catch my breath.

"The meal service is at least one hour from now," a woman's voice said. It was Hula.

A hand reached around to my front side and grabbed onto my cock. "That may have hurt him too much," Tural said.

"No," Hula laughed. "Watch this."

She put her hands around my body and onto my chest. Then she squeezed onto my nipples, gradually squeezing tighter.

"Ah, the slave is not hurt," Tural laughed.

She was probably eyeing my involuntary erection.

"A few of the stations are already being used," said Hula, concern in her voice. "If we start now, we can let him rest while we have the first course of the meal."

"Bring it," Tural told them.

I was unchained from the wall and led along on either side by the women. One of them kept a hand around my hard cock, pulling on it.

"Here?" Tural asked.

"This is perfect!" Hula exclaimed.

What was "perfect"? My view of "perfect" and theirs was likely different.

They stopped and pushed me down to my knees. My legs were spread slightly, and then they were locked into metal restraints. My wrists were released, but then pulled backwards and lifted slightly. They were locked into something. Metal bands then encircled my biceps, and they were moved apart, straining me slightly until I heard something lock. I was arched backwards, on my knees, ankles spread apart.

"I am going to have you," Tural told me. A wet hand latched onto my cock.

"Save part of it for me," Hula complained.

I was slightly taken aback. Torture was one thing, but they were going to have intercourse with me while this many others were present?

A different pair of hands produced a leather strap which was tied around my testicles. Blood filled my erection, and I thrust my hips out slightly.

Behind me to my right came the sounds of a whip cracking, followed immediately by the sharp sound of a frey in pain. There were other things happening all around us, but I was tuning it out of my head.

"Nice. Big," Tural said.

My cock was slapped with an open palm. I shouted and struggled uselessly against the restraints.

I was slapped again as one of the women straddled my chest, her thighs gently squeezing the sides of my exposed chest. Strips of her gladiator-style leather skirt pressed against my skin. She put her hand on the back of my hood and pulled my head forward into her crotch.

She was wet and warm and sweet. The hole in the hood was barely wide enough for me to get my tongue out to lick. I caressed her with long, slow upward strokes.

My erection grew, and I found myself thrusting at the slapping hand even though it hurt.

The pain from the strikes charged my excitement, and I rapidly darted my tongue into my captor.

Her thighs tightened around my chest and squeezed. After a moment, she shuddered and grabbed onto my head with both hands, pushing my lips hard into her. She shuddered again, an Erskan growl coming from deep in her chest.

I was panting, my ears pounding in the hood, musky. On my knees, hooded in leather and chained, the drive to sexual pleasure was overwhelming. Then, instead of slapping my aching erection, one of the women stroked my cock.

I cried out, trying to thrust into her hand. She pulled away for a moment. I bucked, needing to make contact with her.

The woman in front of me moved away as she thrust two wet fingers into my mouth. They were dripping wet of her. Her fingers stroked my tongue. I licked, and then sucked.

"Good slave," Tural said from behind me.

Then I was not being touched.

My body shuddered and an agonizing, long whimper came from my very being.

"Yes, slave?"

"Please, Mistress... Mistresses, please allow me release."

"No, slave." Tural laughed.

Another woman pressed her crotch against my mouth. In an instant I was pleasuring her.

One of the women wrapped both her slick hands around my cock and stroked, slowly. I tried to thrust. She stopped briefly, teasing me, and then slowly moved over the head to the shaft. It was agony. I whimpered again as my tongue explored the captor having complete control over me. She put her hands on my shoulders and scratched her nails into my skin.

I tried to pull away from the woman tormenting my cock. Another hand grabbed firmly around my testicles and held my body in place. The hands around my cock slowly masturbated me.

"Faster," the woman above me ordered. I licked with the flat of my tongue. She was so hot. Her juices flowed down my chin, inside the leather hood, and along my neck. The gorgeous, musky scent was intoxicating.

Then she tightened her legs and dug her nails deep into my shoulders as she came.

My cock was released.

The woman above pushed my head into her for a moment and held me, rubbing the leather laces on the back of the hood. Then she slowly stepped away.

"Ah," I said. My breathing was rapid. My head was hot. My cock was on the verge of ripping apart – it felt so hard.

"Meal time," Hula said cheerfully.

"Go," Tural advised. I will be there in a moment, after I give the slave instructions."

I was panting.

"Slave."

"Yes, yes, Mistress," I managed to reply.

"I will not be late for my dinner."

She was so cruel to leave me on the edge.

"You will have one minute."

One minute? Did I really understand?

I felt Tural move and then her boots brushed the inside of my twitching thighs. She guided my cock up and then backed herself onto me, mounting all of my cock in one slow action.

"Oh, Mistress," I breathed, my voice quivering.

"One minute," she said, her voice melting my mind. "You have permission, if you can."

She was wet and hot. I thrust hard into her. She responded by backing herself into me and pushing back equally as hard. I managed to get one more thrust before she took over the movement and took me, without any build up. She was using me as hard and as fast as she could.

Tural came down over and over as I strained my arms and legs. She was breathing heavily, panting.

She let out her growling sound and that was *it* – I barely managed to say "Thank you, Mistress!" as my hips bucked, and I came.

Tural continued to gyrate herself as my body jerked again and again.

My erection savored the last of it as she pressed down.

Finally, my Mistress pulled away.

I was panting heavily, my head in a swirl.

"Clean me, slave," she said.

Between gasps of air I licked my fluids from hers as she straddled me.

"Good, slave," Tural told me. "Now, we can eat dinner."

My hood was removed and my eyes slowly adjusted to the lighting.

There were at least half a dozen women nearby, most attending to their own slaves while others watched Tural and I.

My breathing was still rapid, but I was almost in control.

I had not been aware that there had been music.

"The palace guards will take you to be cleaned and then bring you to my table. Hurry," she said, "I will not miss the first course!"

*****

The celebration ended six hours later.

The food was spectacular.

The Erskan celebration had been constructed around their grouping of nine. Nine cane strikes, nine "waves" of slaves to dominate and use for torture or for sex, depending on the mood of the women, three items per three courses of the meal, and so on.

At times I was allowed to talk to the frey sitting closest to me. The property of a jurina leading a mounted unit, he had engaged in actual sword fighting for a few seconds until reinforcements arrived. He proudly sported a left forearm dotted with eighteen sutures.

I had been able to get out of a forced-demonstration of the singing capabilities of frey, because I did not know the words to any songs – thankfully.

Several times I crouched under the table, moving from warrior to warrior, providing oral service. This seemed to be one of the primary duties of frey. My throat and tongue were sore after the first hour – but I never gave up. It was a compliment that I had been ordered to come back several times among the warriors.

Or, perhaps, it was because I had been caught maneuvering the order of frey so that Tural was frequently on the receiving end of my devotion.

*****

The door latch clicked as I pushed the door closed.

"Slave, come here," Tural whispered.

I walked to the closest side of the bed. Tural pulled my belt and let my skirt drop to the floor.

"Bend down," she ordered. She pulled the sheet away. I saw her silhouette on the bed.

I bent over, and she hooked a light metal chain to my collar. The other end snaked over to an eyebolt at the center of the bed's headboard. There was nearly no slack in the line. She tugged on the chain until I moved over her and into the middle of the bed. I groaned softly as my sore body creaked in protest from a dozen places.

Hula was on the other side, lightly snoring. I lay down on my back. Tural pulled the covers over myself and then onto her. Then she tugged on my collar to roll toward her.

Naked, we embraced, her arms wrapping around mine. Our legs intertwined.

"My slave," she whispered into my ear. "I am too tired to use you again – I spent the rest of my energy on my lover."

"Yes, Mistress."

I felt Hula's warm skin as she backed into to me. My spine tingled.

"I am happy to be your slave, Mistress."

Tural kissed my lips. "Good. Now, sleep, my slave."

"Yes, Mistress."

About the Author

K. McVey has been a rubber fetishist and BDSM enthusiast since the 1980s. His debut novel blends life-long passions for science fiction and adventure with pulse-pounding erotic dominance & submission.

When not traveling to kink events throughout the world, he collects original fetish art to complement a growing latex and leatherwear wardrobe. K. lives in the USA with pet racing motorcycles.